The
PAUPERS'
GRAVEYARD

GEMMA MAWDSLEY

The
PAUPERS'
GRAVEYARD

MERCIER PRESS

IRISH PUBLISHER – IRISH STORY

MERCIER PRESS
Cork
www. mercierpress.ie

Trade enquiries to CMD,
55A Spruce Avenue, Stillorgan Industrial Park,
Blackrock, County Dublin

ISBN: 978 1 85635 617 6

10 9 8 7 6 5 4 3 2 1

A CIP record for this title is available from the British Library

For George

arts
council
schomhairle
ealaíon

Mercier Press receives financial assistance from the Arts
Council/An Chomhairle Ealaíon

Printed and bound in the EU.

True evil never dies; it just lays dormant,
waiting for the right time to waken.

One

It is the sort of noise that wakes us in the dead of night. A vague sound from somewhere within the house that sets the heart racing. We lie in the dark, alert and waiting for it to come again, panic is barely contained, while seconds tick by like hours, and beads of perspiration break out all over our body.

Gathering strength, we reach for the bedside lamp and, once its comforting yellow glow dispels the dark, it is safe enough to rise and move from room to room, checking locks and window fastenings. Only when closets and under the bed have been searched, to rule out the presence of a knife-wielding maniac or sharp-toothed monster, does our heartbeat begin to regulate. Finally, silently, cursing the night and our own stupid fears, we climb under the warm covers again and turn off the lamp. With a little luck we will soon fall back to sleep and, by morning, the nightmare will be over, forgotten.

Timmy woke to such a sound. At first he thought someone had called his name and he lay in the dark, waiting. In days gone by it would have sent him running to his mother for comfort. Strangely, though, his heart was not pounding as he imagined it should be. It did not seem to be beating at all. There were no beads of sweat on his brow. He was cold, freezing cold. He should have been afraid and yet he was not.

It was only when the sound came again, a child's voice crying out in terror, that he became aware of the weight on his chest and the terrible taste in his mouth. He tried to identify the dry powder that coated his lips, but his tongue refused to move. It felt alien and heavy, and then he realised that it too was weighed down by the same substance. Still he didn't panic, didn't try to take what could have been deep suffocating breaths. Instead, he quietly accepted that he was lying there covered by the earth.

He was aware of others stirring close by. A great wave of restlessness seemed to sweep through the soil and he thrust his arms upward, wanting to be free. The earth parted before him like liquid, as he soared towards the surface.

Bright sunlight startled him and he stood blinking, rubbing his eyes. Thick grass reached almost to his waist, and he could hear rustling and whispers. The grass parted as small shapes scurried all around him. He knew this place well, he had only recently come here to bury Katie, but the grass had been much shorter then. The air smelt fresh, but still held the sting of winter. It was probably early spring and, judging by the sun, late afternoon.

The ground beneath Timmy's feet shook and a roaring came from beyond the trees bordering the field. As he went to investigate, he saw that much of the earth in the graveyard had been dug up. Large chunks had vanished, causing the ground to fall away into a chasm. Jumping, he landed with ease in the deep hole. The freshly dug earth smelt raw, blood sweet, and he was suddenly overcome with a desperate longing, a feeling of loss. His head filled with voices calling out to him, pleading.

A new gateway had been cut into the bushes, and the dents in the fresh earth were alarming. No cart or plough could possibly have made such a track. Giant furrows, almost big enough for him to lie down in, tumbled one into the other. He followed the trail carefully, aware that the others were moving silently behind him through the long grass. He was dreaming; he had to be.

As he walked, he realised that everything was different in this dream world. The grass moving against his arms, caressing his fingers, felt like silk. His steps were languorous. Was he sleepwalking? The very air seemed to move through and within him.

Then he saw the reason for the noise. Was it a monster? No. Be brave, he told himself. It was huge, unlike anything he had even seen before, bigger than a hundred ploughs, but without horses to pull it. The noise alone would frighten the bravest of beasts. It stood shaking and belching smoke, causing the earth beneath his feet to throb. Light glistened off the yellow paintwork, dazzling him. All at once the noise stopped and silence buzzed.

He came out from behind the machine and walked along its length, feeling braver now. There was writing on its side and he traced the big, white letters with his finger. It read 'Earthmover'. This machine was exactly what he had thought, a giant plough. Great steel arms reached out in front of it and he went forward carefully. At the front, instead of a blade, was a gaping mouth with saw-like teeth as big as his arm. Small dark scraps of material were caught between the teeth. Like the grass, the machine felt warm to the touch. The unfamiliar cold of the steel fascinated him, and he moved his fingers across the metal.

'Jesus Christ, will you listen to me, man!'

He spun round at the sound, unsure what to do. Moving back towards the long grass, he crouched and felt the others coming towards him. Soon the children had surrounded him, all familiar, frightened faces. He had buried most of them.

'Timmy.' A little girl came crawling towards him and tiny arms encircled his waist. Katie, she was here.

'Timmy, what's happening? I'm frightened. I want to go home. I want Elizabeth.'

'Hush, Katie, there's nothing to be frightened about. That's just a big plough,' he said, pointing towards the Earthmover. The other children nodded. Timmy was their leader, and he was never wrong.

'Let's go home, Timmy.' Katie could not be pacified.

The others looked to him for an answer, but he had no idea where home was any more. Small faces showed the ravages of disease and famine, with gaunt skin, sunken cheeks and hollowed eyes. Please God help me, Timmy prayed, show me what to do. The voices came again, loud angry mens' voices carrying across the field.

'Stay here,' Timmy ordered, 'I'll go and see who it is.'

The field, once lush and ripe, was now a muddy landscape. The few remaining trees looked to have been uprooted by some dreadful storm; great oaks lay on their side, roots dark and leprous. In some places, there were lines of roofless, brick buildings, in others, roped-off squares.

He ran across the vast expanse of mud into the grass on the edge of the field and towards a group of men gathered beside three blazing fires. Somehow, the fires came from inside barrels that were not burning.

Two men were arguing. One paced, cursing and running his hands through his hair. The other was calmer, more in control. Timmy crawled closer, so that he could hear what they were saying.

'Listen, Paddy, we've had enough delays as it is with the weather. This is all we need.'

'I want the proper authorities informed, Sean, and I don't care how long it takes. I told you yesterday those weren't animal bones. There's too many. Can't you see what's in front of your face? We're digging in a graveyard. We've been burning the bones of the dead! It's desecration!'

Timmy followed his gesture towards the barrels and almost cried out as realisation came. They were digging up the children and tossing them into these great fires. He had to stop it. No one should have to die twice.

The rest of the workmen stood apart from the argument, whispering and casting fearful glances towards the two men. Timmy was about to leave when another machine, somewhat like the Earthmover, came thundering into view. It moved as if by magic – there were no horses pulling it. Sure it would crush the men in its path, he stood up to shout a warning. They either chose to ignore him, or were unable to hear over its noise. No one looked in his direction. It stopped before reaching them and Timmy watched, spellbound, as a man got out of it. It reminded him of Jonah in the belly of the whale.

The man was red-faced, waving his arms about and shouting. He walked to one side gesturing to the man called Paddy and his opponent to follow. Timmy was forced to move even closer to them in order to hear. He was afraid to go too near in case they saw him, so only snatches of the conversation reached him.

'There's only about an hour's more digging needed,' an angry Sean said. 'If we stop now and do as he says,' he glared at Paddy, 'we could be held up for weeks, even months.'

There was more muted conversation between the three before, finally, the new arrival walked towards the other workmen. He called them all together and spoke.

'You all know what's happened here. We've obviously come across an unmarked graveyard. Now, if we report this to the police or local authorities, it could mean weeks of delay, they might even revoke permission to build. Then we'll all be in trouble.'

This sent mutterings through the group. Building work was monotonous at the best of times and the novelty of card playing and drinking tea would soon wear off. Worse still, if the permission to build was revoked, they would have to find another employer.

'On the other hand, if you are prepared to complete the digging that Sean assures me will only take another hour or so, there will be a bonus payment of €300 in all pay packets.'

This last statement gave rise to gasps of surprise and nods of agreement. They could do with the extra money. Anyway, what harm could it do? The people in the graveyard were already dead. This was the consensus of the group. Their employer walked away, sure that the matter was resolved. Money solved everything as far Bob Richards was concerned. Timmy watched as Paddy tried to stop him, to reason with him, but was rudely waved aside as the man got back inside the machine and drove away.

'Okay, everyone back to work,' Sean roared.

Timmy hurried back towards the others. Already the men were advancing up the slope and would soon be upon them.

'Come on,' he whispered, leading the children back the way they had come. They would be safe in the tall grass. They had just made it back to the graveyard when the Earthmover trundled towards the gap in the trees. The children hid, but Timmy stood fast. As the machine came closer it dipped its head and opened wide its huge jaws. He was right in its path, looking up into the black-stained mouth and jagged teeth. They must be able to see him; they were probably trying to frighten him. The head descended jerkily, as though measuring him for size. As the teeth scooped into him he tensed and waited for the bone-crunching that would herald his end. He felt a faint breeze as the mouth passed through him and buried itself in the earth. Stepping back in amazement, he watched as the teeth tore into the soil and the screaming started all over again. He could see the bodies being wrenched from the earth. Small hands holding rotten toys reached out to him, as they ascended skywards, held firm by the jaws of the beast. It swung around, dumping its cargo into a heap, before descending again. With each bite it tore more bodies from their resting places. Men, women, mostly children were wrenched from the ground as the graveyard reverberated with their cries and moans. Timmy covered his ears, trying to block the sounds of torture. It was hopeless … the cries seemed to come from within him.

As quickly as it started, the machine stopped. The cries died away to a sighing that floated into the trees and hung there. As the branches swayed in the breeze, the sound echoed, and became the lament of so many souls in torment. Timmy ran behind the machine to the pile of freshly dug earth. Expecting to find it strewn with bodies he only saw bones. The men were picking them from the dark earth, and stacking them in wheelbarrows ready for burning. The one called Paddy stood by watching as they went about their grim task. He refused to take part in this grave-robbing, even if it meant losing his job.

'Stop!' Timmy's cry shattered the silence, but the men paid him no heed, none except Paddy who brought his hand to his chest in terror. 'Sweet Mother of Jesus,' he said, backing away.

'What's wrong with you now?' Sean stood up from his sorting.

'There's a thing … a boy I think,' Paddy pointed a quivering finger at Timmy.

'Where?' Sean looked straight at Timmy, but saw nothing.

'He's there!' exclaimed Paddy. 'Can't you see? He's right in front of you!'

The others had stopped working and looked where he was pointing. They could see no one either. Some laughed, but there was no merriment in the sound.

'I don't know,' Sean said, scratching his head. 'If this keeps up, Paddy, I'll have to speak to the boss about you. You're getting past it, old man, going soft in the head.'

He turned to the other men, raising his eyes to heaven. Some smiled and nodded in agreement. Others went back to their task, but would say in the months that followed that they had felt something – an overwhelming sense of loss and a desire to run from the field and hide; as it was, they did nothing.

Timmy wrung his hands. 'Why can't they see me? Why don't they listen?' He turned to Paddy. The man shook his head, still too shocked to speak to this … boy. The frightening spectre was the stuff of nightmares. He was unable to see the child. Instead, he saw a near skeleton, its cheekbones protruding against the tightly stretched skin, dark eyes peering from deep hollows and the jet-black hair which death had failed to fade, glowing against the bloodless face.

As he watched this boy-thing move backwards and forwards in front of the men, pleading with them to stop, he almost cried out in pain. What was it? Some sentinel of the dead? A guardian sent by God? Paddy lowered himself to the ground and began to pray aloud. 'Dear God, protect and forgive us for what we do this day.'

This was followed with the rosary and many of the men joined in answering.

Sean sighed in frustration at these stupid, superstitious fools as he reached down to retrieve a bone lying nearby. A small white hand was laid on top of his own brown weather-beaten one. He tried not to scream as he traced his eyes upwards, along the rag-covered arm, up the neck, towards the face.

'Stop, you're killing us!'

Timmy's voice broke the spell, and the man screamed and stumbled back towards the dirt pile. His workmen watched, dumbfounded, as he picked up a shovel and began to beat at the air.

'Get away from me,' he screamed, swinging the shovel at Timmy, but his efforts were in vain as the blade passed right through the boy.

'You can see it?' Paddy cried, wrestling the shovel from the terrified man. Sean stopped and turned to look at him, and then at his workmen who stood open-mouthed. Wiping the sheen of sweat from his forehead with the back of his hand, he answered hoarsely, 'I saw a rat. That's all. We'll finish up for the day. Burn those,' he pointed to the heap of bones, before striding swiftly from the field.

The men picked up the handles of the wheelbarrows and moved towards the gap in the trees. Timmy ran in front begging them to stop, but it was useless. They couldn't hear him.

'Timmy.'

He stopped and turned towards the voice.

'Come here, child.'

Elizabeth stood in the long grass, arms outstretched. The children clustered around vying for her attention. She watched as he ran towards her, sobbing. Once his arms went around her waist and she held him, he knew that he was home. She rocked him as the sobs came from deep within his dried-up heart.

'Hush, child,' she whispered. 'We'll be all right.'

'But where are we?' he asked, looking up into a face that seemed as beautiful as ever to him. 'I know we're in the graveyard, but I don't understand. Why are we here? Are we dead?'

The other children watched, waiting. She gazed down at them, searching for an answer, but she had none. They were dead, they had to be, and the things she had just witnessed were inconceivable. What was the purpose of it all? They had been through so much during the famine. Had they somehow displeased God? Was their suffering to be eternal?

A bellowing laugh came from the other side of the field. The sound of a man delighted with his lot. The children giggled and looked at one another, as the laughter continued, unabated. They stood on tiptoe as Elizabeth and Timmy shaded their eyes against the late afternoon sun, trying to make out who it was. He was in the shadow of the trees, and they waited in anticipation for him to show himself. Slowly, he walked forward and as he did, the smiles disappeared from their faces. Black Jack!

Timmy turned to Elizabeth. She was frozen with fear, but Timmy no longer felt the terror that Black Jack's presence would once have instilled in him. He felt the strange calmness that reconciled him to the fact that his battle with evil was not yet over.

'Elizabeth, we meet again.' Black Jack's voice carried across the quiet of the graveyard, as he bowed mockingly. It was now Timmy's turn to try and give comfort and, taking her hand, he whispered, 'Never mind him, Elizabeth. I don't think he can harm us any more, not here, not in this place.'

She nodded and tried to smile, but he could see the look of fear and confusion in her eyes. The children, sensing her fright, gathered around her for protection. The smaller ones buried their faces in the remnants of her skirts.

'Come now,' she smiled down at them. 'It's been a strange day and we all need some rest. Let's all lie down. I'm sure things will seem much better in the morning.' She sank into the long grass with Timmy on one side, both surrounded by the children. For a while she lay staring up at the darkening sky, listening to the sound of the breeze while the children tossed and turned trying to get comfortable. When at last they had quietened, she turned her face to Timmy and asked, 'Are you afraid?'

'No, are you?'

'A little. I wish I knew why we're here.' She sighed and closed her eyes.

Timmy did likewise and was overcome by velvet darkness as he, along with the others, became absorbed by the earth. The last thing he heard as he drifted away was her voice. 'We are no longer in our own time, of this I am sure. Either that or we are in hell.'

TWO

February 1845

For Charles Fitzwilliam the untimely death of his elder brother, John, was something to celebrate. Not only was he rid of a brother who was considered saintly by many, it also meant that John, having been considerate enough to die without a male heir, passed on to him the title of lord and the privileged estate and monies that went with it.

That his brother had also left a widow and three daughters meant nothing to Charles. They would soon be packed up and sent back to his sister-in-law's family. He had no intention of shouldering that responsibility. As a man of considerable means, he intended to do exactly as he pleased. Once all the nonsense of the funeral was out of the way, his life was going to change for the better.

London society was tiring of Charles' womanising and gambling. He had been aware for some time that it would be prudent for him to seek pastures new. He had never seen Maycroft Hall, having refused to attend the wedding of his brother and 'that woman', but he'd heard it was not at all grand. Certainly not on a par with some of the fine houses he was used to frequenting. His late brother's taste had never been as refined as his, but he was sure that time and money would bring about some great changes. A manager, he believed, took care of the many farms, some six thousand acres and hundreds of tenants. This was just as well, because, unlike his brother, he had no knowledge of farming. So it was in the spring of 1845 that he set sail for Ireland.

As always the Irish Sea had been moody, alternating between periods of calm when they sailed on water as smooth as glass, to giant waves that tossed the ship until he felt that they would surely capsize. If his information was correct, the people of this land were very much like its sea; a most disagreeable bunch, and savage. His fears were confirmed on arrival – only the most uncivilised people would allow the roads to remain in such condition. Roads! These were no more than dirt tracks made by numerous farm carts. How would he survive in such a dreadful place?

As they neared Maycroft, Charles Fitzwilliam studied the many thatched cabins dotting the landscape. The number of children clustered about each door amazed him. Drawn out by the sound of his carriage, they had come to stare at their new landlord. It was late afternoon and there appeared to be very few men or women about, from what he could see, only the old and infirm. The few men that watched him pass, raised their caps to him.

His thoughts were interrupted and he almost fell out of his seat, as the carriage hit another hole. His stomach, which had already been sorely tried by the sea crossing, heaved once more.

It was a great relief when the large ornate gates of the Hall came into view and he knew he would soon be back on solid ground. Once the carriage had come to a halt, he jumped out and leant against the door. The sudden change overwhelmed him and, for a moment, his head swam. When he managed to steady himself, he turned and looked towards the Hall. The servants were lined up and waiting to greet him. Walking towards him was a woman dressed from head to toe in the black of mourning.

'Charles, it is good to meet you at last, but I wish it was under happier circumstances.' Her eyes filled with tears as she grasped his hands in hers. He was taken aback by her looks. Even now, in her worst sorrow, she was utterly beautiful. Although he had never seen her before, Charles had been among the many to scoff at his brother's choice of wife. Untitled and from farming stock, she had seemed at first to be John's only folly, but the years had proved the gossips wrong. She had adjusted to the position of titled lady as though born to it, and if she had one failing, in Charles' eyes, it was her inability to bear his brother a son. But if she had done so, he wouldn't be where he was today. Every cloud, as they say.

'Elizabeth,' he bent and kissed her marble-cold cheek. 'Sorry I wasn't able to attend the funeral, but you understand.'

'Of course,' her smile was icy. She understood only too well how selfish and uncaring her brother-in-law could be. Her husband had never spoken of his brother's shortcomings, but she had noticed him frown, as he read numerous letters from Charles begging for money to get him out of one pickle or another. Even in the wilds of Ireland gossip reached them, and John would shake his head in disappointment at the life his brother was leading. It was at such times that she had felt a sense of dread. Her failure to bear a son meant that there was always the possibility that one day both she and her daughters could be at the mercy of this man. That day had now arrived and she could only wait and see what he had decided to do with them. Her father had explained that she could not return home, as he was unable to feed four extra mouths, not on his meagre income. She had little money of her own and the swiftness of her husband's death meant that he had died without providing for them.

She watched as Charles shook the wrinkles from his cape, more interested in his appearance than in the recent loss of his brother.

'Shall we go in?' he motioned towards the door and the waiting staff, 'or had you planned on staying here a while longer staring at me?'

'Yes, of course, forgive me,' she blushed, bringing her hands to her flaming cheeks; she had been lost in thought.

He took little heed of her and proceeded towards the steps to the house. She raced to catch up with him and automatically named each servant as they walked by. He did not acknowledge any of them, most likely forgetting the names as soon as she had mentioned them, but Elizabeth still felt it was her duty to perform the introductions.

'So, this is Maycroft,' his eyes swept around the cavernous hallway.

GEMMA MAWDSLEY

'I must have a hot bath before dinner,' he said as he strode towards the stairs.

Thomas, the butler, tottered after him. She watched the old man's polite attempts to pass his new master and lead the way to the prepared rooms. She nodded a dismissal to the other servants, who hurried away to fetch water for the bath. Soon the house was in an uproar as maids hurried up and down the stairs with pitchers of hot water following Charles' bellowed orders.

What must the children be thinking, she wondered? She had requested that they stay in the nursery until sent for. Still in shock after the death of their beloved father, they were unsettled, unsure of what would happen next, and she had tried to make the arrival of their uncle a happy, anticipated event. Lucy, the eldest at fourteen and quite the young woman, was not fooled by her mother's smiles and knew that her uncle's presence might mark a turning point in their lives. The others, Becky aged eight and Charlotte six, were not old enough to understand and waited in wonder for him to appear. Perhaps, Elizabeth mused, he would be in better humour after a bath and a hot meal.

The only sound that broke the silence was the swishing of her silk skirts as she paced the drawing-room, waiting for him to reappear. The clock in the hall counted each agonising minute, until the head parlour maid stuck her head around the door.

'Mistress,' she whispered, 'he's in the dining-room.'

'Thank you, Mary,' she smiled, 'I'll be there presently.'

Squaring her shoulders and holding her hand to her stomach to quell the dark butterflies that fluttered there, she left the room. Try as she might to appear brave, Elizabeth couldn't help but notice her hand trembling as she turned the doorknob. He was sitting at the head of the table, in her husband's chair.

'I trust you are feeling better, Charles?' He did not reply, but continued to pick at the food as though it disgusted him. 'Is the food not to your liking? I can have Annie prepare you something else.'

20

He stopped her with a wave of his hand, and then resumed chopping and mashing his potatoes, moulding and heaping them like a spoilt child.

'I appear to have lost my appetite,' he said, pushing the plate away. With a sigh of boredom, he leaned back and draped a leg over the arm of his chair. Still ignoring her, he looked around the room at the black drapes covering the mirrors out of respect for his dead brother.

'It's this house,' he finally spoke. 'It's so gloomy. There's no life in it.'

'There has been a death. You can hardly expect it to look any other way.' She dug her fingernails into her palms, to stop herself saying something she might later regret.

'Yes, I know, but that was weeks ago. It is time to move on. I want all these coverings removed at once.'

'Yes, Charles.' In one short hour she had lost everything, the house was no longer her own, and she knew that there was worse to come.

'I want a drink, whiskey. Do you have any or did the local rabble drink it all at the party?'

'Which party?'

'That thing they have when someone dies in this country. You know, some sort of party.'

The wake! She realised he was talking about the wake.

'It's called a wake, Charles,' she said, calmly. 'It's certainly not a party, but rather a traditional last farewell, held in honour of the dead.'

'Well, whatever it is.'

She grasped the bell pull and rang for Thomas.

'Yes, mistress,' the old man shuffled in and waited for his orders, but before she could answer Charles spoke

'You there, bring me some whiskey, now.'

'Yes, sir.' Thomas bowed and left the room.

Charles drummed his fingers on the arm of his chair until the butler reappeared, carrying a silver tray with a crystal decanter and two glasses. Placing the tray in front of his master, he filled one of the glasses with a generous measure and handed it to him.

'When I ask for a drink I mean a proper drink!' Charles grabbed the decanter and filled the glass almost to the brim. 'One would think that you were paying for this stuff,' he sneered, downing almost a third of the whiskey.

'That will be all, thank you, Thomas.' Elizabeth wanted to get the butler away as quickly as possible. She was mortified at such rudeness. After he left, Charles turned to her.

'Well, Elizabeth, it's time you and I got better acquainted, don't you think? Sit down.' He pushed at the chair nearest to him with his foot. 'You'll join me in a drink, I hope?'

She watched in horror as he filled the other glass before handing it to her. She rarely drank and then only a little wine. How she was expected to drink that much whiskey, she could not imagine.

'To your good health,' he raised his glass and took another swallow, all the time watching her until she was forced to bring the glass to her lips and sip. The whiskey burned her throat and brought tears to her eyes. Her predicament only made Charles laugh and he thumped on the table in glee. 'This will never do, dear sister-in-law. I'll have to train you myself.' She smiled, unsure of what he meant. 'We have a lot to talk about, don't we, so much to learn about one another?'

'I should like to discuss matters with you, Charles.'

'Now, now, let's not rush things. Let's get to know one another first,' he murmured.

She squirmed under his lecherous gaze.

'Really, Charles, I would like to speak to you about my position here.'

'But you don't have a position here, do you, m'dear? None that I'm aware of.'

'Yes,' she wrung her hands, 'that's what I mean. Have you had any thoughts on our future here?'

'Not really. Do you have any plans? I though you would be returning to your family home.'

'I would rather not. The children are used to a certain way of life and I'm sure their father would have wanted it to continue.'

'Possibly … if he were still alive.'

His words stopped her short, and she had to clasp her hands to stop them from trembling.

'Yes,' she whispered, 'if he were still alive.'

'For the time being it suits me that you remain here. You will be valuable as a hostess, I'm sure, and one never knows what time may bring,' his smile sent waves of revulsion through her. 'However, there is one thing I insist upon. Your children; I do not want to hear or see them, especially in the mornings.'

'But, you will meet them, Charles? They are so looking forward to meeting you.'

'I dare say I'll come across them in time, but for now I have no desire to do so.'

She began to speak again, to entreat him to meet his nieces.

'I do not want you to place any demands on me, Elizabeth. I am not my brother.'

He waved his hand to dismiss her and watched as she walked, straight-backed, from the room. He hadn't meant to keep her on, but she was lovely and the nights could be long in a place such as this. She might yet prove her worth, and if she decided to be difficult he could always dispense with her.

Elizabeth leant against the other side of the door and tried to still the sobs of anger and humiliation, as all the loneliness and sorrow of the past few weeks caught up with her.

———

The next few days passed slowly. Keeping the children amused and quiet was a daunting task. She felt as though she were walking on pins as she tiptoed around the house. Like it or not, she knew they were living on borrowed time. The girls had taken their uncle's disinterest fairly well, although Lucy did raise her eyebrows as she listened to her mother's excuses. However, she did her best to keep her sisters outside and as far away as possible from the house.

The air of tension touched everyone. The maids no longer exchanged friendly banter with the grooms and gardeners; flirting and teasing became a thing of the past. Charles, to Elizabeth's relief, chose to eat alone, which meant she was spared his leers and insults. When he tired of the house, he sent for her.

'I take it I have a horse?'

'Well,' she murmured, feeling confused. 'There are the animals that pull the carriage, but they're really only workhorses. Most are used on the farm.'

'And my brother, did he not hunt?'

'There is Lightning,' she whispered, 'but he was John's own mount.'

'Well, he can hardly object to my riding him, can he? Not any more.'

Before she could reply he left the room and she watched from the window as he strode towards the stables. Soon the sound of horses' hooves could be heard on the stable-yard cobbles, and she watched as Timmy, the youngest stable boy, led Lightning and his rider through the gate. She could see Charles talking down at him and Timmy pointing towards the north pasture, probably indicating the best areas for riding. She waited until Charles had disappeared into the distance, before going outside.

Timmy stood rooted to the spot, still watching the rider, who was now no more than a dot on the horizon. It wasn't until she had almost reached him that he became aware of her and turned around with guilty eyes.

'He ordered me to saddle the master's horse, mistress.'

'I know, Timmy, it's all right,' she patted his shoulder. It felt thin beneath her fingers. 'You'll have to eat more, get some flesh on those bones.'

'Yes, mistress. My da says I eat like a horse and look like a greyhound, but I'm strong.'

'I'm sure you are, Timmy.'

She could see why her husband had been so fond of this boy. Always willing and not afraid of hard work John had said, but there was something else too. The very air around him seemed to crackle with energy. He had a thirst for life. Her thoughts were interrupted by a shout from within the stable-yard.

'Timmy, you good-for-nothing wretch, where the hell are you?'

Jack Carey. He was head groom, and the bane of those who worked under him. She watched as Carey walked over to the gate, looking all around him for the boy, who stood mute at her side. On seeing them, he feigned surprise, but walked forward smiling and doffing his cap.

'Good day to you, mistress.'

'Good day, Carey.' She neither smiled, nor looked directly at him. 'I borrowed your young man here,' she smiled down at Timmy. 'He's been a great help in saddling his lordship's mount.'

'His lordship's horse?' He was taken aback, until he realised that she meant his new master. He had wanted to meet him first and get on a good footing before anyone else.

'Thank you, Timmy.' She nodded to them both, and turned towards the house. Stopping before the door, she looked back and watched the man and boy enter the stables. Carey's sheer size was overwhelming; he was over six foot tall and built to match. It was his eyes that made her uncomfortable; they were almost as dark as his hair, a deep, unsettling black. She knew the servants had christened him Black Jack and it was easy for her to see why, she thought, going indoors to summon the children to lunch.

Once out of the mistress's sight, Black Jack grabbed Timmy by the arm, almost lifting him off the ground. 'Why didn't you call me when his lordship came for the horse?'

'I did call you.' Timmy tried to wrestle away from the strong fingers that were biting into his thin flesh. 'But you weren't there, and the master wouldn't wait.'

'Well, the next time, boy, make yourself heard.' He gave the struggling child a hard clip across the ear and watched as he hurried away. He'd make it his business to be here when the master returned. If any of the rumours were true, it might turn out to be quite profitable. He was not averse to a game of cards himself, and when the master sought companions in the sport, he would only be too glad to steer him in the right direction. There were many wealthy farmers in the district who liked a gamble and were not fussy whom they played with, so he would be well thought of for bringing gentry to the table. Yes, he was on his way up. By this time next year he would be a changed man, hadn't his own mother predicted it?

Agnes Carey always predicted great things for her son. He was her world, despite the fact that on many occasions she had to get rid of his 'mistakes'. She was an accomplished abortionist; her knowledge of herbs, along with the aid of a long wire hook, helped keep the population down. And it wasn't just with the poor. Agnes told of many's the fine lady who had willingly lain spread-eagled on the dirty tabletop and allowed her to poke and prod between their legs. That so many died afterwards from shock, loss of blood or infection was of no account to her. She saw herself as a saviour of sorts and made quite a bit of money in the process. Those who did survive soon found that they were in debt to Agnes Carey for the rest of their life. Her silence cost dearly.

Black Jack didn't have long to wait for his master's return. Quickly bored, Charles rode back into the stable in a foul mood. His inspection of his estate had come to an abrupt halt in just over a mile. What he saw depressed him; dirty little cabins with children running around barefoot and barely covered in rags. And as for the women! There wasn't one that caught his eye. But then it was hard to imagine beauty in such filthy circumstances. The smell had been the worst. Many of the hovels had large manure heaps outside, pigs roamed freely and he had even seen them appearing from inside the dwellings! His estimation of these people had been correct; they were no more than pigs themselves. He dismounted almost before Black Jack could catch hold of the reins, and would have stormed away, if the groom hadn't stopped him.

'How do you do, my lord?'

Charles turned, aghast that this upstart was addressing him. Timmy came running from the stable to relieve Black Jack of the struggling horse. Charles walked back to where the man stood, cap in hand.

'Are you addressing me?' He was mortified to find that he had to look up at the man. This made his humour worse, and he was sorely tempted to use his riding crop.

'Yes, my lord, begging your pardon, sir, but I just wanted to welcome you to Maycroft.'

Charles looked on as the man stood twiddling his cap, and decided the fellow was harmless enough. He was, after all, attempting to be sociable, which was more than he could say for the rest of the rabble.

'Yes, indeed, thank you.' He cleared his throat as though the simple sentence was sticking there, and turned to go, but was stopped again as the man spoke.

'If there's anything I can do to help, I'd be glad to.'

'Help! Is it possible to help someone who finds himself in hell?'

'I can understand how this place must seem to you, my lord. There's very little to do. Sure if it wasn't for the odd game of cards, we'd all go mad.' Black Jack could see the gleam of interest in the master's eyes.

'What's your name?'

'Jack Carey, my lord. I'm head groom here. I've been here since I was ten years old. I served your late brother well and I hope I can do the same for you.'

'You may well be of service to me, Carey. Now tell me about these card games.'

Timmy watched as the two men drew closer, but try as he might, he could not hear what they were saying. Whatever it was improved Black Jack's humour and he even allowed Timmy to finish a whole hour early.

THREE

'Timmy!' His brothers and sister came running to meet him, and threw their arms around him.

'Let me breathe,' the twelve-year-old laughed, untangling the numerous arms and trying to answer their questions.

'Why are you so early?' Peter wanted to know from his older brother. 'You didn't lose your position, did you?'

He looked down at the three little faces.

'No, indeed, I didn't.'

They smiled with relief and he hoisted Rose, baby of the family at two, into his arms. Balancing her on his hip, he took six-year-old Tom by the hand, and they walked indoors.

Even in summer the cabin was cold. Built of stone, with two rooms and an old thatched roof, it retained very little warmth. The crude wooden table that stood in the centre of the room had a bench on both sides of it and a wooden chair at the head.

A small cupboard, placed as near to the fire as possible, protected their food from the damp. Two rickety armchairs stood on either side of the large open fire. His mother and father sat there each night, weary after working hard in the fields. Over the fire hung a long black arm with two hooks; these held the cooking utensils, a large black pot and a kettle. A flat griddle pan lay beside the hearth.

After sending Peter to fetch water from the well, Timmy set about preparing the supper. Half-filling the pot with water he carefully counted in the potatoes, six for his father and three for his mother and two for each of the children. He quickly got the turf and sticks to catch fire, and swung the heavy pot over the flame.

Next he set the table with three chipped cups and three small wooden bowls to hold the buttermilk for the younger children. Since starting work he was considered a man and was allowed to use a cup. Three plates, in much the same condition as the cups, followed, with a small bowl of salt. Two bent forks and two knifes, their blades worn away to an arch from constant sharpening, completed the table setting.

Timmy then sat in his mother's chair with Rose on his lap and with his brothers sitting on the floor beside him, he recounted stories about fairies, goblins and wicked witches. They listened in wide-eyed wonder as he told of Tir na nÓg, a magical land where a person never grew old, where there was plenty of food to be had, fish and meat every day if you wanted it, clothes made of gold and silver, and real shoes for your feet. They shook their heads in awe, imagining not having to go barefoot.

The pot was bubbling cheerfully when the door opened. Timmy beamed with pride when his tired mother gazed around the room, taking in the table and the pot on the fire. Then he glanced past her to his father, who was glaring back at him.

'What are you doing home at this time, lad?' Without waiting for an answer, he reached for the stick that was always kept handy in a corner and turned back to Timmy with his hand raised, ready to strike.

'For the love and honour of God, Pat,' his mother stood in front of Timmy, 'let the lad answer.'

'There's nothing wrong, Da. Black Jack just let me finish early, that's all.'

He watched in relief as his father returned the stick to its rightful place. His brothers had been looking on, ashen-faced, and Rose's lower lip was trembling. They had all felt the sting of the stick in the past. Brushing past them, their father slumped into his chair and sat gazing glumly into the fire. Their mother, trying to lighten the mood, chatted gaily as she checked the potatoes, sticking a fork in to see if they were soft enough to eat. Once she was happy, so were her children. She carried the pot outside and, covering the top with a piece of sacking, tilted it to one side to allow the water to drain off. The pot was placed back over the fire for a few minutes, to let the potatoes dry, and the piece of sacking, steaming from the boiling water, was held in front. When it was dry, she placed it in the centre of the table and upturned the pot, allowing a mountain of potatoes to appear. Some tumbled and rolled, and the children laughed, as their mother and Timmy tried to stop them from falling onto the dirt floor.

From a small cupboard she took a covered dish. This, like the cups, was chipped and the flowers on it faded, but it was still her pride and joy, given to her by her mother when the flowers were still bright blue. The same colour as your eyes, her mother had said, as she kissed her goodbye on her wedding day.

She had been fifteen when she married Pat, and now, almost fifteen years later, she was faded, like the bowl. Sometimes she felt as though she had been alive forever. Lifting the lid, she carefully spooned a piece of dried fish onto her husband's plate. His large hand covered hers.

'Take a bit for yourself.'

'I have no appetite, Pat. I'll save it for tomorrow.'

'Eat it now, you're skin and bone as it is.'

She had no choice but to obey, and the children watched her trembling hand spoon out a small piece of the fish and replace the lid.

'Eat,' she nodded at the children, and Timmy picked up a knife and began to peel the potatoes for Tom and Rose. His father and Peter ate them skin and all, but his mother and the younger ones had no stomach for that. The skins did not go to waste though, because they went to feed Nelly, their pig. From a churn his mother scooped up buttermilk, pouring it into each of the cups and bowls. As always, she took the least, and Timmy watched her picking at the piece of fish, pulling it apart, checking for bones. He knew what was coming next, so he turned to his father and started to talk.

'The new master came into the stables today.'

'Did he indeed?' His father was interested. 'They say he's not a patch on his brother, though he was a hard enough man, God knows. Not that it matters to us,' he snorted. 'He'll do little enough to help here.'

Now that Timmy had started his father off about the changes that needed to be made, it allowed his mother some free rein. He watched as she studied her husband, and when she was sure he wasn't looking, she took bits of the flaked fish in her fingers and fed them to Rose and Tom. They opened and closed their mouths soundlessly, reminding Timmy of the fledglings in the trees beside the cabin. He would have loved some of the dried fish and, licking his lips, he tasted the salt from the potatoes and pretended it was from the fish.

Peter watched each mouthful, his eyes as big as saucers. Timmy and Peter knew that the younger ones needed the food more than they did, but it would have been nice to taste it, just this once. His mother caught his eye and winked, he winked back, glad to be sharing a secret with her. They had outwitted his father who was now in full flow, waving his knife in the air and sending bits of potato flying into his hair. Soon it looked as though it had snowed on his head, and she shook her head in warning to them not to laugh. When the meal was finished, his father went outside with the slop bucket to feed the pig.

Timmy and the others helped their mother clear up, and then get ready to wash the younger ones. She placed a chair in front of the fire and took an old enamel basin from a nail in the wall. When his mother had half-filled it with cold water from the bucket, Timmy brought the kettle from the hearth and allowed the hot water to dribble into the basin until it was warm enough. Each of the children squirmed as she scrubbed necks, ears and between sticky fingers with a soapy rag, determined to root out any trace of dirt. We may be poor, she often told them, but that's no excuse for filth.

Timmy was glad he no longer had to endure this nightly ritual. When she had finished with the others, he emptied the bowl. This was refilled as before and handed to him. He took it into the other room, the sleeping place for them all. The beds were planks of wood tied together with rope and covered with straw. One set in the corner for his parents and a larger one for the children. A frayed blanket lay in the centre of each one and this was all the bedding they had. When the weather got too cold, they dragged the beds into the kitchen and slept by the fire. The only other furniture in the room was a stool, and it was on this that he placed the bowl.

The threadbare cloth they used for a towel had hardly enough fabric left in it to dry him; still damp, he carefully manoeuvred the jumper over his head and elbows. There were so many holes in the sleeves, that he once managed to put his head through one, stretching it even further. As he was carrying the basin outside, his father loomed from out of the darkness.

'Hurry to bed, boy, the spring planting has to be done on Saturday. You'll need all your strength for that.' He brushed past his son without looking at him and went inside. Timmy heard him talking to his mother and the tone was sharp.

Timmy did not look forward to spending a full day in the fields with his father, but the planting of the potatoes was the most important event of the year. He waited outside for a while, watching shadows moving within the cabin, caught by the light of the fire. The three small ones went from the kitchen to the bedroom, then the large, lumbering shape of his father, followed them. At last his mother was alone. He crept inside, closing the door as quietly as he could.

His mother brought her fingers to her lips, nodding towards the other room. He understood that they could speak only when they heard the thundering snores of his father. They sat in silence before the fire, his mother trying to darn one old jumper with wool from a more threadbare one. He studied her face as she worked. He found it hard to imagine that she had once been young, except when she smiled; her eyes lit up and then she seemed like someone else, not like his mother at all.

As the sounds from the bedroom signalled their release, she put aside the jumper. Timmy knew what to do. They had been doing the same thing for over a year, since he had grown old enough to be trusted.

He crept to the turf pile, moved aside a few sods and felt for the loose brick. After prising it out, he reached inside and pulled out a package wrapped in old rags. This he placed on his mother's lap and watched as she opened it. The book inside was so old, the pages had come loose, but that didn't matter. It was the words that were important and also the stories they told.

'We'll start on a new one tonight.' She smiled at him, moving to one side of the chair, and allowing him to squeeze in beside her.

Slowly he moved his fingers across the page, sounding out in a whisper the more difficult words, until he had finished the first paragraph. He was pleased and looked at his mother for approval. She was gazing at him with an odd look in her eyes, a sort of sadness. But she kissed his forehead and told him how well he was doing, and warned him, as always, that he must never speak to anyone about the book. She told him that the strange, musty scent from within the book was the smell of freedom, that one day he would understand. For now all the words and wonderful things he learned must remain a secret, to be whispered between them late at night, while the others were asleep.

He hid the book again, replacing the brick and piling the turf back against it. Squeezing back into the chair, he laid his head on his mother's shoulder and felt her thin arm encircle him, stroking his hair. He was far too old, he knew, to need cuddling, but he let her, for her sake.

'What's he like?' she asked.

He was puzzled, 'Who?'

'The new master, what's he like?'

He knew he could be truthful with his mother.

'He's a bit cross and strange-looking.'

GEMMA MAWDSLEY

Her laugh startled him. There was little that made her laugh and he felt powerful for having done so. Trying to outdo himself, Timmy continued, 'He walks like a girl as well. I'll show you.' He minced his way across the floor exaggerating the master's walk, hands held in a foppish manner. This was too much for his mother, who roared with laughter and he joined in, delighted. It took them a moment to realise that their noise had awoken his father, who was now glaring at them from the doorway.

'What in the love and honour of Christ do you think you're doing?' He looked from one to the other. The sight of his red-rimmed eyes and angry face was usually enough to frighten them, but now they looked at each other and burst out laughing once more. This made his temper even worse and he lurched towards the corner that held the stick.

'You see this?' He waved it in front of their faces. 'I'll use it on the both of you in a minute.'

The laughter died. He threw the stick aside and it landed with a clatter on the floor.

'Now get to bed and don't have me tell you again.'

They set about preparing the room for the following day. His mother steeped the oatmeal for the breakfast porridge, as Timmy filled the kettle and placed it near the hearth. When there was nothing more they could do, they went grudgingly to bed. His father was snoring again and Timmy lay beside his brothers and sister enjoying their warmth.

Tonight, for the first time, he realised how much he hated his father. If the look in his mother's eyes was anything to go by, she felt the same. He wondered, as he drifted off to sleep, what made his father so bitter. Martin, his best friend, had six brothers and sisters and his family was even poorer than them, but his father had a smile and a good word for everyone. Life was very strange, he decided.

FOUR

July 2003

If Timmy's life had seemed strange his death was proving to be stranger still. Endless days blended one into the other, no finality, no peace, and it was not at all like the afterlife he had been expecting. He was awakened each morning by the thundering of the great machines. The replanting of the fallen bushes and trees had cordoned off his part of the graveyard.

Sometimes the smaller children grew bored and ventured into the next field. They could walk and run unnoticed among the living, and took great pleasure in playing jokes on the frightened workmen. A coat would fall from the seat of a machine, pulled by invisible hands, then be dragged through the mud and bushes, its owner watching open-mouthed in amazement. No one dared to follow, afraid of what might lie beyond the boundary. Many voiced their fears to the manager, only to be laughed at and waved away. But Timmy noticed that he avoided looking towards the bushes after that first time.

Elizabeth spent most of the time in deep thought, although she feigned normality. Sometimes, as the dark closed in, she would walk to the edge of the field and gaze across to the road and the lights of the machines that passed. Some even flew through the air, and for the first few weeks they all ducked down in case one fell on top of them. The children, though still wary of Black Jack, mostly ignored him. They adjusted well to their situation. Many of them had not known him in the other time. They didn't fear him, even though his face was frightening. Strangulation had discoloured his skin more than the soil and its insects could ever have done. The loss of blood had turned it to black-blue. The pupils of his eyes were still as dark as ever, but, with every blood vessel burst, they could be seen at night, glowing red, all the way across the graveyard.

Black Jack kept very much to himself, and for this they were all grateful. He, like Elizabeth, spent much time in thought. Sometimes, when he grew bored, Jack moved among the workmen and stroked the cheek of one of them. He watched with pleasure as the man shivered, drawing back, sensing his freezing touch, but unable to see what it was that had touched him. He was a fast learner and, after seeing Timmy's performance on the day they first awoke, he knew there was a lot to master. One could reveal oneself to the living. Already they could feel his touch, and it wouldn't be long until … Never mind, there was plenty of time.

Soon, each roped site contained a building in progress. No one stayed long, although others soon replaced workers who left suddenly. The boss grew frustrated at the men's unwillingness to see the job through, in spite of him offering inflated pay rates. But even he had to admit that there was strangeness to the place; a feeling of uneasiness, with a heavy, cloying scent in the air. He was not one to be frightened by ghost stories, and God knows Ireland abounded with them. Utter nonsense, these stories of whisperings and figures in the trees.

Timmy hated the nights most. Even though he disliked the daytime roaring of the machines and the muffled shouts of workers, he dreaded the silence. When the men finished for the day, a gloom descended with the darkness. The noise made it hard to think, but the quiet brought memories. His throat tightened when he thought of his family. His mother, brothers and sister were not in this place. But there were others, like Martin, his best friend, who was there, but had failed to waken. Martin's father and Mick were here. He had buried them, he could not be mistaken. Why could they not come to him now? Perhaps Elizabeth was right, maybe they were in hell.

A stirring in the darkened field beyond the bushes interrupted his thoughts. Urgent whispering and the sound of running feet reached him. Soon a light appeared in the window of one of the buildings and the crackling of a fire could be heard. Elizabeth and the children had all returned to their dark sanctuary and there was no sign of Black Jack. The small fire lit up the night sky, outlining all the buildings. He really wanted to investigate these newcomers, to see if some weary travellers had chosen this place to rest for the night. Perhaps it was someone who would not be afraid and would talk to him. He was about to crawl through the bushes, when a movement stopped him. Black Jack was striding purposefully towards the light. His tattered frock coat waved about him as he walked, but his footsteps made no sound.

Timmy started to follow and was only a few feet behind him, when Black Jack turned. 'Stay out of my way, Walsh,' he warned, 'or I'll crush you like the bothersome insect you are.'

'Oh and how do you think you will do that? You have no power here.'

Black Jack hit out at him and growled with frustration, as his clenched fist encountered nothing but air.

'Give me time, Walsh. I'll find a way; I always do, as you well know.' He turned and walked towards the light, without noticing the look of fear that crossed the boy's face.

Timmy peeped through a window, as Black Jack marched straight inside. The blazing fire cast shadows on the bare bricks and made giants of the people moving about. He knew nothing was beyond Black Jack, there was no stopping the devil's offspring. He saw a group of boys, dressed alike in jumpers and baggy trousers. Each had a hood pulled over his face. Timmy had to climb inside the house to get a better look at them. They seemed no older than he was, had been, in that time long ago. Black Jack stood in one corner of the room, his blood-red eyes narrowed, watching. Their language was hard to understand.

'This is good shit,' one of the boys said, taking a shiny packet from his pocket. 'Almost pure.'

He hunched in front of the fire and the others joined him. Each held out a silver spoon and he divided the powder between them. Timmy squeezed in beside them and watched as the spoons were held over the flames and the powder melted into liquid. Even Black Jack had drawn closer. Next they took a tube with a needle attached to it. The tip of the needle was placed in the bubbles and the liquid sucked into the tube. The first one rolled up a sleeve and tied a string around his forearm. He held the needle as it punctured the skin in the crook of his arm and a small amount of blood appeared to mix with the liquid. Timmy watched in amazement as it all disappeared inside him. One by one his companions repeated the ceremony. Timmy pulled back as they fell away from the fire and slumped against the wall. Each wore the same stupid smile, and their voices now sounded different, slurred. After a while they began to move.

The banging of metal sounded as they pulled silver canisters from their bags. Timmy hunched closer to one of the boys, their noses almost touching, as he pulled a ring on the top of the canister. Suddenly, with a sharp hiss, the air was filled with the scent of ale. Black Jack came forward, licking his lips, and tried to pick up one of the canisters, but it was useless. It just passed through his fingers, and he swore loudly, before stalking away.

Timmy stayed to try and find out where he was, what year he was in. But it was difficult. They spoke of bitches, but he could see no dogs. They seemed to be religious as they used the name of Christ often in their speech.

'This fuckin' place is A-1, man,' one of them said. 'No watchman, no security guards, fuckin' happenin',' he looked around, and the others mumbled their agreement. 'Anyway, who'd want to come way out here, to the arsehole of nowhere, to knock off that shit?' He pointed to the bricks.

Their speech grew duller, their movements slowed, as the hours passed. Timmy grew tired of their company and decided to return to the graveyard. He had seen enough of the living for now, it was time to go back to his own kind. The light from the fire glinted off one of the tubes that littered the floor and he bent to pick it up. He held the fine plastic between his finger and thumb, amazed at its smoothness, lightness and craftsmanship.

'What the fuck is that?'

He spun around to find one of the boys pointing in his direction.

'It's floating, man,' answered another, 'flying.' Flapping his arms, he mimicked a bird.

'No, that other thing; it's some sort of scarecrow. Look at it.' The others tried to focus on where he was pointing.

'Hey, you,' the first one spoke to Timmy, 'get the fuck out of here.' He aimed one of the empty canisters at him. The others joined in, and though the missiles sailed past, Timmy was afraid and started to run, the boy's voice following him.

'And stay the fuck out.'

Timmy could still hear their hysterical laughter as he ran through the bushes to be confronted by Black Jack.

'How did you do it, Walsh? How did you pick it up?'

'I don't know.'

'If you're hiding something from me, some sort of secret, I'll find out, and then there'll be hell to pay.'

'There's no secret.'

'If there is, I'll learn about it soon enough. I can wait. I have all eternity.'

Timmy sank down into the grass. He would have much to tell Elizabeth come morning.

———

There was great confusion and shouting the next day when the workmen discovered the remains of the fire. By nightfall a small cabin had been placed at the end of the building site. When work finished for the day, a machine drove up and a man got out. He wore a uniform with a peaked cap that reminded the children of the officers they had seen in the workhouse. He went inside the cabin and immediately it lit up. He came back out and went to his machine. Doors on its back opened and two large dogs leapt out.

The children jumped about with excitement at the prospect of new playmates. Elizabeth had to stop them from running forward to embrace the animals, whose huge mouths and sharp teeth could have easily snapped their thin bodies in two. Instead she made them wait as a chain was hooked to each of the dog's collars and the man began to walk them around the site.

Black Jack went right up to the animals and was delighted by their reaction. They snarled and growled, their hair standing straight, eyes wide with fear, as they backed away, dragging the man with them.

'Butch, Sandy, what's wrong?' He spoke firmly, his eyes scanning the field for whatever was upsetting them. Black Jack stood inches away from him, laughing. Then, turning to the dogs, he stamped his foot at them. Instantly they cowered and the man had to drag them on their bellies back to the cabin. They almost knocked him over in their haste to get inside. The children ran to the windows to see what was happening. Both dogs were hiding under a table and no amount of coaxing from the man would get them to come out. After a while he gave up and took to patrolling the site alone.

Black Jack had grown bored with tormenting the dogs and walked back to the graveyard. He would have to think about this. The dogs could see him, but not the man. He stood behind the bushes and watched as the children went inside. He heard them talking softly and petting the animals. Soon they came out, closely followed by the dogs whose eyes darted furtively around the site as they sniffed the air. When they realised there was nothing to fear, they lay down and allowed the children to rub and hug them. The animals licked at the ravished hands and faces as though they were living, breathing children.

Black Jack didn't understand. Why weren't the animals afraid of them? He studied the children's hands as they glided over the soft hair, wondered as they picked up small sticks and threw them for the dogs to fetch. He tried to pick up a twig time and time again, but was unable to. There had to be a way. Groaning with anger and frustration, he brushed at a moth that fluttered by his face. His hand came in contact with the soft wings and the moth fell injured at his feet. He had touched it. Without even trying, he had touched it. Kneeling down, he ran his fingers lightly over the injured insect. He could feel its wings soft as gossamer beneath his fingers, feel its tiny heart throbbing in terror. He allowed his hand to glide over the twig and gasped as it appeared between his fingers.

Timmy and Elizabeth watched as Black Jack stood, triumphant, and crushed the moth with his foot. He had just learned what they had known from the start. They belonged to the soil, were one with the air and could become part of anything they chose. For the next few hours he roamed the graveyard picking up whatever he found lying about, growing bolder and more confident with each new action. He threw stones against the trunk of the trees and revelled in the small thunking noise their contact made.

Elizabeth called to the children and they came running. It was best that they should not witness this, and she had seen quite enough. Squealing children flew through the bushes, closely followed by the dogs. She could hear their owner calling, but they paid no heed.

'Look, Elizabeth,' Katie ran up to her, 'we've got doggies.'

'Yes, indeed,' she laughed at the dogs sniffing around her and Timmy.

'Watch this,' one of the boys climbed on a dog's back. 'See, they're almost as big as a pony.'

The other children clapped and screamed with laughter as he rode up and down the field.

'Well, well, what have we got here?' Black Jack asked.

Instantly the dogs' behaviour changed. They cowered down, stiffening and whimpering.

'Doggies, look!' Katie was too caught up in the excitement to be worried about him. But the others were already backing away, crowding around Elizabeth.

'So I see,' his smile at the child was one of pure malice. 'May I stroke them?'

'Oh, yes, do,' Katie smiled.

'Katie, come here.' Elizabeth held out her hand, and with just a backward glance, the child ran to her.

The sighing in the trees became louder and the wind whipped against them as Black Jack knelt down and buried his hands in the hair of one of the dogs. The terrified animal whimpered, its cries mingling with those circling the air. From outside the boundary hedge they could hear the dogs' master calling to them, trying to be heard above the noise of the wind.

The creatures drew courage from his voice, baring their teeth and emitting menacing growls. He had taught them to stand and fight when need be, but they had never faced anything as evil as this.

'Butch, Sandy, where are you?'

Elizabeth tried to tear her eyes away from those of the animals, tried to call out to the man from the living world, but it was useless. Black Jack, who had been momentarily startled by the man's voice, turned back to his game. He looked up at Elizabeth, winked, and broke the dog's neck.

The sighing had turned to a scream.

'No!' Timmy ran towards Black Jack, as the sound of snapping bones still hung in the air. Black Jack knocked him aside as easily as he had the moth.

The children cried and covered their ears against the screams around them. The other dog lay frozen, awaiting its fate. Its whimpering sounded childlike. Elizabeth noticed that the hair beneath the eye nearest to her was matted and wet. The dog was crying. Black Jack turned to finish his dire task. Timmy jumped on his back, beating him with his fist, but Black Jack easily shook him off. It lasted for an instant, but it gave Elizabeth time to act.

'Let's save the dog,' she called, running forward and throwing herself at Black Jack, who was knocked on his back by the suddenness of her action. At once the children were all over him, biting, scratching, and pulling his hair.

'Get the dog away,' Elizabeth called to Timmy.

Dragging the terrified animal over to the bushes Timmy pushed him through.

Once outside the graveyard, the animal took flight and ran back to its owner, who would spend the rest of the night comforting it and calling for its mate. The screaming of the wind ceased.

When they realised the dog was safe, the children drew back from Black Jack, who was covered in teeth and nail marks. He sat rubbing his wounds and swearing. 'I'll get the other dog, mark my words.'

'Do that,' Timmy warned him, 'and we'll get you.'

Black Jack watched as they sank down into the grass. The children lay clustered around Elizabeth. The smaller ones sniffled and sobbed over the dog's death, while the older ones tried to cheer them.

'Did you see Black Jack's face when I bit him on the ankle?' asked one. 'I think I pulled his nose off,' offered another. But secretly they were all afraid, and glad when the dark veil of earth covered them.

'I'll stay behind and bury him,' Timmy whispered to Elizabeth. 'It's best that the dog be gone when the children awake.'

'You're a good boy, Timmy Walsh. I hope you know that.'

'And you're a good woman, Lady Elizabeth Fitzwilliam,' he replied with a grin. She smiled at his cheekiness and closed her eyes, wondering if there was anything worse than the fear of the unknown?

FIVE

May 1845

Lying fearfully in her bed in Maycroft, Elizabeth was pondering the same thought. Each day now held new terrors for her. During the week someone had tried several times to open her bedroom door. She had taken to locking it and the nursery door, since Charles had dismissed the nanny as a needless expense.

At night she watched the door handle from her bed as it slowly, soundlessly, turned and held for a moment, until the unseen hand allowed it to fall back into place. Sometimes she crept to the door and listened to the heavy, unsteady breathing.

In daylight Charles had gone no further than to leer at her and make crude suggestions, but she knew it was only a matter of time until things got out of hand. That morning she had found him in the nursery talking to Lucy, admiring her waist-length hair, while the child stood blushing. She looked delighted that her uncle was finally paying attention to her and unaware of how threatening his behaviour was. He smiled on seeing Elizabeth and remarked on how lovely Lucy was and quite the young woman. It had taken every ounce of her strength to give him a civil answer, before hurrying her daughter away from his wanton gaze.

There was nothing else for it, she decided, but to go to her father and beg for his protection. After all, John had been generous to him when he was alive. Surely he could find it in his heart to give them shelter? Her eyes felt sore from unshed tears, but she knew that if she started to cry now, she would never stop.

Charles was in better humour when she went down to breakfast. She had no idea of his plans to attend a card game that night, but just thanked God for whatever it was had cheered him. He had rigorously cut back on the number of staff. A house the size of Maycroft needed at least sixteen servants, but the new owner had decided they would manage on just two, so Elizabeth was now in sole charge of the children's washing and ironing. Only Thomas and Annie, the cook, remained. At least her days passed much quicker now that she had also taken over the duties of governess. In Charles' opinion, girls did not need a formal education, because the only skills required of them were in the ballroom and the bedroom.

Elizabeth's daughters were delighted that they were to visit their grandfather, as it was an excuse to get away from their books. They walked the two miles to his house.

Her father's farmyard was very busy, as heaps of tubers, the seed potatoes to be planted, filled cart after cart. She failed to recognise at least three of the casual labourers hired for the planting, but her father's full-time men, Jim and Matt, saluted her and Mick called out to her as always, 'Hello there, Miss Lizzy.'

She smiled, the others had taken to calling her your ladyship, but she would always be Miss Lizzy to him.

'Hello, Mick.'

She hitched up her skirts and ordered the girls to do the same. While they carefully picked their way across the yard to the house, she went over to Mick.

'How are you, Mick?' She smiled into the familiar weather-beaten face.

'Sad times for you, Miss Lizzy.' It was a statement, not a question.

'Yes, indeed, Mick, sad times.'

'Himself is inside, and there's no telling as to his humour.'

'Thank you, I'll go right in. Say a prayer for me.'

'Always, girl, always.'

Mick watched as she walked towards the open door and was swallowed up by the darkness of the hallway. He knew she was there to ask for help, having seen it coming ever since he'd run into that Fitzwilliam in one of the local taverns.

Elizabeth found her father at the kitchen table with his granddaughters sitting around him in silence. He looked up on Elizabeth's arrival, but there was no word of welcome, no smile to soften the hardness in his eyes.

'Hello, Father, I trust I find you in good health?'

'Well enough, and too busy to receive visitors.'

'I can see that, Father. I just wanted a word with you in private. It will only take a moment.' She nodded to Lucy, who took this as her cue to take her sisters outside. When they were safely out of earshot she said, 'I need your help.'

He held up a hand.

'If this help, as you call it, means taking you and your young ones in, you know where I stand. I've enough to do without having four more mouths to feed.'

'But you're doing well, Father. I saw three more labourers in the yard, and there's a room lying empty at the top of the house. We won't take up much space and I can help in the house.'

'Mrs Riordan sees to all that.' The daily help, if the rumours were to be believed, was far more than a housekeeper.

'Then you could get rid of her. Save that wage.'

'I'll not get rid of her, indeed! I thought I was rid of you, and now you want to come back and with three more along with you! I'm not having you back here. Haven't you a grand roof over your heads as it is? You don't like your new master? Well, get used to it, my girl. There's better than you have had to.' He was red with anger.

'He comes to my room at night, Father, tries to open the door.' She felt so mortified at having to speak to her father of such things.

'And?'

'He tries to come in.'

'Well let him in and maybe he'll treat you better.'

'Are you saying I should sell myself for a place to live, Father? Would you make a whore out of your only child?'

'Enough,' he banged the table with his fist. 'You've said enough, madam.'

'I've only started! My husband was good to you while he lived. It was he who gave you the horses that pull your plough.'

'All that's in the past; no good can come from bringing the dead into it. Your husband can't help you now. Go on your way and don't trouble me again.'

'You have my word on that,' she said, shaking with temper. 'I'll never see you again.'

'Good.'

The children were looking at the spring lambs when she called to them. Without waiting, she walked through the yard gate and out onto the track that would lead her back to Maycroft. Catching Mick's eye, she shook her head and turned away, afraid he would see the tears.

The children were breathless when they finally caught up with her.

'Did it not go well with grandfather?' Lucy asked.

Elizabeth drew her close.

'I asked if we could come and live with him, but he refused.'

'Has Uncle Charles asked us to leave?'

'No, it's just that I've been unsettled since your father died. I'd prefer to find a place of our own, one without so many memories.'

'You don't like Uncle Charles do you, Mamma?'

'Well, it's not that I don't like him,' she lied. 'We have different ideas and tastes and it is difficult to live with someone with whom you have nothing in common.'

'I don't like him either. I know you think I'm still a child, but I'm not really. I hate the way he looks at me. I always feel he's going to bite me.'

Becky and Charlotte came running past, shouting at their sister to play with them.

'We must look out for one another from now on,' Elizabeth said.

'Yes, Mamma.'

They walked back to the Hall an arm around each other's waist, and for the first time in weeks, Elizabeth did not feel quite so alone.

———

It was well into May and as yet there was no sign of summer. It rained for days on end and the children had begun to behave like caged animals, fighting and arguing all the time. Their noise brought Charles bellowing from his study on a number of occasions. Elizabeth was spending most of her time in the nursery and was unaware of his many visits to the stables. She was thankful that he stayed out each night until almost dawn and returned too tired to pay her any unwelcome visits.

———

For Charles the past few weeks of gambling were beginning to tell financially as well as physically. Carey and his fellow players might be having a run of luck, but he assured himself, it was only a matter of time until his turn came. In the meantime his coffers needed replenishing. With an estate the size of Maycroft, there must be many ways of doing this. He would send for Ryan, the estate manager and set him the task. Feeling very sorry for himself, he drank almost a decanter of whiskey.

SIX

Endless days of rain were bad enough, but it was the cold and damp that bothered Timmy's mother most. She needed to keep a fire going constantly and this used up most of the turf. Since her husband was working in the fields and Timmy in the stables, it was up to her to cut more in the bog. Turf-cutting mostly depended on the weather. In dry weather the turf was at least clean. Now, with the constant rain, it was proving to be a nightmare.

Her back had been bad since the birth of Rose, a breech that had almost cost her life. She had paid a high price for her labour, taking weeks to recover. Weeks when her husband shouted at her to get up from the bed, berating her for what he saw as laziness. It was loss of blood that kept her there, and the pain that shot like fire along her lower back. Even afterwards, when he turned to her at night and she begged to be left alone, he paid no heed. Four children to feed and he still only cared for his own needs. The priests were worse for filling men's heads with their nonsense. Increase and multiply, fill the earth. Aye, the men took them at their word.

She had gone to see Father O'Reilly once, begged him to speak to Pat for the sake of her health and that of the children. Instead, he berated her and sent her away with her head bowed in what he though was disgrace, but was, in fact, despair.

'Where there's life there's hope, woman. Go home and do your duty as a wife and, if that means you're to bear more children, then so be it. It's God's will, and he will see you through.'

See her through, she thought, as she heaved the old wicker basket over her shoulder. He was taking his time.

Peter carried the spade as he walked beside her. They would have to make at least ten trips before there was enough turf to last the week. The rain had turned the bog into a soggy, puddle-dotted, swamp. The spade sliced through easily enough, but it was hoisting the water-logged peat that hurt the most. Each sod seemed to weigh a ton as she tore it from the earth, and her sweat mingled with the rain, so that she was soaked through within minutes. Twice during the day, she slipped and fell in the mud, wrenching and pulling her back. She had to lie breathless and allow waves of pain to wash over her until, finally, she was once again able to stand. Peter tried to do as much of the digging as possible, but the spade was too big for his hands and he was more of a hindrance than a help.

It was late evening when they collected the last load and she was glad of the pelting rain. At least the child could not see the tears that ran down her cheeks, making tracks through the dirt on her face. She knew that there would be four hungry mouths waiting at the cabin when they got there. Despite three of them working, there was little left to spend each week on food. They put aside a large amount for rent, more for seeds, and Pat drank what she didn't manage to get from him. It was only by going through his pockets when he fell into a drunken stupor, that she got the odd shilling or sixpence. He never mentioned its loss to her, imagining that it had fallen from his pocket in the tavern.

Was it a wonder so many men drank, working all the hours God sent and for what? A cabin that is no more than a hovel, hoards of hungry children to feed and growing old before their time. And if they did manage to scrimp and save, what could they ever hope to buy, to own? The gentry made sure that land was out of their reach. A Catholic owning land, and maybe doing as well as them!

But, to hear the priests tell it, they were blessed; theirs was the One True Faith. Hungry men, women and children filled the pews each week and listened to the words that kept them downtrodden. Work hard, they preached, have more children, honour God, but fear him more. Fear him more? She almost laughed. She feared everything. She feared the coming of each day, feared the look of want in her children and the knowledge that it would only get worse. It was lucky that the women of Ireland did not take to the bottle, for then the country would surely collapse.

Once inside she dropped the heavy basket and got Peter out of his wet clothes. She took the blanket off one of the beds and wrapped it around his shivering body. She wiped at his hair with a piece of cloth to remove as much of the rainwater as she could, unaware of the sodden skirt clinging to her legs. Peter, as usual, was ravenous and wolfed down the four potatoes Timmy put in front of him, along with a bowl of buttermilk.

Her husband sat coldly watching without saying a word. It was only when Timmy took the last basket of turf to the pile in the corner and upended it onto the growing mound that he finally spoke.

'That stuff is so wet, you'll be lucky if it dries enough to burn.'

Peter stopped eating for a minute to stare at his father, Timmy stood with one leg on the turf pile in stony silence, and their mother, who was holding out her steaming skirt in front of the fire, just glared at him. It was probably the hatred in her eyes that sent him away to bed without another word.

She had to bite her bottom lip to stop herself crying again. What would it cost him to say something kind? Even one small word could help to lighten the darkness for her and the children.

Timmy laid a hand on her shoulder. 'Ma, sit down. I'll make you some tea. That'll warm you up in no time.'

She allowed him to lead her to the chair and watched as he set about mashing the old tea-leaves, trying to beat some flavour from the damp, black clump, before pouring steaming water over them.

'There's to be a killing up at the Hall tomorrow,' he told her. 'The herdsman said I should bring a sack, and maybe there'll be some offal and bones left over.' He hadn't meant to tell her, wanting it to be a surprise, but he was glad that he did, when the sadness faded from her eyes. Bones meant beef broth and nourishment for them all, especially the younger ones. He handed her the cup and she gazed down into the weak, amber liquid, sighing.

'Aye that would be grand, lad, a sup of beef tea would drive the cold from all our bones.'

Peter's head drooped as he nodded off from the heat of the fire. She motioned to Timmy to help him to bed. After he had done so he came back and knelt before her. 'Will you try and eat something, Ma, just a bit of bread?'

'No, son, I'm tired out, and I don't want to waste it. You can take some of it to work with you tomorrow. Lord, but I'm tired,' she whispered into the flames.

Timmy reached up and felt her forehead.

'Ah, I'm all right, son,' she stroked his cheek. 'Just old and tired, that's all.'

But Timmy was worried. He knew that his mother wasn't old. She was about the same age as Martin's mother, a plump and jolly woman.

His mother was thin and sick-looking, and rarely smiled. He wanted to ask her so many questions. Why, with the three of them working, was there so little to eat? Perhaps he already knew the answer. Wasn't it plain to see in the fine trap and horses that Mick Dwyer, the local tavern owner, drove? Profiting from the weakness of the men, many said, and Timmy knew it was true in their case. Sometimes he wished his family were like Martin's. There were many times, when he called in to see his friend on the way home from work, that he was greeted with a cup of tea and a hot bit of griddlecake with the butter dripping off it. He'd sit around the table with Martin and his mother, and tell them all the latest gossip from the Hall. They would listen wide-eyed in wonder to the stories about the gentry and Martin's mother would refill his cup and cut him another slice of cake, as she urged him to tell her more. His favourite time of all was being there when Martin's father came home. Tired from a day of casual toiling he would still come smiling through the door.

'God bless all here,' he'd call and be greeted by his wife and a flurry of children. On seeing Timmy, he'd ruffle his hair. 'And how's the big man? Still keeping that Hall in running order are you?' Timmy would laugh and say he was only a stable boy, but Martin's father would have none of it. 'Go on with you, I heard you run that place single-handed. They say it would go to rack and ruin without you.'

Before he sat, Martin's father put what he had earned that day into an old china teapot on the mantelpiece. 'That will see us through another day, Maisie,' he'd wink at Martin's mother, and Timmy would feel himself grow warm inside with the look she gave her husband. There was no hatred in her eyes, just the proud look of a woman well thought of by the man she loved. Now looking at his mother and remembering this, brought tears to Timmy's eyes. His mother noticed and pulled him towards her. She smelt damp and the hand that stroked his face was rough and bumpy with calluses, but it was his mother's hand.

'I'm fine, son. You're not to worry.'

She had mistaken his tear-filled eyes for worry about her, and worried he was. No matter what it took, if it meant going down on his knees, he would get the unwanted offal and bones from the herdsman the next day. 'You'll have to get out of these wet clothes, Ma,' he whispered. 'You'll catch your death.'

'I'll do that, son, I've a shift hanging on the back of the door. I'll put that on and hang these in front of the fire. They'll be dry come morning.'

'I'll go to bed.' He got up knowing she needed her privacy and sorry that, for the first time in over a year, there would be no reading that night. Just before he left the room, a thought crossed his mind, and he stopped and turned around. She thought he had gone and was peeling off the wet clothes. Her back was towards him and he was aghast at how thin she really was. He could have counted every bone in her back, and her once snow-white skin was covered with large yellow and black bruises. How had she come by these? His father hadn't beaten her of late. She tugged at the piece of rag that tied up her hair and pulled it free. Her hair tumbled past her waist, reddish-brown in the light of the fire. Just for a moment, he was able to imagine how beautiful she had once been.

Timmy crept into bed and lay down beside the others. Only then he remembered what he had meant to say to her ... it was that the rain would stop soon and the bushes and shrubs would be filled with wool. There had been so many new lambs born that year that, at times, it looked as though it had snowed on the fields. They could gather the wool in the evenings after work, and Martin's mother would let her use the spinning wheel. They would have lots of wool and his mother could make them all new jumpers and a shawl for herself. That was what he had wanted to tell her and she would have smiled.

SEVEN

The rain did eventually stop, but it was a very poor summer that year. Things went from bad to worse at the Hall. Charles Fitzwilliam had been spending even more time in the company of Black Jack and his friends, losing heavily. His gambling debts were now in the thousands. Carey laughed it off, and let him sign ever more promissory notes. After all, he regularly assured Charles, what was a few thousand between friends?

As his debts grew, Charles' drinking increased, until the wine merchant's account was outstanding to such an extent, that he refused to supply the Hall until it was settled. Charles had sold many fine paintings and priceless heirlooms were occasionally dispatched to Dublin for a few hundred pounds. The family silver shared this fate. He had descended to such a muddled state that he no longer knew what assets he had left.

When Elizabeth realised this, though it went against all her beliefs, she started to steal little trinkets, silver snuffboxes and ivory miniatures that she knew he would not miss. On her rare trips to town, she sold these to a jeweller known for his discretion. She got only about a tenth of what they were worth, but she was saving as much as she could. Charles' moods and outbursts were becoming worse, and twice she had to stop him from hitting the children. Lucy had grown out of almost all her dresses, but Charles refused to buy her more. Elizabeth spent days cutting and sewing some of her own things to fit the girl. The children's education was suffering too, but she just didn't have the heart to teach.

August was almost out and the few fine days they had were heavy and humid. Faint breezes did nothing to dispel the stifling heat that hung about the rooms like heavy curtains. The place had been in an uproar all day. Ger Ryan, the farm manager, had been in to complain that things were not as they should be.

Charles had completely neglected to buy seeds and new equipment. He refused to buy in any new stock. After the sale of the spring lambs and most of the ewes, there would be very little to sell the next year. But he wasn't interested in next year, she heard him yell at Ryan, nor the year after that.

'You're the damned manager!' he'd roared. 'So manage. Now get out.'

Elizabeth watched as Ryan came out of the study and knew from the man's expression that if Charles didn't mend his ways, it would be disastrous.

She was surprised to receive a summons to his study later that day. They had taken to avoiding each other and speaking only when necessary. He still made the odd attempt on her bedroom doorknob, but other than that he left her alone. She walked tentatively toward the door and knocked.

'Enter.'

'You wished to see me, Charles?'

'Yes, yes,' he waved her to a chair and she perched herself on the edge of it. 'I want you to organise a small dinner party for me. There will be just four of us dining, unless you would care to join us?'

She did not reply.

'No?'

Her silence said it all.

'I thought not.'

'Is this dinner party to be attended by anyone I know?' she asked, hoping he had made friends with the local gentry.

'Yes, as a matter of fact. I believe you may be acquainted with one of the gentlemen. We shall wait and see.'

'Very well, when is this party to be?' She wasn't sure what they had in the larder.

'Tonight.'

'Tonight!'

'Is that a problem? After all, that's why I keep you here. You're no use to me if you can't even arrange a small gathering.'

'No, Charles, it's not a problem. I'm sure I'll find something for Annie to prepare.'

'Nothing too fancy, mind,' he called after her.

Elizabeth rushed to the kitchen and told Annie the news. There was a lot of head-shaking and sighing, before they finally decided on a beef broth with veal pie for the main course, and some cheese and biscuits for after. They were limited to what could be grown or killed on the farm, because Charles had not paid the grocer's bills either. Elizabeth helped Thomas and Annie to prepare the food, and it was almost eight o'clock before they were ready. She emerged from the kitchen flushed from the heat and was about to go to wash when Charles called to her.

'You'd better hurry and change,' he said, pleased by her surprised expression. 'I've decided you are to join us after all.'

'Yes, Charles,' she nodded and went upstairs. Any argument would be futile. While she was dressing, she heard the main door open and the sound of loud voices from the hallway. She smiled at Lucy, who was doing her hair, twisting and curling until she was pleased with the results.

Elizabeth had chosen a pale blue, lace dress with a scooped neck-line that wasn't too revealing, and would not give Charles any reason to make rude remarks. Around her neck she fastened a single sapphire on a gold chain and clipped on matching earrings. This was all the jewellery she had left besides her wedding ring and a gold locket with a picture of John and herself. Everything else had been sold. This set had been his engagement gift.

'You look lovely,' said Lucy, looking her over from head to toe.

'Do I?' Elizabeth smiled, realising she no longer thought about how she looked. There was very little reason to care since John's death. Before going downstairs, she ordered the girls to lock their door and the connecting one to her room; she was taking no chances.

She stopped for a moment outside the dining-room and forced a smile that she hoped looked welcoming. When she opened the door and saw who the guests were, she almost fainted. Charles sat at the head of the table. On his left there were two rough-looking men she had never seen before, but it was the man sitting on his right who shocked her most. Black Jack sat smiling smugly at her, and she almost fell into the chair that the butler held out for her. None of the men had stood up when she entered.

'Well now, isn't this pleasant?' Charles laughed. 'I believe you know Jack Carey here,' he tapped Carey playfully on the arm.

'Yes, of course,' she managed to find her voice. 'Good evening Mr Carey.'

'And a good evening to you, your ladyship,' he gave a mocking bow from his seated position.

'These other scamps are Willie Ryan and Tommy Cusack.'

The men acknowledged her respectfully, and she could see they too were uncomfortable in her presence and the unfamiliar surroundings.

When Thomas served the meal, she picked at the food and tried not to listen to the conversation at the other end of the table. These men were rough and coarse and Charles sounded as though he belonged in their company. The jokes were filthy and intermingled with swear words. Charles glanced at her occasionally and appeared pleased to see her blushing. Bottle followed bottle and, as the drink took effect, Black Jack stared at her, refusing to look away, even when she glared at him. Charles dismissed Thomas once the coffee had been served and she panicked when she realised that she would be left alone with them.

'Perhaps I should retire too, Charles, to allow you gentlemen some time to yourselves.'

'Not at all, my dear. I insist you stay, if not for your brilliant conversational skills, then for your ornamental value.'

Her cheeks blazed in mortification and she knew that Carey was laughing at her. She let her mind wander to block out their words, and was unaware that Charles was speaking to her until he raised his voice.

'Elizabeth, are you listening to me?'

She looked up, startled, 'I'm sorry, Charles.'

'I merely asked that you earn your keep by refilling our glasses.' He pointed to his empty glass, and to the one that Black Jack was twiddling between his fingers. The delicate stem looked even more fragile in his huge hands.

'Should I call the butler?'

'No, I told you to do it.'

'Very well,' she replied, walking to the sideboard. She picked up the decanter and offered it first to the two men nearest to her. They thanked her, but refused. As she refilled his glass, Charles winked at her. She walked around to where Carey was sitting and leaned over to fill his. Her hand shook at the thought of serving him and how he would boast about it the next day to all and sundry, her ladyship being reduced to no more than a serving wench.

'That's a very nice dress you're wearing, my lady.'

She looked at him in surprise.

'But it's what's in it, that interests me more.'

Before she could retort to such brazen words, she was shocked to feel his hand move up and pat her bottom.

'How dare you!' She hit Carey in the face with the decanter and watched in horror as the flesh opened and blood gushed from a wound on his cheek. For a moment no one spoke.

Elizabeth ran. Behind her chairs were knocked over, and she was not sure if the men were following her, or rushing to Carey's aid.

'Come back here!' Charles bellowed, but she kept running. She took the stairs two at a time and ran to her room. Locking the door behind her, she threw herself down on the bed, sobbing. She'd really done it this time.

After what seemed like hours, she drifted into a troubled sleep, and was surprised when Lucy shook her awake. It was morning.

'Mamma, you're still in your evening dress.'

Elizabeth sat up and looked down at the dress in a daze.

'Has Uncle Charles gone out?' she grabbed Lucy's arm.

'Ouch, Mamma, you're hurting me.'

'I'm sorry, I didn't mean to be so rough. Just tell me, has he gone out?'

'I'm not sure. Did you have another argument with him?'

'Yes,' Elizabeth whispered, 'and it was a bad one this time.'

'What are we to do?' Lucy sat beside her. 'Will he throw us out?'

'He may well do. We'll just have to wait and see.'

Elizabeth stayed in her room all morning refusing to eat, afraid she would be sick. It was late afternoon when he sent for her. There was no going back now, but she wasn't going without a fight.

Charles was stretched on a couch in the drawing-room. 'Well, well, well,' he laughed. 'So the cat has claws.'

'What do you want, Charles?'

'What I want, m'lady, is that you and your children vacate my house.' He got up quickly, but had to sit again, as the effects of the previous night's drinking caught up with him.

'It was our house before it was yours, Charles, but the way you're going, it won't belong to any of us for much longer.'

'What do you mean?'

'You know exactly what I mean. You owe money to everyone in the town. There is not a grocer or wine merchant who will supply us. The farm is gone to rack and ruin. Look at this room,' she waved her hand at the patches on the walls, where paintings had once hung. 'The house has become a ghost, a shadow of its former self; there's nothing left worth selling.'

His face, already flushed from drinking, was purple in anger. 'I'll remind you, madam, that it was only through the greatest kindness that I left you and those, those ...' he pointed to the ceiling, unable to think properly.

'Children,' she screamed at him. 'They're called children, and like it or not you are of the same blood. And don't you dare speak to me of kindness. From the day you entered this house you made our lives hell. You are not a scrap on your brother. He would never have treated a woman in such a disgraceful and demeaning way.'

'My damned brother! That's all I've heard since I got here. Well, I'm sick of it, do you hear me? Once I'm rid of you, I'll no longer have to hear about what a saint he was!' He was dribbling and had lost all self-control. 'I have one thing that he can't have, and that is life. He's dead, Elizabeth, rotting in the ground even as we speak, and I'm glad he's there. I hope he rots in hell.'

She hit him and he fell back, stunned by the blow.

'You have two weeks to find somewhere else to live. After that, I never want to see you or your wretched children again. Do I make myself clear?'

'Perfectly.'

'We'll see how clever you'll be then, madam. Even your own father refuses to have you under his roof!' He delighted in her expression of shock. 'Yes, indeed, I've known for some time.'

'I'll find a place to stay. Anywhere would be preferable to living here, and being degraded the way I was last night. Only a beast would stand by and allow that to happen. You should be ashamed of yourself.' She turned and walked out.

'Remember,' he called after her, 'two weeks, and take only your clothes, nothing else.'

Her stomach was churning as she walked up to the nursery. Where could she go? Whatever money she had managed to save would not last very long and what then? They were almost into September and, if the summer was anything to go by, the winter would be a bad one. She had little time to plan, but she would not let the girls see how worried she was.

EIGHT

The walk to work seemed longer than usual for Timmy. He had slept badly after waking during the night to the sound of crying. He sat up, unsure of what he was hearing, and tried to isolate the sound above the thunderous snores of his father. No, he had been right, it was the sound of someone crying. At first he was afraid and looked over to where his parents were sleeping, trying to make out, in the darkness, if they were both there. It was impossible to see, so he got up and crept over to the door. It came again a sad, mournful sound that chilled him to the bone. Could it be his mother crying? He had never seen her do so in all his twelve years. Even when his father beat her, she refused to cry. He edged his way farther through the doorway and peeped into the kitchen. Only the dying embers of the fire lit the room, but he could make out her shape huddled up in the chair with her head in her hands and crying as though her heart would break.

'Ma?'

'Timmy, lad, I'm sorry. Did I wake you? Oh, I'm so sorry.' She put her head down and the crying started again.

'Ma, what is it, what's wrong?' He shivered in the cold, pre-dawn air. 'Ma, tell me.'

'I'm frightened child, so frightened.' Her hands muffled the words.

'Why, Ma, why?'

She must have heard the panic in his voice, for she sat up and bought the back of her hand across her face, wiping away the tears.

She put her arms around his shoulders and pulled him towards her. 'Listen to me, child, and mind you listen well. I'd never for all the world want to frighten you. You know that, don't you?'

He nodded.

'But there's something bad about to happen. I don't know what it is, but it frightens me. I feel as though I've lost you all. That my children are gone from me.'

'No, Ma, we'll never leave you.'

'Ah, child,' she kissed his forehead. 'I'm not afraid of you leaving me. You'll do that anyway in time, but there's a force greater than anything I've ever felt abroad tonight.'

Timmy knew his mother had always been fey, it was as though she could see the future. Stupid old wives' tales, his father called them, but she was always right in her predictions.

'I have four children,' she continued. 'All as healthy as the times allow and of the four, you were the only one who was in a hurry to get here. You came from my womb crying lustily and with clenched fists ready to take on the world. So I'm telling you this, child. If all around you are dying you must stay alive to take care of the other children. Promise me that you'll live.'

'I promise Ma, but I don't understand. I'm only twelve. Why would I die?'

'Because I heard it today, as clear and sharp as the death-knell.'

'What did you hear?'

'The wind, child, the wind called my name. You know how it was today with the gusts so sharp and cutting. From early morning it beat itself against the door and I knew that it would be a cold night. So, late this afternoon, I went to gather dry kindling. As I walked about the fields I heard it. At first I wasn't sure, I had to stop and listen, and then it came again. It was a voice I knew, a well-loved voice that has long been silent and had come to warn me.'

She said no more, and he lay there for a while with his head on her breast, listening to the beating of her heart, until the cold got to them and she sent him to bed. 'You'll remember my words, won't you, child, remember what I've asked of you?'

'I'll not forget Ma, I'll do as you ask.'

Had her powers of prediction been greater, she would never have asked of him the thing she did.

———·——

He noticed the strange smell on his way to work the next morning. It seemed to be all around him. He stopped and sniffed the still air; he had never smelt anything like it before – it was really bad, putrid. It followed him all the way to the Hall.

The stable-yard was unusually quiet and he could hear murmuring coming from the door leading into the kitchen. He wanted to go and ask what was happening, but was afraid that Black Jack might be there and his curiosity would earn him a clip across the ear.

As he walked towards the kitchen door, the voices inside grew louder, but they made no sense, just a droning. Then he realised that they were praying. His heart thudded as he edged his way down the hallway and into the big room. Everyone was there. The few farm hands that were left, Mr Ryan the estate manager and even the butler, who in normal times would have shooed him away, took no notice of him. Some of them held rosary beads, which clacked together as they passed them through their fingers. Someone must have died, he thought, perhaps it was the master. He hoped it wasn't her ladyship or one of the children.

Annie was crying and some of the men seemed near to tears as well. They would hardly be crying if it were the master. He waited with head bowed in reverence for the prayers to end, but when they did, no one spoke for a few moments. With some effort Annie stood and went to the range, filling the large black teapot with boiling water. He watched her place extra cups on the table and fill each one with the blackest tea he had ever seen. The farm hands sat down at the big wooden table as though born to it, and he moved slowly over as one of them beckoned him to sit. He took the cup and sipped the scalding liquid, all the while watching the others. There was a plate of bread and butter in the middle of the table, but no one moved to take any of it. He was hungry, as always, and would have loved some. The old man sitting next to him reached over, took a slice and handed it to him as though reading his thoughts.

'I dare say you'll eat that, lad.'

'Thank you.' Timmy took the bread and bit into the thick crust.

Still no one spoke, and his curiosity finally got the better of him.

'Who's dead?' The whisper seemed like a shout in the quiet of the kitchen and they all turned and looked at him.

'Ireland, lad,' the old man said. 'It's Mother Ireland that's dying. Can't you smell it in the air around us?'

They all murmured in agreement, and went quiet again, until Mr Ryan spoke.

'You're all to go home.'

The men began to rise and Timmy, unsure of what to do, asked, 'Me, sir, should I go too?'

'Yes, lad,' Mr Ryan stopped and ruffled his hair, 'you go too.'

Timmy was delighted, although the old man's words were strange and everyone was so miserable. He had been given his first day off work.

It wasn't until he was clear of the Hall and getting near to the cabins that haphazardly dotted his world, that Timmy stopped smiling. The smell was worse there, and from the hill where he was standing, he could see all his neighbours running into the fields where the lazy-beds were. His mother's words came back to him now and he, too, started to run. He found the cabin empty, but he knew exactly where to go.

His mother and brothers were busy digging in the plot behind the cabin, as little Rose sat watching. There was nothing sinister in this; it was the sight of his father on his knees raking the earth with his fingers that chilled his blood. His father never came in from the fields during the day. Even when his mother had been near death in childbirth, his father had refused to come. When Father O'Reilly had sent for him with the message that she could be breathing her last, he still stayed at his work. Now there he was and the sun barely up, digging with his bare hands. Without asking, Timmy took the shovel and waited to be told what to do. His mother was on her knees pulling at the stalks, and he could see her fingers bleeding from the effort.

'Ma, let me do it.'

The earth released the first group of potatoes almost gladly, and he watched as she leapt upon them and rubbed away the soil. The first one she picked did not please her and she moved on to the next. It was the same with this; it was cast aside, as she scrabbled in the dirt for another one. Timmy didn't know what to think. He reached for the potato she was holding. She was staring at it as though it was a foreign object. He almost had to prise it from her hand, and gasped in disgust, as he felt his fingers sink into its slimy, stinking softness. Standing up, he looked at the sodden mass, and for the first time realised what had happened.

'Is this it, Ma? Is this what you felt?'

'Yes, child, this is what I felt, though I never in all my life thought it would be this bad. I imagined some loss of life, but this is death for all of us.'

A shadow blocked the sun. His father was standing over them. Usually he would berate them for slacking and Timmy waited for the chastisement. But instead of his fearsome father, there was a broken human being, holding a fistful of decaying potatoes in front of him. Tears rolled down his cheeks as he looked at his wife for words of comfort, anything that could appease the terror he was feeling.

She got up, and for the first time, Timmy saw his mother take his father in her arms. 'I know, Pat, I know,' she murmured.

The potatoes were bad, but did that really matter so much? Two-thirds had already been dug up, and were still stored in the deep pits, until needed. What did it matter if some had died? More would grow next year. They could plant the good ones, and the following harvest would surely yield a better crop.

He became aware of the sounds coming from the other fields. At first it seemed like a low keening, which he had heard many times before at wakes, when the women cried for the loss of a loved one. Then it intensified in volume until it filled the air. Timmy gathered his siblings closer to him and they huddled together, listening. The keening gave way to screaming, and little Rose tried to burrow beneath his jumper in fright. His mother hurried them from the field.

Once inside the cabin, she started to light the fire, although she usually did this only when it was cold or to cook. Timmy went over to the turf pile, took some sods from it and carried them back to the fireside. She was kneeling on the hearth blowing the kindling to help it catch fire, and his hand brushed against hers as he laid the turf beside her. She felt cold and her skin was whiter than usual. His father sat in his chair and said nothing, but his eyes had a faraway, haunted look. The children were mute; they knew there was something wrong, but had no idea what it was. Placing the sods carefully on top of the kindling, she watched until she was sure they would light. Then she went to the pile of potatoes in the corner and picked out enough to feed them, carefully looking at each one as though weighing and measuring it to assess its value. She scrubbed them free of dirt, before sending Timmy to the well. He took the bucket and ran off, glad to be free of the overpowering silence. He returned quickly and his mother emptied half of the water into the large black pot. She laid the potatoes inside before finally hanging the pot on the blackened firearm and swinging it over the blaze. They all listened to the crackling of the fire and watched as flames reached up and caressed the pot's sooty bottom. His mother also watched from her chair, mesmerised by an action she had seen countless times before.

If Timmy had closed his eyes, this could be any normal day and the events of the past hours only a dream. But there was a fire lighting, when there should not have been and they were going to eat at a time when they never did. The meal was eaten in silence. When they had finished, Timmy got up and started to clear the table, but his mother stopped him.

'Be a good boy and take your brothers and sister for a walk.'

His brothers were up in a flash, but Rose was cranky. She wanted to sleep; the unexpected meal had made her content and drowsy, and she wanted to cuddle up with her mother.

'Come on, lazybones,' he teased her. 'We can go to the stream and see if there are any fish there. You'd like that, wouldn't you?'

She looked up at him doubtfully.

'Listen,' he draped an old scarf around her shoulders and knotted it beneath her chin, 'we might even see a fairy fish with golden scales and a silver tail. Wouldn't you like that?'

She smiled happily. Timmy led her outside and they started across the fields towards the stream. He made up stories about fairies and imps and faraway lands as they walked. His father said that Timmy did too much dreaming, and that he could not imagine how he found his way home at times with his head so far up in the clouds. His mother insisted there was nothing wrong with dreaming, and that some of the best things ever had started with a dream.

It seemed that many of the other parents had the same idea, as Martin called out to him to wait. He had his six siblings in tow, and Timmy could see other children walking towards them across the fields.

'So,' Martin caught up with him, 'they sent you out too?'

'Yes, they seem to be very upset by the loss of the potatoes.'

'By God,' Martin snorted, 'you'd think the world was coming to an end.'

'Did you save most of your crop?'

'Yes, that was done over a month ago. That's why I can't understand it.'

Reaching their favourite spot on the bank, they sat down. The smaller children threw stones or trailed branches in the water, while the bigger ones climbed trees and swung upside down from the branches. The older ones came and sat beside Timmy and Martin and all the questions were the same. What was going on? How did it happen? Where did it come from? They frightened each other with stories of potato rot and famine. Many had heard these words bandied about by parents, who were so out of their mind with worry, they no longer cared if the children had overheard. They all thought Timmy would have the answer. Wasn't it he who calmed their fears when they first heard the fearsome tale of the headless coachman? The dark coach, it was said, that roamed the roads by night in search of the dying. Some of the smaller ones had snivelled in fear and even the bigger ones gulped loudly.

'Comes to collect you when you're dying?' Timmy had scoffed. 'How can he see where he is going when he has no head?' He had laughed loudly at the idea, and that had shattered the tension. From then on, if something was wrong, Timmy was expected to provide the answers. But on this day he had nothing to say, he was as much in the dark as anyone. They played and talked for hours until hunger and cold sent them hurrying home.

They were greeted by the delicious smell of newly made potato cakes. There was no sign of their father, and Timmy guessed that he had gone to the tavern. Whenever there was trouble, be it sickness or shortage of money, his father always seemed to have enough for a pint and found great consolation in its depths. Their mother greeted them warmly, although her eyes still had that frightened look. She tutted and fussed over the baby, taking her to be changed in the other room. Timmy washed his hands and had to bully his brothers into doing the same. They had set the table and were sitting expectantly when she came back and placed the baby on the bench next to Timmy.

The smell of this favourite food made their stomachs rumble. Their mother smiled and cut into the first one. They could see that it was more flour than potato, but it smelled lovely. She cut it into four triangles and placed a slice before each of them. Small pieces were broken off and stuffed into impatient mouths. This was washed down with buttermilk, and when all were finished, they began to get up from the table.

'Would you like another bit?' their mother asked.

They looked at one another before sitting back down, and watched in awe as she brought the second cake and shared it out in the same way. Rose had already had enough and her second slice lay untouched when the boys had finished eating. Before his mother could offer it to them, Timmy spoke.

'Have some yourself, Ma. We're full up and it will only go to waste.' He glared at his brothers, who eyed the slice like hawks.

'Well, maybe I'll eat it later.'

'Have it now, Ma, while it's still hot,' insisted Timmy. 'I'll make you a cup of tea to go along with it.'

He swung the kettle over the fire. Rose's head was drooping, so he motioned to Tom to take her to bed and for Peter to follow. The kettle was soon boiling and he used fresh leaves to make the tea. He could hear the sound of Peter singing softly to the children, who were probably already asleep. The lullaby drifted in from the next room and his mother joined in humming. Taking the cup, he left it beside her on the hearth and placed the slice of potato cake on her lap.

'Eat it, Ma, please.'

She broke off a piece and placed it in her mouth. She just let it sit there for a while, too tired to chew and swallow.

'Come on, Ma, have another bite.'

She picked up the cup with shaking hands and brought it to her lips. Timmy noticed a crumb on her cheek and reached over to brush it away. His gentle touch opened the floodgates.

'Is it that bad, Ma?' His mother was crying for the second time in two days!

'It's worse than you could ever imagine,' she gulped between sobs. 'We're in terrible trouble. Only a miracle can help us now.'

'But, Ma, we've saved most of the potatoes. We can replant the good tubers in the spring.'

'Listen, child, you're too young to understand how bad this is, but I'll have to try and make you see.' She took a deep breath. 'What was left in the ground was meant to see us through next spring and summer, with enough left over for planting. The potatoes stored in the pits will last only until Christmas and then what? There's nothing. Nothing, but hunger awaits us.'

'What about, Nelly?' His thoughts went to the fat pig in the yard. 'We can eat her, and then there's our wages.'

'Most of the wages go on rent,' she explained, reaching out and stroking his cheek. 'There's little left over for food. Nelly will be our last resort, for your father was planning on selling her and buying two calves. He said we'd at least have some milk and cheese from them when they were older. So she'll be the last to go, you can be sure of that. But there's other families will be worse off than us, God knows.'

It sounded bad, much more serious than he had imagined. Finally he asked, 'What will happen when the potatoes run out?'

'We'll starve, child.'

He knew his mother was speaking the truth. She never lied to him and she wasn't the kind that found pleasure in frightening him. 'There'll be rabbits, Ma, and fish. There are pheasants and wild duck. Some families have chickens and geese.'

'Yes, but for how long? There won't be many birds around in the thick of winter and what rabbits there are will soon disappear. Anyway it would mean jail or worse if we were caught poaching. I dare say there will be many of the richer families that will survive, aye, and there'll be many that prosper by what misery is yet to come. But for us, child, and our kind, there'll be nothing but want.'

'It's not fair, Ma,' his eyes filled with tears. He thought of his

brothers and little sister in the next room. He was big and could mud-
dle though somehow; they were so small and already hungry at times.
And his precious mother was only skin and bone as it was … how
would she survive?

Walking to the table, he stood with his back to her, hands pressed
firmly on the rough wood. His mother must not see him like this, weak
and childlike in his fear. He tried to stifle the tears that were building
up inside him, but it was no use, they came anyway. Loud angry sobs
racked his thin frame until he thought he would be sick.

'There now, child,' he felt her arms go around him. 'Don't take on
so. Many will survive, I'll swear to that this very night. We'll find a way.
Between us, we'll keep you and your brothers and sister alive. Come,
child, sit by me and listen well.' He let her guide him back to the fire.
She pulled his father's chair over beside hers.

'As in all such times,' she continued, 'it's the strongest who survive,
and that is what we must do – make you all strong enough to fight the
hunger when it comes.'

He understood the second slice of cake now.

'Take everything that is offered to you from now on, child. Don't
turn down one morsel of food, no matter what it is.'

He thought of Martin's mother and her offer to him to call any
time he was passing. Well, she would have little to give him now.

'What about da?'

'What about him?'

'Will he still go to the tavern?'

'You be respectful when you speak of your father.'

'I didn't mean it the way it came out.'

'Ah, I know you didn't,' she said, taking his hand again. 'There will
be many changes from now on, we'll just have to wait and see. Now off
to bed with you before your father gets home and keeps us up all night
with his talk of rebellion.'

Timmy got up smiling. They knew his father was very brave when he was drunk. He laid awake thinking that sleep would never come, and wondering what tales his friends would have when they all met the next evening. He thought of how God sent down manna to His people when they were starving, and how He could turn one loaf of bread into thousands. Perhaps tomorrow there would be ten pigs in the garden instead of one and ten more the day after that. After all, God did lots of miracles. Maybe He would do one for them. It didn't have to be a big one, just enough food to stay alive.

NINE

August 2003

The murder of the dog had upset the children far more than Elizabeth could have imagined. They had become terrified of Black Jack, and the slightest look from him sent them running to her for protection. They had taken to spending more time beneath the earth, hiding. Black Jack, on the other hand, was growing stronger and bolder by the day.

The last of the houses were almost completed. Most of the builders had finished and been replaced by plumbers, electricians and landscapers. A stream of security men came and went, but no one stayed for long. Most did not last the night and the boss was completely frustrated trying to coax men into taking the job.

When the latest recruit arrived, Timmy and the others went to see what he was like. They watched him hang up his coat and unpack his bag. He placed a container and cup on the desk along with a paper-wrapped bundle. Turning to the bag, he took another parcel from it and a hammer. With this, he fixed a nail high on the wall opposite the desk. Soon a sad-eyed Christ gazed down at them. The light from inside was dazzling, and it was only when he put his coat on and came outside to do his hourly inspection that they were able to get a proper look at him. He stood in the doorway, pulling on gloves, and was almost frightened senseless to hear his name whispered.

'Paddy!'

Timmy was amazed to see it was the man called Paddy. The same man who had tried to stop the digging.

'Jesus Christ!' exclaimed Paddy.

Timmy walked slowly towards him followed by the others.

Paddy had lowered himself onto the doorstep. His first instinct had been flight, but he was not sure that his legs were capable of it. He watched the advancing group, eyes darting from the crucifix on the wall to the only weapon available, the hammer. The children stopped just feet from him and eyed him warily. For the hundredth time that night he cursed his decision to take this job. He had known of the boy-thing's existence. Had heard the stories going around about the site and yet he had felt compelled to come. As if some magnetic force was drawing him to this place, to his destiny. He wasn't a coward, far from it, but looking at the ragged group of skeletons standing before him made him quiver in terror. Raising his hand to his forehead he began to make the sign of the cross, and watched fascinated as the assembled group did the same. As suddenly as it had come, the fear left.

'There's more than one of you, then?'

The children looked at one another in wonder and the whisper went about, 'he can see us'. A girl pushed her way from the centre of the group and faced him. 'My name is Katie.'

Paddy had to remind himself again not to scream, as he looked into the sunken eyes of the dead child. From inside the cordoned-off section of the graveyard he could hear someone calling and the children reacted at once.

'Katie, come on!' the boy-thing came forward and pulled her back. They turned as one and started to walk away.

'I mean you no harm,' Paddy called after the retreating figures. He watched as they walked towards the boundary, wondered if there was a small gap in the thicket where they could get through. The light was fading and it was difficult to see, but he held his breath as he watched them disappear, one by one. Only the boy turned and looked back at him, before he too blended into the greenery.

Elizabeth listened in awe to their stories about the man who could see them. She looked at Timmy for confirmation of this and he nodded.

The children lay down in the grass and cuddled together. Timmy and Elizabeth stood listening until the chattering and laughter faded away and the earth and its darkness once again welcomed them.

'So,' she put her arm around his shoulders, 'tell me about this man.'

He told her the man's name and about how he had seen Timmy on that first day.

'Will you talk to him?' she smiled, already knowing the answer to this.

He laughed in reply.

'I thought as much. But do take care. There is still so much we don't understand.'

'I will.'

He went back towards the bushes and walked through them. Only then did she lie down in the grass and stare up into the starlit sky. There had been no sign of Black Jack all day. He was probably inside the houses or foraging around the site. He behaved like a magpie, stealing anything shiny, or whatever took his fancy.

The place that marked his grave resembled a dump with pieces of broken pipe and old rope piled in a clutter. Still, she was glad of the peace and, closing her eyes, surrendered to the dark.

Timmy crept up to the security cabin. He could see the man inside, seated at his desk. Climbing up onto the step, he peeped through the window. The man was pouring liquid from the container into the mug. Steam rose into the air, and for the first time in years, Timmy smelled the leafy aroma of tea.

'There's enough for two.'

He almost lost his footing in surprise, and waited for a moment before pushing open the door and stepping in.

'Sit down.' The man pointed to a chair beside the desk. 'I won't bite, and I hope you'll do me the same courtesy?'

'I don't bite!'

'Would you like some?' The man asked, indicating the bread and meat before him. 'I mean if you can eat. No, I mean … God, I don't know what I mean.'

Timmy noticed how his hand shook as he brought the mug to his lips. 'No, thank you. I'm not hungry, not any more.'

'Aye, well, I seem to have lost my appetite as well,' the man said, throwing the food back into its container.

'What year is this, please?' asked Timmy. He gasped at the reply. Almost two centuries had passed. He had been dead for more than a hundred and fifty years. He asked question after question of the man, who answered each one patiently. In turn, Timmy told him about his life, about Elizabeth and the other children, and finally about Black Jack. He told stories of famine days that only an eyewitness could know.

The man listened as Timmy's words tumbled from him, telling of the horrors he and the others endured, and about the fear that each day brought as they wandered in this new world, this limbo. The first fingers of light were streaking across the sky when he got up to leave. He had finished his story and wanted to be back with his own kind.

'Come again tomorrow night,' Paddy said. 'I'll bring you some books. Show you all the wonderful things that have happened since … your time.'

'Yes I will. Thank you,' Timmy called, as he melted into the early morning mist.

———

Paddy was as good as his word and arrived with armloads of books the next night. Timmy spent hours leafing through the pages and calling out in wonder at some of the things he found there. 'Could I take these to show the others?'

'Of course you can, boy. Keep them. They're yours.'

Timmy couldn't believe it. How could anyone part with such precious things as books? He accepted the gift and carried them back to the graveyard. Paddy watched him go, shaking his head in wonder. He was surprised at how easily he accepted the boy who had just the night before frightened him rigid. There was goodness about the youngster, a goodness that transcended his fearsome features. He had been right after all, in taking this job, Paddy decided as he went about his work.

———

The drug addicts returned and were disgusted to find a security man guarding the site. Still, the night was dry and they lit their fire on the opposite side of the graveyard, well hidden from prying eyes. They shared out the stash the same as before and soon all were high and feeling no pain. Each one slumped down onto the grass lost in a drug-induced fantasy world, as time slipped away from him.

'Shit, what was that?' asked one of the boys, sitting up and rubbing the back of his head. Turning onto his knees, he searched the grass. 'Wow! Cool!' he exclaimed, holding the object up for the others to see. The skull glowed in the light of the fire.

'Toss it here. Let's have a better look,' called one of the others.

The skull was passed around until it finally arrived back in the hands of its finder. 'I wonder if she gave good head?' He brought the mouth close to his crotch, shaking with laughter.

'She almost broke your head, wanker,' added someone else.

'Yeah, fuck it,' he said gruffly. He threw it hard against a tree trunk, and grinned as the force reduced the skull almost to dust.

'Hey,' one of his friends came over and leaned on his shoulder, 'it kind of reminds me of that bitch we did last night.'

Black Jack listened, as they recounted how they had broken into the home of an elderly woman and beaten her and robbed her of her savings. He found these boys to be fearless, amazing in those so young. They could be of use to him, he decided, before walking through the bushes.

'Who or what the fuck is that!' one of the boys uttered in horror.

They drew back initially, startled by Black Jack's blood-red eyes and blackened skin, but the drugs coursing through their blood quickly helped them to overcome any fear.

'Yeah, who the fuck are you?' challenged another one of them, swaggering towards the spectre.

'Look at his clothes,' another sneered. 'What are you? Some sort of sissy, huh? Hey, lads,' he called to his friends, 'I bet he's a shirt-lifter.'

'Are you?' the one nearest to him laughed. 'What's the matter, nancy boy? Can't you speak?'

Black Jack realised he had been wrong in imagining that these boys could be of use. The pleasure he had felt at first was quickly being replaced by a growing anger at their mocking and jeers. He walked back into the graveyard, unnoticed by the boys who were falling about laughing at their own jokes. Stalking over to where he kept his latest acquisitions, he pulled some lengths of rope from the pile. These he fashioned into six nooses, biting and tearing them into shape with his hands and teeth.

The children and Elizabeth sat clustered around Timmy looking at the picture books. They could hear Jack swearing and talking to himself, but that was nothing new.

When he was finished, Black Jack strode back to the next field. The boys were now hunched beside the fire. Worn out by the laughter they dozed in and out of consciousness, and were too far gone to react, when a noose was slipped over each head and tightened. They had no time to scream, before he gathered the ropes and dragged them, pack-like, through the bushes and trees.

The boys clawed at the nooses that were slowly strangling them, oblivious to the thorns and branches that tore at their clothes, shredding their skin.

Timmy was forced to hold the pages of the book down as the wind whipped up sending them into a flurry. Elizabeth stood as the sighing increased around the graveyard, and cried out when she saw what Black Jack was doing. 'Children, lie down. Do it now.'

They huddled together, fearful of the cries around them, and glad to return to the dark earth.

Timmy dropped his books and ran after Elizabeth. They tried to wrestle the ropes from Black Jack, but were no match for his demonic fury and strength. He pushed them aside and continued dragging the struggling boys over to the highest tree in the graveyard. Allowing the wind to lift him he sailed over a strong branch taking the ropes with him and landed smoothly in front of the terrified boys. Four of them stood on tiptoe trying to stop themselves from being strangled. The other two had lost consciousness either from fear or asphyxiation, and swayed drunkenly from side to side. The only thing keeping them upright was Black Jack's grip on the rope.

'Please, Mister,' one croaked. 'Please. Let us go. We'll do whatever you want.'

The others sobbed as he laughed at their misery and the wet patches on the front of their trousers. Time after time Elizabeth and Timmy tried to take the ropes from his hands, only to be thrown aside.

'Get the book-man,' Elizabeth whispered to Timmy as she made another assault on Black Jack. Timmy raced through the bushes and returned with the man in tow. It took Paddy a few minutes to force his way through the tangle of branches and during that time, Black Jack pulled on the ropes and sent the screaming, wriggling bodies skywards. The voices in the wind screamed louder, mourning the loss of so many young lives.

Nothing could have prepared Paddy for the sight that met him when he finally broke through. Black Jack stood like some monstrous puppeteer holding the ropes of the thrashing boys who jerked and kicked in a crazed dance of death. Eyes bulging from sockets, swollen, protruding tongues that were turning black.

'Oh Jesus, Jesus!' Paddy stumbled forward, his heart pounding.

Sensing his approach Black Jack turned and, for the first time, Paddy saw what the devil looked like.

'Stay back or join them,' he warned.

Paddy tried to be brave, to save the boys, but his heart had never been very strong and couldn't take any more. As he reached the tree he felt it slow to a dull thud as pain exploded in his chest. The crying of the wind faded as he fell against the trunk and slid to the ground. He lay staring up at the tangle of loosely hanging legs above him and watched the leaves tossing in the wind, sometimes allowing a star to peep through. He gasped just once, as his heart gave up and the darkness descended.

TEN

December 1845

Charles had revoked his order of eviction on Elizabeth and the children. He was worried by what was happening, and thought she could prove useful to him through her knowledge of the land and its people. He spoke of little else other than the collection of rents, and she was worn out from having to explain the enormity of what this potato rot meant to the country.

'Now, listen carefully, Charles,' she sighed, in one last attempt to reach him. 'You own most of the land around here. In order to run a successful estate this size you have hundreds of tenants. Each one has a small cabin and a half-acre or more of land with which to feed his family. For this they pay an annual rent, and that is what keeps you in whiskey and good food.'

He was about to argue about her reference to his drinking, when she silenced him. 'Wait, I am not finished. The people here have very little, and what they have goes on the rent and feeding their families. They rely on potatoes, because they're easy to grow and take very little looking after. If the crop has failed, they will have nothing to eat. The price of food will soar and the money they would normally pay to you for rent will have to be spent on food. Do you understand? You will have no money coming in.'

He was flabbergasted, no money? What was he supposed to do? He had debts, pledges to meet, and he was a man of honour.

'They will simply have to pay their rent. There are no two ways about it. They'll pay or I'll have them out.'

'And where will that get you? If they have no money what will you have to gain by evicting them?'

'When are the rents due?' he asked.

'Early in the spring.'

'I'll wait until then, and we'll see what happens.'

―――――

The following months were the hardest Elizabeth had ever known. What little food they had was soon used up and the larder was empty. Costs had gone up, and their credit had run out with every shopkeeper in the vicinity. She had to travel far and wide in search of one who had not, as yet, heard of Charles' inability to pay his debts. Many tradesmen had called in person to the Hall, to simply be told that his lord and her ladyship were not available. A very drunken Charles, threatening to loose the dogs if they were not off his land immediately, met the truly unlucky ones. Warnings of returning with the bailiffs fell on deaf ears.

Each day more tales of terror reached Elizabeth from the surrounding countryside. They could no longer afford to pay the staff. Thomas and Annie stayed on, only because they had nowhere else to go after spending a lifetime in service. Charles, to her disgust, had even taken to borrowing what little savings they had.

As predicted, the winter was severe. They stayed inside and spent most days huddled around the fire. Elizabeth was almost distracted at the children's constant complaints of hunger. She was well aware that other gentlefolk in the district were not as hard up as they were, and she cursed Charles for his careless ways. If only John had lived he would have done something to alleviate the suffering she saw each day from her window.

When they did go outside, they walked only as far as the main gate. This was now kept locked and chained in order to deter any more creditors from calling, and also to keep out the growing number of beggars who came pleading for food. The children had been so frightened by grey spectres reaching skeletal arms out to them, that even these walks had to stop. She kept the curtains closed most of the time, in the vain hope of shutting out the world with all its misery and suffering.

———

Besides the horror of possible starvation there was a more immediate threat to her family: Jack Carey. He now had free run of the house and could come and go as he pleased. Charles was always glad to see him, as he came bearing gifts, usually of whiskey or brandy, but sometimes he brought food as well. She was grateful for this, and tried not to think about what means he had used to obtain it.

As Charles' drinking worsened, Carey's decreased. He now dressed in much finer clothes, and although nothing could hide the fact that he was a ruffian, his manner had changed. He imitated Charles' speech and mannerisms, and no longer leered at her, but expected to be treated as an equal.

From the very beginning he had advised Charles to dismiss his estate manager, Ger Ryan, and put him in sole charge instead. Ryan, he said, was allowing the people to poach rabbits. Elizabeth knew that this was true. He saw their suffering and turned a blind eye to the scurrying shapes of the poachers. Carey introduced other ideas too and, as always, Charles went along with whatever he said.

Of course she had no idea how deeply her brother-in-law was in debt to the man. Only seven weeks remained before the estate rents fell due and she dreaded this time. It was plain to see the tenants had nothing, but that did not deter Charles in his expectations. His days were increasingly spent in an alcohol-induced stupor and he refused to acknowledge what was happening.

He ate little, his stomach now unable to take food, thereby fooling himself into believing that things were not as bad as Elizabeth said.

She was trying to reason with him one day when Carey appeared and interrupted the conversation.

'May I speak to you outside, Elizabeth?'

His free use of her christian name astounded her, but she followed him into the hallway. 'How dare you address me in such a familiar way, Carey!' she snapped. 'I am her ladyship to you, and don't forget it in future. I don't know what relationship you have with my brother-in-law, but whatever it is, it does not entitle you to make so bold with me. Do you understand?'

'It's you who does not understand, Elizabeth. It is I who allows you and your children to remain here, not your brother-in-law. Surprised?' he laughed. 'Well you should be.' Fumbling beneath his coat he withdrew a sheaf of papers. 'These,' he held them out, 'are promissory notes, quite a collection, don't you think?'

She stared at the odd assortment of papers that had Charles' handwriting on them.

'There is enough here for me to buy this place twice over, so be warned,' he threatened. 'It would benefit you to be nicer to me in future. After all I can have you, your children and that drunken layabout you call a brother-in-law, evicted at a moment's notice.'

'Then why don't you?'

'I'm biding my time, Elizabeth. It suits me to have you all here for the present, but I have plans, make no mistake about that.'

Looking into his eyes sent a shiver through her. There was no light in them, nothing, but a vast emptiness. As she began to move away, he caught her elbow and pulled her towards him.

'You would also do well to remember where you came from. You weren't born a lady. All those airs and graces were learned from another. You're exactly the same as me, nothing more, nothing less.'

'Thankfully I am nothing like you,' she said, trying to pull away.

'Time will tell,' he glared at her. 'Time alone will surely tell.'

He pushed her away with such force that she flew across the hall and landed in a heap at the foot of the stairs. She banged her hip and sat there for a moment, shaking with shock. He turned and walked towards the study without a glance. The pain made her gasp when she tried to stand, but she managed to haul herself up using the bannister for support.

Lucy came out of the nursery with the others and ran to help her mother. 'Mamma, what has happened?'

'It is nothing, child,' she crawled onto her bed. 'I just had a little fall, that's all.'

'A fall, how?'

'I lost my footing. I'll be fine once I have rested, I promise.'

'Are you sure, Mamma?'

'Yes, you run along and play, and I'll have a little nap,' she waved them away, wanting to be alone to inspect the damage. Her daughters left and she struggled to sit up. She was surprised to find her dress and petticoat torn. The flesh on her hip was already turning blue and she saw at once what was causing her such pain. A large splinter of wood from the stair had torn through her clothes and embedded itself in her side.

She tried to remove with her nails, but it was hopeless, every attempt she made caused even more pain. Surely something in her sewing basket would do the job? The wood dug deeper as she inched her way across the room. Throwing back the basket lid, she fumbled about among lace and threads, and finally found a small pair of scissors. Opening the blades just enough for them to catch hold of the wood, she pulled, and cried out in pain as the splinter tore from her flesh. Blood seeped darkly from the wound and she pressed a shawl onto it to stem the bleeding.

Her cry brought Lucy running, and the child's eyes darted from the bloodstained scissors in her mother's hands to the shawl at her side that was rapidly turning crimson. She didn't stop to ask questions, but led her mother back to the bed and ran to fetch water and a dressing. She cleaned the wound in silence and Elizabeth, who had propped herself up on some pillows, watched as the water in the basin turned red. Only when she had finished putting on the dressing did Lucy speak.

'Really, Mamma, you should see a doctor.'

'I'll be fine, dearest.'

Elizabeth knew she could not afford a doctor. She was not even sure if there was still one in the district, as most of the well-to-do were leaving the country in droves. Lucy hurried from the room and quickly returned with a large measure of brandy.

'Here, Mamma, drink this. It will ease the pain and help you get some sleep.'

Elizabeth took the glass and sipped at the pungent liquid. It tasted foul, but she could feel it warm her and she managed to drink almost half of it. Lucy brought her nightgown and helped her to slip it on.

'Thank you, Lucy dear. I'm so sorry,' murmured Elizabeth.

'It's not your fault, Mamma. It's these terrible times and us being so poor.'

When she left Elizabeth had to bite her lip to keep from crying. She would have to do something soon to save her daughters; once Carey took over they would be in dire trouble. Around sixteen pounds remained in her savings and she had been keeping that for an emergency.

A plan had formed in her mind over the past few weeks. She had a cousin, Andrew, in America. He was doing well, and though married for many years, was childless. He would surely find it in his heart to take her in with the children. Like it or not she wasn't going to give him the chance to refuse. This is it, she thought, as the effects of the brandy took hold, they would get passage on a ship and sail to America. Just as soon as her hip was healed, they would leave Maycroft Hall forever.

ELEVEN

Timmy woke up in a panic. He couldn't breathe properly. Despite the freezing cold of the room he was sweating. His throat felt dry and sore and every bone in his body ached. It felt as though the skin at the back of his throat tore each time he tried to call out to this mother. His legs were unable to take his weight and he realised he would have to crawl. They had all taken to sleeping in the kitchen for the past few months, in the hope that the fire would keep them warm.

It must be almost morning, he thought, although it was hard to tell as the wooden shutters on the window had been closed tight. This didn't stop the cold from seeping inside and icy patterns, like silver spider webs, had formed on each shutter. The fire was out and only the milky-white light that squeezed between the slats of wood lighted the room. Its ghostly glow seemed as thick as fog in places, and he felt he could reach out and touch it.

Sweat dripped down his face as he crawled and the freezing stones of the floor burned beneath his fingers. The room that had always seemed too small to accommodate the six of them, now felt as big as an acre field, and he was panting when he reached where she slept. Reaching out, he grasped her sleeve and shook her awake. She opened her eyes, looked at him and smiled. He tried again to speak, but it was too painful. Her smile disappeared as she sat up.

'Sweet Mother of Jesus,' she pulled him to her, 'you're burning up.'

His mother rose and wiped the sweat from his forehead before laying him in her place. She pulled the dress over her shift.

'I'll get some fresh water from the well. It'll cool you and you'll feel better.' She looked down at him, wringing her hands and repeating the same thing over again like a prayer to still her pounding heart. 'Yes, you'll soon feel better.'

Timmy felt odd, hazy and dreamlike. Always sensitive to sights and sounds, his senses were now heightened even further. The snap of the door opening was a pistol shot. The icy blast that swept inside hovered around him, but he was not aware of its chill. He listened to spiders scurrying in the turf pile and, from somewhere close by, the scratching of a mouse. His father's thunderous snores shook the bed.

His head was lifted and he felt the cold cup against his lips, but he had not the strength to drink from it. He wanted to sleep; he was falling, falling, warmth engulfing him. He wanted to surrender to its folds, to sink into its softness, but instead he was shaken towards wakefulness as something was pushed between his teeth. A trickle of cold water ran over his parched tongue and burned the back of his throat. He spluttered and tried to protest, but the spoon was refilled again as his mother allowed it to drip between his lips. His mother lay next to him and held him. She was singing and he felt a dampness on his face, but it didn't bother him as he relaxed to the lullaby from long ago. He was drifting deeper and soon could no longer feel his mother's tears on his skin.

Next came the jolting of a cart. Timmy was bundled up and lying on his mother's shoulder as they trundled along. He tried to open his eyes and see whose cart it was, as they didn't know anyone who owned one.

Unbeknown to him, it had started snowing before dawn. The glare of sun on snow was too much for his eyes, and mercifully he was forced to keep them shut. They were on their way to the infirmary in the funeral cart, their seats the empty coffins.

When Timmy woke again he was in a strange bed and the helpers told him he had slept for many days. He was barely able to lift his head and was tormented with a great thirst. He asked for jug upon jug of water and drifted from day to day, waking only to relieve himself into a pot beside the bed, or to drink more icy water that tasted sweet as honey. The moans and screams of his fellow sufferers were no more to him than vague, nightmarish sounds that disturbed his sleep. Slowly, the mist lifted, and he struggled to rejoin the world of the living.

When he was well enough to sit up Timmy realised, with horror, that the dreadful visions of his fevered dreams were real. The tortured creatures, whose cries and smells permeated his sleep, surrounded him. He hugged the foul-smelling blanket as he gazed in terror around the large room, counting some thirty beds, with two or three people in each. He thought how lucky it was that he had a bed all to himself, but it was too small to fit anyone else. No one stopped to answer his questions, as he huddled beneath the blanket trying not to cry. A sound beside his bed made him look up and he caught the eye of a woman who was emptying his urine pot into a large bucket. The stench was sickening, and he held the blanket over his nose and tried not to breathe too deeply.

'Well, you're back with us, are you?' she asked, dropping the pot back into its place. She moved to the end of his bed before pausing to look back at him. The smell was not as bad now that she had moved away. 'You're one of the lucky ones, God knows,' she continued. 'There's not many recover. Most only leave this place like that poor soul,' she gestured to where a body was being lifted onto a makeshift stretcher. Timmy watched wide-eyed as the thing that had once been a man was carried by. Its chin hung down almost to its chest and the mouth stretched open in a manic leer. Eyes were only hollows in a face that was swollen and misshapen. They watched the small procession as the body, accompanied by a praying priest, left the room.

'Ah, sure, he's better off out of this,' the woman said. 'His suffering is over, and here we are still awaiting our fate. God know it's the dead that are the lucky ones.' She bent once again to pick up her putrid cargo.

'Please, missus.'

She looked quizzically at him 'Well, what do you want, boy? I haven't all day to be chatting. There's plenty more besides you that need seeing to,' she placed her hands on her hips and painfully straightened up.

'What day is it?' asked Timmy.

'Well, b'God is that all you want to know? What day it is?'

'No,' he stammered.

'It's a Thursday, boy. The month is March and the year, God help us, is 1846. Is that enough information for you?'

March! He couldn't believe it. He had gone to sleep in mid December! Could he really have been ill all that time? She could see how puzzled he was, and although there had been many times over the past few months, when she believed she could no longer feel compassion for anyone, his plight moved her. Walking around the bed, she dropped wearily onto it.

'Has my mother been here in all that time?'

'There's no one allowed to visit here, boy. It's the sickness you see; it's easily caught. Like you, I've had it and got over it. For some reason God, in his infinite wisdom, didn't take me. He took my husband though, with our two sweet children, and left me, Maggie, all alone.'

Timmy reached out his hand and placed it on top of hers. She stroked the skin that felt soft beneath her calluses.

'I've nothing left, boy, that's why I stay here. That and the bit of food they throw me from time to time. In truth I'm waiting for death, and when it comes I'll welcome it with open arms. That's the way 'tis, I'll not lie to you, but enough of my old guff. What about you, eh? Tell me about your mother and family.'

Maggie listened as he told her about his brothers and sister and their cabin. He made it sound like a palace with its roaring fire and comfortable chairs. Most of all he talked about his mother, how beautiful she was, and how he would some day buy her a shop-bought dress and shawl. He spoke about the stream, his friend Martin, their games and stories. He realised that, as she listened, her eyes lost their anguish and a smile crept to her worn features. He told her all about his mother's special dish with the blue flowers on it and then, because of the fever, or perhaps because of the feeling of happiness his old memories gave him, he told her about the reading lessons.

Maggie's eyes grew wide at this information, and she held up a hand to silence him while furtively looking around to see if anyone had heard, 'You can read, boy?'

'Yes, and write too.'

She brought a hand to her mouth to still a cry. Wasn't that exactly what she had been doing with her own children, teaching them to read and write? There were many more like her. Women, that in the dead of night and with the aid of a lone candle, taught their children to read, so that they might better themselves and not remain slaves like their parents. She had often wondered, if women the world over felt the same about words or if it were just the Irish. Her dreams had died with her family, until now. Here, amid the stench of urine and vomit, she had found a gem. A boy with a spark that rekindled the fire in her heart, and in such a place as this, where hope had long been abandoned.

With Maggie's careful tending Timmy got better. She begged, stole, did whatever she had to, to get food. She did things she couldn't bear to think about and had this been normal times she would have felt shame. But, these were not normal times, and if one need could feed another, then so be it. Her boy, her Timmy, was thriving. Although his body still showed the telltale signs of typhus and he still scratched at the angry red rash that covered him, the fever was gone.

Soon Timmy was up and about. The doctors wanted him to leave, as they feared a relapse. With a heavy heart Maggie sent him on his way with bread, meat and cheese from the kitchen bundled up in her shawl.

'God speed you, child,' she said, kissing his forehead. 'Stay to the fields, avoid the roads.'

He understood what she meant. She had spent the last few days warning him about the new danger that stalked the land. More virulent than typhus, this disease was starvation.

Knowing he had many miles to go, Timmy walked slowly on in the morning sunshine. Something had been bothering him since he left the hospital, and it wasn't until now that he realised what it was ... the silence. Usually there would be cattle lowing and sheep bleating. He couldn't hear anything of nature. Even birdsong was missing. It felt as though the whole world was holding its breath.

He shivered and pulled the neck of his jumper closer to his chin. He looked to his left and right, hoping to see or hear someone or something. There was nothing, other than a faint breeze stirring the grass and the sound of his breathing.

Timmy was relieved to finally find a laneway. This rough, dirt track meant he was bound to meet people. And it was not long before he did. But the people were not what he expected. Each one was more frightening than the last. Skeletons with gaping mouths and sunken cheeks passed by him, unseeing. They walked with outstretched hands, pleading for something, anything, to appease the terrible hunger. Most were naked, although others still had some rags hanging off their jutting bones. Briars, bushes and the elements made short work of their clothes. He thought these were monsters or some hideous undead things that had crawled from the bowels of the earth to invade his world. He hid in ditches when he saw them coming in the distance, and covered his ears to block out the horror of their moans and shuffling feet that raked the earth before them.

He saw the carcasses of many burnt cabins littering the landscape. Remnants of furniture or broken pots were the only proof that anyone had ever inhabited them. He walked over bridges and heard voices from beneath; the sound of women and children crying seeped through his toes. Makeshift shelters were everywhere, in ditches or under trees. The occupants crawled out as he passed and he shied back in horror. What little flesh remained on their bones was yellow or black.

Small black puddles stained the road where the dead were piled. The smell of rotting meat made him retch and, moving closer, he saw that the puddles were large clots of blood. The worst sight of all awaited him as he rounded the last hill before home. A group of children huddled together around the fallen body of what he imagined was their mother.

'Are you all right, can I help in any way?' He touched the shoulder of the child nearest to him. It turned, snarling, and he stared in disbelief at the bloodstained mouth. They were feeding off the corpse.

'No!' he screamed, 'no, this is not happening!'

The children watched him as he took the food from the shawl and broke it into chunks. These he scattered on the road as though he were feeding hens, and watched as the children dived on the food. They grabbed and tore at one another as they crammed the morsels into their mouths. They behaved and looked like wild beasts with dirty, limp hair hanging around their faces and nails as long as talons. When they had finished they turned to him for more, and he held up his hands to show he had nothing. They didn't seem to believe him and advanced until they circled him.

'Look,' he held up the shawl. 'This is all I have left and you can't eat that.'

The smallest child reached out to take it from him and he drew back, hugging it to his chest. This was all he had left of Maggie, and he wasn't going to give it up without a fight. If, however, they decided to attack he would be finished. A sound from behind him drew their attention away. One of them was vomiting. The food had been too rich for its stomach and the child was spewing onto the ground. The others ran over and for an instant he thought there was some streak of humanity left in them. That they were hurrying to the aid of a sibling. Instead they fought one another for the vomit. So bad was the hunger that even the child who had been sick, tried to push it back into its mouth.

Timmy started to run away from this awful scene. Sobbing and blinded by tears, he tripped and fell onto the grass verge. Empty retching shook his body and he realised, to his shame, that he had wet himself. When the retching stopped he lay face down upon the grass and waited for his head to clear. He was nearly home, he reminded himself. He was in hell now, but soon he would be home. There was a movement beside him and he sat up quickly, afraid that the wild children had followed him. It was a man, holding something out to him.

'What do you want?' he asked the creature who stood before him, head drooping.

There was no reply. Instead it held out its hand and offered what was in it. Timmy moved closer, puzzled, the bony fingers were closed over whatever it held. Grass, it was just grass!

'I don't understand. What do you want me to do with this?'

The man tried to lift his head; it was taking what little strength he had left to do so. Slowly a face emerged from out of the hair and Timmy gasped at the green-stained mouth.

'I can't,' he said, starting to back away from the hand. How could he be expected to eat grass? It was for animals and sick dogs, not for people.

He must get home, he reminded himself, taking to the road again.

At last the cabin came into view. He was relieved to find it still standing and with a curl of smoke rising from the chimney. He ran towards it. The pig was no longer furrowing in the yard, the cabin door was locked and not a sound came from within.

'Ma,' he called, banging against the door. 'Ma, it's me, Timmy, I've come home.'

The shutter on the kitchen opened slightly and he recognised his father's voice.

'Go away, be off with you now. You're no longer welcome here.'

'Da, it's me Timmy! Look!'

'You heard what I said, boy, be off with you.'

He was frightened by the words from the disembodied voice, but before he could say any more the shutter slammed shut. He tried to peer through the wooden slats, but it was impossible to see anything in the gloom.

'Pat!' Inside, his mother was on her knees. 'In the love and honour of God, Pat, let the boy come in.'

'He has the fever, woman, do you want him to kill us all?'

'He's cured, Pat. Why else would the doctor have sent him home?'

'Please, Da,' the children begged, 'let Timmy come in.'

'He'll not enter this house, not while I still have breath in my body.'

Their father picked up the stick and waved it at them, but it was no longer a threat. He could barely lift it; in place of the once strong man, stood a bony skeleton. Most of his teeth had fallen out from the scurvy and the rags that he wore were hanging from his body.

'He'll die if you leave him outside,' cried his wife.

'Then he'll die. It's coming to all of us soon.'

'I'll go to him,' she said, but her husband caught her and held on.

'Look around you, woman. Look at your children and think.'

She turned to her two sons and small daughter who stood huddled together by the fire. They, like their father, were no more than skeletons.

'If you go out, catch the fever and die, what'll become of them? I'm not long for this world myself, and then what, who will fend for them?'

'Better we all catch it and go together, than leave my child to die alone.'

'I'll kill you here and now, if you try to go outside.'

She knew he would. Frail as he was, he was still a lot stronger than her.

'Let me speak to him then. Just a few words and I promise I'll not try to leave.'

'You can speak to him from the window.'

She nodded and he let go of her. Moving to the window, she opened it a little.

'Timmy!' she called. 'Timmy, come here, son.'

'Ma!' he cried.

She could not speak for a moment. He looked so well, so strong compared to his siblings.

'Timmy, you can't come in. I'm sorry, son,' she said, trying not to cry. 'You have to leave for a while. Go to the workhouse. Tell them you're an orphan and they'll take you in.'

'The workhouse, Ma, why?' He knew this awful place was only for the destitute, the paupers.

'Just do as I ask, child. They'll feed you and God knows there's nothing here for you. We're starving ourselves, and will probably join you there soon.'

'But I can help. I can find work now that I'm well again.'

'There's no work, child, nothing. The potatoes failed again.'

'Heed your mother, boy,' his father said. 'Be on your way.'

The shutter closed and he was alone again.

His mother ran into the bedroom. Flinging open the shutters, she screamed. 'Timmy!'

He ran back and grabbed hold of her outstretched hand. Her fingers slipped from his as his father caught hold of her and tried to drag her back. She fought him like a tigress with one hand, while holding on to the sill with the other.

Timmy watched the struggle in amazement. His parents looked like the others he had met along the road. They twisted and turned in an unholy dance like the marionettes he'd once seen at the Hall, finally, her strength gave way and she was hauled back inside. Her words echoed away as the shutters were closed with a bang.

'Stay well, child, and remember your promise.'

'I will, Ma,' he sobbed, resting his forehead against the cool dried mud of the cabin walls. 'I'll never forget, and I'll never let you down.'

TWELVE

Elizabeth had learned of a ship sailing on the twenty-ninth of March and she was going to get them a passage on it. The dock was more than two hours drive away; they would need to leave a day early to walk the distance and find overnight lodgings. She would also need to buy enough dry food to keep them all during the month-long voyage; ship's rations were not to be trusted.

Her savings had been drained of two pounds and ten shillings, due to the wound in her side becoming septic and requiring the services of a doctor. It had taken months to recover and she now had just fourteen pounds left.

The day before they departed, she packed two canvas bags, taking only what could be easily carried between herself and Lucy. Up until now she hadn't told the children anything about her plans, being too afraid they might let it slip when speaking to their uncle. Not that he would have minded their going, but if he knew she had money he would try to take it from her. It was Carey she was most afraid of. He would do everything in his power to stop her.

The night before departure she gathered the children in her room and whispered her plan to them. Becky and Charlotte jumped up and down, squealing with excitement. The prospect of a sea voyage was a big adventure to them, and they had no idea they were fleeing from famine. Lucy nodded sadly. Elizabeth could understand how upsetting this was for her. She was old enough to be aware of leaving everything familiar. The next hour was filled with questions, and after a while, even Lucy got caught up in the chatter.

Becky and Charlotte wanted to bring their dolls and sulked when they were told they could only take one each. This sent them hurrying to the nursery to choose and gave Elizabeth and Lucy some time on their own.

'It's not going to be easy, leaving here and starting out anew, but we have no choice.'

'I understand, Mamma and I'm not really sad. It's just that I will miss this place.'

'So will I. I'll miss the memory of what it once was.'

Next morning they waited until Charles and Carey had gone before starting out on the deserted road, pausing only to say goodbye at John's grave. Elizabeth was amazed that there were so many freshly dug graves. After a moment of prayer, she ushered the children away. Closing the gate, she stopped for a moment and looked across the graveyard. The trees towered above the graves, silent sentinels amid the awfulness of so many new mounds.

'Goodbye, my love,' she whispered.

They walked for miles and seemed no closer to town. She had hoped that a passing cart might give them a lift, but there were none. Their first encounter with one of the living skeletons caused considerable upset. It was a small child. It crawled out from a ditch, moaning, hands outstretched. Charlotte had screamed on seeing it and it took Elizabeth all her strength to loosen the little girl's fingers from her skirts. The others stood mute with shock at the terrible figure before them, and once she had calmed Charlotte, Elizabeth hurried them away. She had no food to offer the starving creature and could do nothing to help.

They walked on in silence save for the sound of Charlotte's sniffling. No taverns or lodging houses were open to welcome them; most of the business people had left the country, and what taverns there had been were boarded up or looted. Elizabeth knew they would not make the town before nightfall. The smaller girls were already complaining about the cold. There was no choice, she decided, they would have to spend the night in the open. Luckily the sky was clear, and she doubted if it would rain. Catching sight of what she took to be an abandoned cabin, she ordered the girls to wait, until she checked that it was safe.

The roof had all but caved in, but there was still enough standing to give them shelter. The inside smelt of damp and something sickly-sweet. Broken utensils and chairs littered the room. She was just about to go outside and call the girls, when a movement from a dark corner stopped her. As her eyes adjusted she saw, with terror, at least five corpses in varying degrees of decomposition, huddled under a single blanket. Each wore an expression of unrepressed agony, mouth open in a silent scream.

She backed away, shaking. But there had been movement; maybe one of them was still alive. It was impossible to tell in the gathering darkness. She searched for a light and soon found a small stub of a candle and some dry flint. This she struck on the metal bar over the long-dead fire and was relieved when it caught. Cupping her hands over the flame, she moved back towards the corner. There it was again, the movement. Maybe there was a small child or baby under the foul smelling blanket. She picked up the edge and pulled it back. The reason for the movement became clear and she stumbled back, retching.

A black swarm of rats fed on the corpses. Elizabeth was paralysed, as she watched them move, as one, over the bones of their victims. It wasn't until Lucy called her name that she managed to shrug off her revulsion and hurry back outside.

'Is it all right, Mamma?'

She shook her head, unable to answer, she herded them away. No matter how many more cabins they came across, she would not try to enter one again. For months afterwards she would wake screaming, having once again heard the shuffling and terrible scraping of the claws.

They walked on, until finally they found shelter beneath the branches of a giant oak. Elizabeth was relieved to find a hollow big

enough for them to crawl into at the base of the tree. This would protect them from the elements and they were out of sight of any passing
strangers. Her mind was filled with thoughts of the child she had seen
that day. If she didn't have the money for the voyage, that could have
been one of her children.

They woke cramped and cold at first light. It was another clear day
and she was thankful for this. They had walked only a short distance
before the children started asking for something to eat.

'Mamma, my stomach hurts,' Charlotte whimpered.

Elizabeth assured them that they would soon be in the town and
perhaps they could pick berries on the way. But all the bushes had been
picked clean. She was relieved when the masts of the ships came into
view on the horizon.

The town was a mass of humanity. People lay dead in the streets and
hundreds begged at the workhouse gates. She led her family down back
lanes and through side streets, but there was no way she could protect
them from the horror. The quayside was crowded with emigrants. The rich
sat stiffly in their carriages and looked down their noses at the wretches
sitting fearfully on the road. Large leather-studded trunks contrasted
poignantly with the bundles of rags being carried by the poor.

Elizabeth knew many of these were tenants being sent abroad by
landlords who found it more economical to pay their passage across
the ocean than to leave them on the land. This action cleansed the
lands of the unwanted and left it clear for the planting of wheat, oats
and barley. Most tenants were in the charge of an overseer, paid by
the landlord to make sure they went. People who had never set foot
outside their village were being dispatched to the other side of the
world.

Elizabeth pushed her way through the crowds to reach the captain
of the ship she required. He was bartering with the overseers, and it
took her some time to attract his attention.

'I need passage on your ship for my children and myself. What will it cost?' she enquired. She could see the demand was great, and where there is such demand there are usually higher prices.

'Six pounds a head.'

'Surely not for children as well?'

'Let's see them.'

She waved to Lucy who was standing on the edge of the crowd to bring the others. He looked them carefully up and down, rubbing his beard in thought.

'I'll take the two smaller ones for the price of an adult. It will be eighteen pounds for all of you. That's in the hold mind, not in a cabin.'

'How much for a cabin?'

'An extra four pounds. But it'll be worth it for the children's sake.'

She had only fourteen pounds. That would pay for the children, but she still needed another eight for her own fare and for the cabin. Then there was the food to buy for the voyage.

'I don't have enough money for us all, but I have jewels.'

'Sorry, ma'am,' he held up a hand, 'but I can only accept cash.'

'Here,' she handed him twelve pounds as a deposit. 'We'll take the cabin, and I'll be back soon with the remainder of the money.'

'Very well,' he pocketed the notes, 'we sail in two hours.'

'I'd like to take the children on board now, if I may. I have things to see to in the town and they would be safer here.'

'Mr Williams,' he called to his first mate, 'will you take this lady and her children aboard?'

The man nodded and they followed him up the wooden gangplank onto the ship. Even in the dock it felt shaky beneath their feet, and she wondered what it would be like on the high seas.

'Is it a cabin for you and the little ones, madam?' he asked.

'Yes, that's right.'

He led them up a flight of stairs and along a corridor lined with doors. 'You're lucky to be the first passengers on board. All cabins are supposed to be the same, but this is the best one, I think.'

It was larger than she had imagined and lined with bunk beds on each side. A small porthole lit the room and prevented it from being suffocating. At least they would have a bunk each, and turning back the covers, she was pleased to find the linen was clean. A small table stood between the bunks with a chair either side of it. On it there were four tin mugs and plates, but no forks or knives. A box held candles, a piece of flint, and a small oil lamp hung from the ceiling.

'Well, this isn't too bad, is it?' she asked the children. But they were already climbing onto the bunks and peeping through the porthole.

'I have to go out,' she told Lucy. 'Pack away the bags as best you can and lock the door once I'm gone. Don't worry. I'll be back in plenty of time for the trip.'

She went outside before they could ask any questions, and once she heard the bolt slam shut, hurried from the ship. She would have to find a jeweller or pawnbroker quickly to sell her sapphires. The two pounds she had left would buy the food, but she would have to get at least ten pounds more. The necklace alone was worth a hundred and with the matching earrings she would have enough left over to give them a start in the New World. She finally found an open jeweller's and went inside. The bell over the door jingled in the dusty quiet of the shop. An old man came from behind a curtained door and stood waiting for her to state her business.

'I would like to sell these,' she took a cloth from the pocket of her dress and spread it on the counter. The sapphires glittered in the dim light as he picked up the necklace and examined it, then the earrings.

'I'll give you four pounds for the lot.'

She looked at him in amazement. Four pounds for something so valuable!

'Are you serious?'

'These are hard times, lady.'

Folding the cloth over the jewellery, she started to put them back in her pocket.

'I'm the only one buying in the town.'

She stopped short. Even if she took his ridiculous offer she still would not have enough for her fare. Placing the bundle back down, she put her hands behind her neck and unclasped the chain the held the locket bearing her and John's images.

'How much for this?' She laid the heavy, gold piece on the counter.

He was sure of his game and moved in for the kill. 'One pound.'

'A pound!'

'Take it or leave it, lady. I'm a busy man.'

She looked around the empty shop, he was busy indeed, feeding off the misery and suffering of others. Still, the four pounds would pay for the cabin. The children would not survive in the hold, and the two pounds she had left would feed them. But they would have to go without her.

Picking up the locket, she refastened it about her neck. 'I'll accept your offer for the sapphires,' she said, pushing the cloth towards him.

He took it and walked back behind the curtain. She heard the clang of a steel door and he re-emerged counting out the money. Selling the locket would have been pointless, as a pound mattered little in the scale of things. As she was about to leave the shop she stopped and turned back. She had to say something to this horrid, grasping man. He waited as she tried to think of some words that would fit.

'There will come a time for all of us when we have to stand before the Lord and be counted. What will you answer when he asks you what you did to help your fellow man?'

'I'm doing the same as many others, so I'll be in good company.'

'Perhaps, but unfortunately for you, you can't buy your way into heaven.'

She went in search of a grocer and arrived back at the ship laden down with bags. After taking the food to the cabin and ordering the girls to pack it away, she went again to see the captain. Following direction from one of the crew, she found him in his cabin going through a list of passengers.

He looked up when she knocked and bade her enter, 'You have the rest of the money?'

She took the four pounds from her pocket and laid it down on his table.

'What is this?'

'That's to pay for the cabin. I haven't enough for my fare. I have also supplied the children with food, so there will be no need of the ship's rations.'

'Then they will be travelling alone, I take it?'

'Yes, unless …?'

'There is no room on this ship for those who cannot pay their way.'

'I can work for my fare. I'm a good cook and I can nurse the sick … if you'll just let me try.'

He turned from his paperwork and caught her hands. She tried to pull back, but he held her fast as he examined the skin on her fingers and palms.

'These hands have never seen a day's hard work,' he pushed her away in disgust. 'You'd be of no help to me.'

'Please, sir, my children will have to arrive alone in a completely new land.'

He took her by the arm and led her to the door. Pointing to the quayside and the mass of people huddled there, he explained, 'There are two hundred and fifty seven of them that will board this ship in under an hour. Of that two hundred and fifty seven, there are forty-one orphans. Who do you think will be there to greet them? Go away, woman, and consider your children lucky to have a fine cabin and food enough for the journey.'

She knew it was no use arguing with him. This famine had made everyone hard.

The children were waiting expectantly for her return and rushed to greet her. Lucy could tell there was something wrong and held out a chair. Elizabeth sat and motioned for them to do the same. There wasn't a sound within the cabin as they waited for her to speak.

'I sold my sapphire necklace and earrings today.' She held up a hand to stop their protestations of regret. 'It had to be done, but that's not the problem. I haven't got enough money to pay for my own fare on this voyage.'

There were gasps of dismay and Charlotte started to cry. Taking her on her lap, Elizabeth continued, 'Remember when your father died and I asked you all to be brave?' They nodded in unison. 'Well, I'm asking you again. You must sail without me and I'll follow on later.'

'Mamma! No!' Lucy threw her arms around her neck and Becky knelt at her feet, burying her face in her mother's lap, sobbing.

'My cousin Andrew is a good man and will welcome you with open arms. He has no children of his own and will be good to you. If asked, he will send the money for my fare. Lucy, you will have to take over my job and see your sisters safely to their new home. It's not going to be easy, I know, but you must be brave for my sake.'

'Oh, darling Mamma, is there no other way?'

'No, there is no other way. I'll be fine knowing you are safe, and it won't be long until we are all together again.'

'Mamma,' Charlotte sobbed, 'I have a pain in my heart.'

'We all have, my darling, but we must try to be brave.'

She sat holding them for a while until the clanging of the ship bell roused her. Looking outside, she could see that the loading had begun and it would soon be time to leave.

'Get me the bags of clothes, please,' she asked, watching as they pulled them from under the bunks.

She searched inside, until she located what she was looking for. Taking out a small, leather-bound book she handed it to Lucy. It was a book of love poems that had been given to her by her husband on their wedding day. Inside, under his inscription of love, she had written Andrew's full name and address.

'This is where you must go when you arrive,' she pointed to her writing. 'Ask the way at the docks, then speak to no one and above all trust no one, no matter how kind they seem. It will be a different world there. You must be careful. Tell my cousin who you are and what is happening here, understand?'

'Yes, Mamma.' Lucy took the book and stared at the familiar handwriting, hoping to find some salvation in the words.

'Now, you two,' Elizabeth said, pulling the younger ones close, 'you do as your sister tells you and be very, very good. I don't want to have to scold you the next time we meet.'

They tried to smile through their tears.

'As soon as the ship sets sail bolt the door,' she ordered Lucy, 'and keep it bolted at all times. The journey can take up to a month, and there's enough food to last that long if you are careful. Go outside only to empty the pot and to get water.'

A sudden knock on the door startled them. It was Mr Williams. He had been sent to take her ashore. 'I'm sorry, madam, but the captain says you have to leave. We sail in ten minutes.'

'Just one more minute,' she begged.

Unclasping her locket, she placed it around Lucy's neck. 'Keep that with you always. It's all I have left to give you, my darling.'

'I'll keep it safe until I see you again, Mamma. Then I will return it to you.'

'Madam, please.'

He could wait no longer. Turning to the children, who were by now all sobbing again, she whispered, 'I've loved you all from the moment I knew of your existence. I will love you unto eternity.'

'We love you, Mamma,' Lucy answered for them all. 'I'll keep them safe until you come for us.'

'I know you will, child, and you'll always be in my thoughts and prayers. Remember everything I told you and bolt the door.'

With this she hurried away and had to be helped down the gangplank in her distress. Standing again on the quayside, she looked up at the huge ship that was taking her children, her very life from her.

'Madam?'

The first mate was beside her. 'I begged the captain to let you sail. If I had the money I'd willingly pay for your passage, but I haven't. I don't see how it would matter if you came. One more wouldn't sink us. These are strange times, and it's not only hunger that's killing people, but the hardening of hearts of those who could help.'

'Thank you. You're very kind.'

'I'll promise you one thing. I'll look out for your children and see that they are safe.'

'God bless you, sir.' She started to cry and he helped her over to a capstan.

'Have you friends or family in America?'

'Yes, I have a cousin. They are going to live with him. They have his address. It's not far from where you will dock.'

'Then I'll take them there myself.'

'You will?'

'I give you my word. There's many below deck that'll not survive this long trip, packed away as they are like cattle. But your children will and they'll thrive and prosper, just you wait and see.' A shout from the deck sent him running, but he stopped at the gangplank and called back to her, 'I won't let you down, trust me.'

He was no sooner on board than the crew cast off. The ship moved slowly as, one by one, sails unfurled and were fastened in place. As the mainsail caught the wind and ballooned out, the vessel picked up speed and slid out of the harbour.

Elizabeth watched until the ship faded into the distance, its lamps shrinking to pinpoints of light against a black sky. In another time bystanders would have been struck by the absence of well-wishers waving it off and the sight of a lone woman hunched over and sobbing as though her heart would break.

THIRTEEN

The walk to the workhouse was terrifying for Timmy. The victims he had encountered on his way from the hospital were nothing compared to the hundreds lying diseased or dying at the entrance to the town. Many had fallen only yards from the workhouse gates, too weak to make it those last few steps. Although it was just over a year since the blight had struck, and the famine had not as yet reached its height, the workhouse was under severe strain. In the absence of any other aid, hundreds flocked to the gates each day. The tenants were the first to be affected by the blight, with so many already living in poverty. Now it was spreading its cloak over every part of the community. The rich were affected, not just by the famine, but also by the spread of disease. The smell of the blight was being replaced by the intolerable stench of disease.

In the overcrowded conditions sickness spread quickly. Without potatoes the inmates also developed scurvy, which caused teeth to drop out and joints to swell. In spite of these horrors contained within its walls, the workhouse was still the best chance of survival for many.

It took Timmy some time to squeeze his way to the gates. Uniformed officers armed with sticks beat at the bars, and at any stray hands that dared to protrude between them. Crowds of people were begging for food for loved ones fallen by the wayside, but they were sent away empty-handed. While there were vacancies within the workhouse no outside aid would be given. The officers tried as best they could to sort out the most needy cases. Timmy stood mute under the waving arms of the adults. He was sickened by the smell of their sweat, and his ears rang with their pleadings.

'You, boy. What's your name?'

He looked up at the man behind the gates. 'Timmy Walsh, sir.'

'Where's your family, boy?'

'Dead, sir.'

The huge gates opened a fraction and strong arms reached out to pull him inside and away from the surging crowd. He felt as though he had entered another world.

'See that door on the right, son? Go in there.'

Timmy nodded and started to walk towards the building. As an afterthought he stopped, turned, and addressed his saviour. 'Excuse me, sir?'

'What is it, boy? Can't you see that I'm busy? Any questions you may have will be answered by those inside,' he turned back to the gates, shouting orders to those both inside and out.

Timmy walked back and tugged the leather belt at the man's waist. The officer's hand automatically reached for the holster containing his gun, before swirling around. Timmy jumped back and held up a hand to show he meant no harm. 'I just wanted to say, thank you.'

The man nodded. 'Save your thanks, boy. I'm not sure if I'm doing you any favour by letting you in here.'

'Well, thanks all the same,' Timmy walked away towards his designated door, and the watching man scratched his head in wonder. His thoughts were soon interrupted by a shout from the gates, and he was forced to resume his position of command.

Timmy made his way across the courtyard. The entrance to the workhouse was like two large houses joined together by an archway. Others queued at the door. He studied them while waiting his turn. There were women with children in tow and bundles of rags under their arms, whole families and groups of lone children. All showed the signs of hunger in their gaunt faces and deeply shadowed eyes.

The woman in front of him turned around. 'Are you on your own, lad?'

'Yes, missus.'

'All your people dead?'

'Yes, missus.'

'Sad times, eh lad, sad times.' She shook her head, and hoisted the child on her hip higher.

Timmy winked and the little one poked his tongue out at him. The few minutes spent waiting turned into a game of face-pulling that soon had the other children joining in. There was much giggling and laughter and the adults smiled at one another in appreciation at the sound.

'What the hell is going on here?'

A man appeared in the open doorway and stood with hands on hips. All laughter ceased and smiles were replaced by worried frowns.

'Do you find all this funny?' he looked around at the adults, and they answered solemnly, 'No sir, it's not, sir, sorry, sir.' He glared at them again before going back inside.

'Old bastard,' one of the women whispered. 'Tormented by the sound of children's laughter.'

'Ah, sure you'd be the same yourself if you looked like him, missus,' a man spoke up. 'Sure hasn't he a face like a slapped arse.'

This sent the children into fits of giggles that were quickly stifled by adult hands.

Timmy's turn came. He peeped around the door before entering and saw four tables, with an officer seated behind each one. He walked over to the officer who signalled him.

'What's your name, boy?'

'Timmy Walsh, sir.'

This was scribbled down. 'Where are your family?'

'Dead, sir.'

'Was it the fever, boy?'

'No, sir. The hunger.'

'But you look well enough. How can that be?'

'I had the fever, sir. I was sick in the hospital for a long time.'

'I see,' he noted this in the book. 'They were dead when you returned?'

'Yes,' Timmy whispered, 'they were all dead to me.'

'How old are you, boy?'

'Nearly thirteen, sir.'

He raised his eyebrows doubtfully.

'I am, sir, really. I was born late summer of '33.'

'Very well. What did you father work at?'

'He was a tenant, sir. Over at Maycroft Hall, Sir Charles Fitzwilliam's place, sir.'

'Oh, yes, indeed,' nodded the officer, writing again in the book. When he had finished he looked up at the boy. 'Listen to me, boy. In here anyone over twelve is considered fit for man's work. You don't look big or strong enough to survive breaking stones. I am putting down here,' he tapped his pen on the book, 'that you are eleven.'

'But I'm willing to work for my keep, sir.'

'Oh, you'll work all right, boy, but it won't be as back-breaking or dangerous. Remember from now on you are only eleven. I can get into terrible trouble for falsifying documents.'

Timmy nodded.

'Go through that door.'

Timmy saw people standing in lines and he turned once to nod at the officer who was watching him with a strange look on his face. If he could have read the man's thoughts he would have understood. Hundreds had passed before the man, but for some reason this small boy's plight had touched him the most.

Outside, men, women and children were divided into lines. Men and women were to live in one part of the workhouse, the children in another. It took some time for the orderlies to get all the adults sorted. Pitiful cries and shouts echoed as they were dragged across the yard to their designated blocks. Young children who were left behind stood in shocked silence or sobbed inconsolably, the bigger boys tried to brave it out, whistling as if this was an everyday occurrence. Their eyes, however, told a different story. Toddlers held tightly to sibling's hands as they were led away.

Timmy joined the procession as it moved towards another building. Each one was stopped and questioned at the entrance.

'Have you family in here?' asked the woman at the door.

'No, missus.'

'Dead, are they?'

'Yes, missus.'

'Stand inside the door there and wait for me.' She pushed him and he stumbled into a cool, dark hallway. Children who had entered before him were nowhere to be seen. It was as though they had melted into the walls. There was not a sound, no sniffling and no calling out, nothing. He watched as others walked by him and were led either up the stairs, or to the back of the house.

It was huge inside; the stairway seemed to climb upward for miles and the sound of bare feet on wooden steps faded quickly. The back of the house unfurled into vast cavernous corridors; that would explain the children vanishing.

He wondered why the woman had asked him to wait. Did she realise that he was older than he'd said? He decided just to say he had lied when asked his age ... there was no sense in involving the kind officer.

When the last child was sent off into the gloom, the woman came inside and slammed the door. Taking a large key that hung from her waist on a chain, she locked the door and allowed the key to drop and be hidden in the folds of her skirt. She tried the door once, to make sure it was securely locked and, seeming pleased that it was, turned to Timmy. 'So you're alone in the world, boy.'

'Yes, missus.'

She studied him. 'There's many more like you in here, and I'm worn out from them all. Some are so small they don't even know their own names. I'll put you to work helping with their care. Are you good with children?'

'Yes, missus, very good; I have two brothers and a sister and …' his voice trailed off.

She did not question his reply. A sudden pounding on the door made her groan with annoyance, before pushing back a latch and peering out. Sighing, she unlocked the door and stepped back, as a small child was propelled inside.

'Found this one hiding in the yard,' a gruff male voice came from outside.

Without replying she shut and locked the door again before turning to the offending child. It was a little girl, about five years old, and very thin. She wore a dress that was almost transparent and her bare feet were red and scratched. She peeped at Timmy, before looking down again.

'Well, so what's your name?' demanded the woman.

The child mumbled something and, noticing the woman was losing patience, Timmy bent down to hear.

'What did you say your name was?'

'Katie,' she whispered.

'I'm Timmy.'

'Enough of the introductions,' barked the woman, 'come with me.'

Timmy took the child by the hand and they followed her. It would have been easy to lose sight of the woman in the darkened corridors. She led them to a room very much like the infirmary, but this one was full of children. All seemed to be aged between two and ten and there were as many as six to a bed.

'This is where you will live,' she said to Timmy. 'You're a bit old for this section, so consider yourself mother and father to this lot from now on.'

He looked around the room at the faces, hoping to see someone he recognised.

'I'll find you a bed and come morning I'll explain the rules to you. It is your responsibility to make sure they are obeyed at all times, understand?'

He nodded, but he had no idea how to deal with so many children. After she left, Timmy was at a loss what to say or do, until he felt the gentle tugging on his hand. He had forgotten about the child, Katie. He bent down and was startled by her question.

'Are you my new da?'

He had to think for a moment before answering. 'I suppose I am in a way.'

'Are you my da as well?' He looked down at the little boy asking the question and gulped. One by one, the children were getting up from the beds and walking towards him.

The woman returned to find Timmy sitting on the floor surrounded by the children. A grunting, puffing man who carried the wooden base of what was to be Timmy's bed, followed her. He dumped it with a loud clatter. The noise startled the children and some of the youngest ones whimpered. Timmy shushed them as best he could, and waved away the dust that had risen. She went out again and returned with two blankets and straw-filled sacks to serve as his mattress.

'This is a list of rules,' she thrust a sheet of paper towards him. 'Though God knows you're probably like most of your kind and not able to read. Still, I'll leave it here and I'll go through it with you in the morning.' She jammed the notice onto a nail by the door and called, 'Mind you keep those children quiet now!'

He was once again alone with his charges. Taking the sack, he flattened them down as best he could. The blankets were better than he'd been used to at home, although the wool was rough against his skin. Katie lay on the newly-made bed and sucked her thumb. The upset of the day had been too much for such a little child, and Timmy had no sooner covered her than she fell fast asleep. The light was fading as he moved around the room, tucking in and cuddling a child here and there. He was about read the notice where a movement from one of the beds caught his eye. A small boy was waving him over. 'What is it?' Timmy whispered, not wanting to wake his sleeping charges.

'You'll be here when I wake up, won't you?'

'Yes, I'll be here. I promise I won't leave you.'

'I was a bit afraid until you came.'

'Don't worry,' he motioned to the child to lie down, 'it'll be all right now. What's your name?'

'Peter.'

Timmy smiled; it was the same name as his brother.

'You go to sleep now, Peter, and we'll talk again in the morning.'

A full moon lit the room. A harvest moon his father would have called it. Sometimes it was so big that it seemed to sit on top of the hill near his home. Taking the note from off the nail, he went to the window to read it. He smiled at his own jokes on each item.

No alcohol (good!)

No bad language (damn and blast!)

No laziness, disobedience or malingering (he had no idea what that was)

Meals to be eaten in silence

Work was breaking stones for men, knitting for women and industrial training for children. Timmy looked around the darkened room and smiled. Most of the children here could hardly walk, let alone work.

Lying down beside Katie, he filled his head with plans for the next day. He closed his eyes and prayed for sleep. Somewhere deep within the house a door banged, voices floated in from outside and an owl hooted its greeting to the night.

'Everyone up! Up! Up!'

He sat up, amazed that it was already morning. The woman was walking through the rows of beds pulling blankets from the sleeping children.

Some refused to move and tried to return to a dream world, where everything was happy. Instead they received a sharp slap on the legs and sat up howling.

'No, missus,' Timmy ran to stop this.

'Who do you think you are boy, telling me what to do?'

'No, what I mean is, missus, I'll wake them up for you. I know how busy you must be, and I want to help in any way I can.'

She looked at him for a moment before deciding that perhaps he was right. She took no pleasure in coming into this room, especially as the stench was worse in the morning. As she read the list of rules to him, he nodded, as if hearing them for the first time. Before she had a chance to leave, he begged for the use of a brush and something to kill the smell.

'There's a brush in the kitchen and some lime in the outhouses. Mix that with water and throw it on the floor.'

He thanked her and she grunted. 'You're wasting your time, you know. This lot are like animals, shitting on the floor, pigs all of them. You,' she shouted to one of the boys, 'show him the way to the kitchens.'

The child jumped to attention and she glared once more around the room before going outside. When she left the children ran to him. Some showed him the red marks on their legs, left behind by her stinging slap. He rubbed the redness on the older children and kissed the smaller ones on the offending mark. A bell rang outside in the corridor and the children rushed for the door.

'Wait, what does the bell mean?'

'Food,' they chorused, hopping up and down.

He looked at the sea of hopeful faces before him. The woman's words rang in his ears and he was surprised to find he was shaking in anger. Pigs were they, these tiny helpless children?

'Line up,' he ordered.

No one moved.

'Get into a line and we'll walk one after the other to the kitchen.'

They did as he asked. At his request some of the older children carried the younger ones. When he was satisfied there was some sort of order they set off. Peter led the way, pleased to be of such help to Timmy.

The kitchen was enormous, long wooden tables with benches on either side seemed to stretch for miles. Each place was set with a wooden bowl and spoon. Dozens of silent children took their places at the tables. At the head of the room was a huge fire and over it hung giant, black cauldrons.

When Timmy led his band inside, a woman pointed to one of the tables. Once they were seated, the children nearest to the fire got up and, taking their bowls, stood in line before each pot. A ladle descended into the pot's dark innards, was withdrawn and its gluey contents slopped into each waiting bowl.

When their turn came, Timmy led his children forward and waited until each had been served before taking his own food.

'Thank you,' he said, smiling at the serving woman who was sweating profusely from the heat of the fire. She was taken aback.

'You're welcome lad, I wish it was more.'

He walked back to the table where the children were already gulping down the hot porridge. At home, his mother would have sprinkled salt on it for flavour or, when things were good, a slurp of milk. Still, he was grateful for what he had and surprised at how hungry he felt. He looked down the table, watching the children as he ate. Smiles appeared as the food filled and warmed empty bellies. He winked at one or two and was rewarded with a crooked or gapped smile. Many had held the bowl to their faces, trying to lick any stray bit of porridge that might lurk inside, with the result that it was sticking to their hair or in their ears. He was surprised to see a couple of women moving down the rows of tables; each carried a bucket full of milk and basket of bread. A tin cup was filled with milk and poured into the now empty bowls. The slice of bread thrust down beside each child disappeared instantly. The milk, he discovered, was half water and the bread hard. Still, it filled a gap.

When they were finished each took their bowl to one of the large stone sinks in the room and washed it out. Some of his girls were ordered to stay behind and help in the kitchen, while the older boys were to fetch wood for the fires throughout the building.

Timmy was instructed to take the younger ones to their room and keep them there. This would have been a daunting task, if it were not for the fact that the children were weakened from hunger. Many wanted to just lie down on their beds and sleep, but he wouldn't allow it. There was a room to clean and beds to air, anyone who was big enough helped to shake and fold the blankets. The straw-filled sacks were pounded until no trace of dust was left. The smaller ones enjoyed this, jumping and rolling on each one.

He went back to the kitchen and asked for the broom. The woman who handed it to him was amazed. He asked the way to the outhouses to get the lime. These were three small sheds at the back of the house that were converted to lavatories. These consisted of wooden boxes with a hole cut in each. Next to it stood a pile of lime and a small shovel with which the user covered his body waste. The lime was to burn the waste and to disguise the smell. There were so many people using the toilets, that the treatment didn't have time to take effect. The stench was overpowering.

Timmy pulled his jumper up over his nose and held his breath, but it was useless and he had to run outside gulping for air. It took him three tries before he could fill the shovel and empty it into the bucket he'd found standing outside. This would have to be enough, as he was already retching.

The women in the kitchen stopped working as he passed and each wondered at this strange boy. He arrived in the room like a lone pilgrim returning from his travels. Small faces showed relief on seeing him.

Timmy opened the windows to shift the clouds of dust hanging in the air. Upending each bed, he stood it against the wall and jumped back in horror as black rats ran from beneath two of the beds. Without thinking, he swore out loud and threw the brush at the vermin.

'Rats, rats, rats,' the children chorused, chasing them as though they were puppies.

The rats, like many of their kind, were quick to escape and disappeared into holes in the corners of the room. Once the place was swept clean, he threw the liquid lime on the floor and brushed it in all over. Its effect was swift in quelling the smell, but its fumes burned the throats of the young ones, making them cough and gag, until Timmy stood them next to the open windows.

When he was finished, the beds were put back in place and the sacks covered with the blankets. The children were delighted with the results and little hands smoothed and fussed over each bed. Timmy realised he was sweating and needed a bath. They could all do with a wash. There was bound to be a tin bath somewhere. He was about to go back to the kitchens, when he noticed one of the smaller children squatting down in a corner.

'No! Stop!' he cried, running towards the child, who whimpered in fear. 'You must use this.' And picking her up, he placed her over the bucket. When she was finished he turned to all the children. 'From now on you must use this bucket, understand? We have to keep the place clean, so that we won't get sick.' They nodded and he called Peter to him. If there were a bath, he would need some help carrying it. Back in the kitchens the women listened to his request in wide-eyed wonder.

'Proper little lord we have here,' one of them jeered. The woman, who had served his porridge, quickly silenced her. 'Leave him be. He's to be proud of, not sneered at. I'll show you where it's kept, son.'

Timmy and his helper followed her to what had been the stables, where she pointed to a rusty tin bath hanging on a nail. The familiar smell of hay and horses pained him. He helped the woman to lift the bath down and carry it outside.

'Half fill it from the well,' she instructed, 'then come inside and I'll heat it with some water from the pots.'

They did as she asked and struggled back into the kitchen with the massive weight. Her ladles of hot water were barely able to heat the freezing water, but it was soon tepid enough for washing. She also found him a bit of soap and a number of rags. The boys thanked her, as they struggled away with their bounty. She watched them go, shaking her head in wonder.

The next hour passed in a haze of soapsuds and squealing children. Ears that had not been washed in weeks were thoroughly cleaned, as were crevices between fingers and toes. Hair that had been dull and lank now shone and flowed. The older ones wished to wash in private and he made a screen from an upturned bed to save their modesty.

Though still ragged, it was a much-improved group who sat to eat at the evening table. The woman who had helped him winked as she served his soup, and he beamed up at her. She felt a lump rise in her throat as he walked away. There was a boy who could become a great man, given the chance.

Timmy used some of the rags to block the holes where the rats had run through. The others were kept for washing, now a twice-weekly ritual. The room was swept and washed each day. Rumours reached him of a fever that was raging in other parts of the workhouse, and he became obsessed with cleaning. Try as he might, he was unable to completely rid the children's hair of lice. One of the women had given him a comb and he spent hours grooming and picking them from heads. The beds were also harbouring fleas. No matter how many times they took the blankets outside and beat them against the walls, the fleas returned. It was a losing battle, though diligently fought.

Timmy and his numerous fairy tales kept up the children's spirits. Each night, before they fell asleep, he would tell tales of a wonderful land where everything was beautiful and there was lots of food. No matter how many times he recounted this story they listened in rapture, as he described clothes made of gold and fairies that rode on white horses. As the atrocity of the famine increased outside the walls, inside, in Timmy's room, each child fell asleep with visions of magic, instead of the horror that was reality.

FOURTEEN

September 2003

The story about the group suicide had spread throughout the country. The scene drew its usual share of ghouls that seemed to revel in such things, and for a while the tree became a place of pilgrimage. Flowers and stuffed toys were laid against the trunk, as the families gathered to mourn their loss. For weeks afterwards the tear-stained faces of the mothers could be seen on television screen and in tabloids, lamenting the death of their sons, sons that had become more precious in death than they ever were in life.

There were many that saw it as a just end for the boys; they were drug addicts in a climate that would no longer tolerate such things. Those who sat in judgement dismissed the fact that these young boys had once been sons and brothers, that their glazed eyes had sparkled with hope, until life had driven them onto the streets, where they developed their nocturnal habits. Preferring to regard them as predators, many kept their pity for the security man who, it was said, had died of shock.

The muttering from the workmen that the site was cursed was also drawing a lot of attention, and Bob Richards, the developer, alternated between threats and offers of pay increases in order to keep them quiet. By the time the members of the local archaeology society arrived en masse, claiming to have heard rumours that he was building on a famine graveyard, he was almost tearing his hair out in frustration. Though suspicious at first, and loath to accept his explanation that the bones they had heard about had been animal carcasses, the society was self-funded and the offer of a donation to make up for wasting their time was grudgingly accepted. It was only when the news crews had lost interest and moved on to another story, that he was able to clear away all signs of the graves. He even went as far as chopping down the tree and throwing away the toys and small gifts that had been left there. Such sentiments would not touch a man who was prepared to burn the bones of the dead.

When the first occupants collected the keys to their new homes a few weeks later, there was no sign that anything had ever been amiss. If they had read about the boys, and it was hard to believe that they had not, they made no mention of it. Once the last house was occupied, Bob could finally sit back and count his blessings. He had averted another disaster and, other than the odd complaint about cracks appearing as the houses settled, he expected to hear very little from the residents of Hillcrest.

The housing estate came to life as furniture vans arrived and were unloaded. Lights appeared in the houses and children ran laughing and shouting as they familiarised themselves with their new homes. The dead children watched from behind the bushes, amazed by the wonder of it all.

Timmy and Elizabeth were too busy watching Black Jack to join in the general excitement. By nightfall most of the houses had been visited. Yellow light streamed from the windows and the shapes of the people moving around inside could be clearly seen. Most of the new owners only stayed for a while, preferring to come back the next day to complete the move. The children's attention was focused mainly on the last three houses, the ones that had been erected on the graveyard. They sat and watched as the removal men carried furniture and boxes inside. Black Jack was biding his time as he too watched. Once the three houses were fully occupied, the children moved forward, to get a better look at their new neighbours.

Joe Mahoney had never considered himself a lucky man. His job, though well paid, was boring. Senior partner in an accounting firm was hardly a thrilling occupation, but for the most part he had been content, if not a little lonely. That was all in the past. When Helen Earls walked into his office, to apply for the post as his private secretary, something told him that his life was about to change forever. As a single mother with a young daughter she was anxious to get the job, and he was soon won over by her enthusiasm and winning smile. The fact that she was an unmarried mother was unfortunate. He had always considered himself a man of high moral principles and frowned on such things, but within weeks of their meeting, he was prepared to overlook what he saw as her past lapse.

Now, only ten months later, he was a married man, stepfather to seven-year-old Jenny and a father-to-be. Helen had been very persuasive and, despite his high morals, they had become lovers soon after their first meeting. Jenny, though timid at first, was warming to him, and there were even times when she admitted to 'kind of' liking him. The role of stepfather came easy to him, and he treasured the time he spent with his new family. His bachelor flat had been a tight squeeze for the three of them and it was out of the question that he would share Helen's council house. Now, they had their first real home and, at last, they would have some much-needed space. The only thing that marred his new-found happiness was Helen's moods. He hoped that these were down to her advanced state of pregnancy and the upset of the move.

'Joe, come and help me,' Jenny called from upstairs.

He put down the box he was carrying and took the stairs two at a time. He had screwed a number of small hooks into her bedroom ceiling to accommodate her collection of model rockets and spaceships. She was standing on the bed trying to attach the strings to each hook.

'My arms are too short,' she looked up at the ceiling.

He took the strings and hung each one on a hook.

'Well, what do you think?' he asked.

They looked up to survey his work.

'Cool.'

'Yes, indeed.'

They stayed like that for a while, watching the swirling models and their mesmerising silver, gold, blue and red paint.

His wife's call from below broke the spell and they both hurried down the stairs. She was in the kitchen, pulling various items from the many cardboard boxes that surrounded her and placing them on the shiny new work surfaces.

'I don't know where to start,' she waved around the room.

'I know,' Joe rubbed her back. 'Why don't you have a lie down and we'll make a start?'

'Yes, perhaps I will,' she agreed.

He didn't notice the glare she gave her daughter or the way the child shrank from her gaze and none of them were aware of the stares of the many watching eyes that were hidden by the shadows of the trees.

After Helen had gone upstairs, Joe continued with the unpacking. As Jenny emptied the cutlery into the designated drawer, he thought about his wife and the way she had changed towards him. Now that they were spending even more time together, he had come to realise that what he had once mistaken for self-confidence on her part, was actually narcissism.

Upstairs, Helen threw herself down on the unmade bed. The neatly folded sheets and pillowcases that Joe had stacked there were kicked onto the floor, as she tucked a pillow under her head and tried to get comfortable. She was tired of being pregnant, her huge stomach ruined the line of her clothes, and she felt frumpy and unattractive. This baby, she patted her bump, was another accident, but at least this time she was married. Biting down hard on her lip, trying not to cry, she closed her eyes and thought back over the last few months. If someone had told her a year ago that she would one day be living in a house like this, she would have laughed. Since the birth of her daughter, life had been a constant struggle to make ends meet. True, she could have done as her friends advised and got rid of the baby, but that had not been an option. She may have been many things, but she could not kill the life within her. It was out of the question.

A clatter of falling utensils from below signalled that the bottom had fallen out of another carton and she smiled at Joe's mutter of irritation. He was a good man, she thought, and kind to both of them; what more could she ask for? Well, a lot more, really. It was true that she had settled for Joe. She had realised during the first few weeks they worked together that he was trustworthy. The fact that he was financially secure had made him seem even more attractive. She had access to his personal computer and had used one of her lunch hours to check up on his bank and stock options. It was an hour well spent.

So here she was, in what had once been her dream home, with a man she cared very little for. She was old enough and wise enough to realise that there would never be a knight on a white charger for her kind. That dream belonged to those privileged enough to grow up surrounded by the comforts only money could buy. Yet now she was trapped. There was no way out for her and the baby that moved inside her signalled that this was indeed the case. Still, once it was born she could go back to work. Not for Joe, God no. It was enough to see him at night, without having to be around him all day. Of course, he had no idea of what she was planning, as she had been looking forward to staying at home. But the past few months had shown her how boring housework could be and the novelty of not being controlled by the alarm clock had soon worn off. She had envisioned the life of a kept woman, but the reality was something else. The dinner parties that had played such a vital role in her fantasy, had not come to fruition, as she found it difficult to mix with Joe's snooty friends. They looked down their noses at her and she knew that they whispered behind her back that she was a gold-digger. Well, let them say what they liked, she thumped the pillow, it would not be long until the birth and then she would really give them something to talk about.

————

Next door, at number 26, a similar operation as Joe's was being carried out with military precision. Mike Byrne had been an army sergeant for over thirty years and ruled his home with the same attitude that he used on his men. Rules were there to be obeyed. Without them there was no order and without order there was anarchy. This was his mantra and he lived by it. His young recruits wondered if his sex life, if he had one, was carried out with the same precision and tried to imagine the role his wife played in this. They mimicked what they thought would be his foreplay, 'stand by your bed, knickers down, assume the position,' and dissolved into fits of laughter. Had he known that the fun was at his expense, they would have paid dearly for it.

Ruth, his wife, picked up another carefully marked box and searched for its designated area. She pulled savagely at the label that marked the space, glad that he was not there to order her about. He had gone for a walk with Brutus, his dog. At least she had some peace while they were out of the house. They say that people start to resemble their pets and they weren't far wrong in Mike's case. He and the rottweiler had the same hanging jowls and sulky scowl. She grinned, as she imagined them side by side. Theirs was certainly not a case of beauty and the beast.

A movement outside the window caught her attention and she walked over to the sink. Pressing her face against the glass, she tried to make out what it was, but the fading light made it difficult to see anything. She put it down to a cat or the movement of the many trees and bushes at the bottom of the garden.

'Are you finished yet?' She hadn't heard the front door open.

'Almost, just a few more boxes.'

'Good, I'm starving and Brutus needs feeding.'

The sound of the television drifted in and she knew that he had put his feet up. He must be tired from doing nothing, she thought.

It was hard getting used to this new kitchen. She missed her old cooker and the familiarity of the worn knobs and jets. She missed the small, dark house that had been their home for so many years. Every nook and cranny had a comfortable feel and scent. This new place had a clinical, plastic smell of polish and new wood. The large amount that Mike had saved, coupled with his army pension, meant that they could afford this bigger place, and she knew that she should be thankful and try to adjust.

Another movement outside caught her eye. She smiled at the young woman in the next garden, who waved at her. A pretty young thing, Ruth thought, and happy in her marriage. She waved back and watched as they unpacked their belongings from an old farm trailer.

She was right about the couple next door in number 25. Tom and Sheila Ryan were almost newly-weds. They were just weeks short of their first wedding anniversary and at last things were starting to improve for them. After eleven months of living in a grotty apartment, they were now in heaven. The house had been a stroke of unbelievable luck. Tom had been offered a job as systems analyst for a new and fast-moving computer company, with a salary far exceeding anything they had ever imagined. It would involve quite a bit of travelling for him at first, but Sheila would get used to that and hopefully the neighbours would be friendly.

Besides, Sheila's teaching exam results had come through and they were overjoyed to find that she had passed with honours. By coincidence, an old friend called to say that she was leaving her post as junior teacher in a local school and did Sheila want to be recommended for the post? So she had found herself only days later, sitting before a panel of school governors with her purse clutched nervously in her lap, answering their questions. They must have liked what they heard and she had accepted the offered position.

She smiled and waved at her new neighbour. The woman waved back and Sheila wondered if it was the bare bulb that made her eyes look so sad and hollow. She shivered and hurried back inside. Tom would be back soon with their Chinese takeaway and she had a nice bottle of chablis chilling in the fridge. She had been too tired to cook, and he had offered to drive into town, even though it was quite a way off. She turned on the oven and put two plates in to heat. Taking a duvet cover, she spread it on the dining-room floor as a makeshift tablecloth. Having little furniture, their first meal would be eaten picnic style. She put two candles in the centre of the 'tablecloth' and set glasses and cutlery on either side. Pleased with her work, she lit the candles and sat watching the flickering flames. She smiled, the candlelight reflecting off the specks of gold in her eyes.

She was unaware that she now had an admirer. Black Jack watched as she sat enveloped by the light. Death had diminished none of his primal urges. He wanted to drink real ale again, smell the perfume of a woman's body, sink his fingers into skin and taste the salty wetness of the flesh. Why should these people have the happiness he had been denied? Still there was plenty of time to change all that and the woman's look of joy would soon be replaced by one of terror. He was tired of the dark and the never-ending night. He wanted to walk in the light again and deserved to have these basic things. Nothing was going to stand in his way.

Sheila looked up, puzzled by a vague unease, but he slipped back into the shadows. She must not see him, not until he was ready.

The residents of Hillcrest were not conscious of the unwelcome visitor that roamed through their homes that night. Some tossed and turned, sensing the figure that was standing over them, but no one woke.

FIFTEEN

April 1846

Elizabeth had no idea how long it had taken her to reach Maycroft. When she arrived, Thomas and Annie helped her inside and up to her room. They told her how upset the master had been when he had discovered she had left. She knew it was not Charles, but Black Jack who had been most upset.

The servants pleaded with her to bathe and change her clothes. She obeyed, and afterwards sat in her bedroom awaiting whatever punishment she would receive. She had had no choice, but to return to Maycroft. When Andrew sent the money for her fare to the New World, she could not chance missing his letter.

Besides, she had nowhere else to go. She heard from a woman in the town of the death of her father. He had married his housekeeper and left his entire fortune to his new wife. She stared at the ceiling as shadows lengthened and evening drew in. She strained her ears for the sound of hoofs on the cobbles below. Although exhausted, sleep was beyond her.

She thought about all that she had seen on her journey. The figures on the road no longer frightened her, so absorbed was she in her own private nightmare. Sleep finally overtook her as the moon's beams crept across the room.

'What the hell did you think you were doing?' She jumped, as her bedroom door was flung open and thudded against the wall. Charles stood there, face contorted like a wild creature. Bloodshot eyes blazed in a face that was sunken and devoid of colour.

'Leave me alone,' she said curtly.

'I want some answers from you, woman, and I want them now,' he approached the bed and spittle flew against her face as he spoke.

'I sent the children to America.'

'You did what?' He steadied himself against one of the bedposts and looked at her, mouth agape.

'You heard me. I sent my children away.'

'But how, why?'

'So they would be safe. I sent them to a cousin who will take care of them.'

'Why didn't you go with them?'

She swung her legs onto the floor and paced the room.

'Don't you think I wanted to go? I would have given anything to be with them, but I hadn't enough money.'

'I would have helped.'

'You!'

'I could have paid your way.'

She looked into his face thinking he was teasing or tormenting her, but she could see no trace of malice.

'Have you some money now?' she asked. 'Six pounds is all I need and I'd gladly repay you when I can.'

'Well,' he thought for a moment. 'I haven't exactly got any money, but I'm sure Carey will lend me some.'

With these words any hope she had died.

'Thank you, Charles, but that will not be necessary. I'll find some other way.'

'Very well,' he went to leave. 'You'll join us for dinner?'

The thought of seeing Carey again filled her with dread, but her stomach hurt from the hunger, and she replied,

'Yes, thank you. I'll be down shortly.'

She went downstairs and entered the dining-room. Everything felt alien now, as though she was part of some giant tableau where movement had no meaning. Carey was sitting at the head of the table and dressed in the finest clothes she had ever seen.

'Elizabeth, welcome home.'

As he stood to greet her, she inwardly wondered what had happened in her absence to improve his demeanour, manners and fortune. She nodded and took her usual place.

She sipped at the soup, savouring every mouthful. Thomas had placed a large platter containing a joint of roast beef on the serving trolley nearby. The smell made her mouth water and she felt guilty at what she saw as a betrayal of her sorrow. Still, she must keep up her strength for the voyage, and it could be months before she received the money from Andrew.

A plate was placed in front of her, filled with carved beef, carrots and bread. Once she tasted the food she wanted more. Nothing had ever tasted that good. The juice trapped within the fleshy meat leaked out, bathing and caressing her tongue. In her hurry, she swallowed chunks that momentarily stuck in her throat. Thomas refilled her plate twice and she blushed at her lust for food. Once, when she inadvertently caught Carey's eye, he winked and remarked, 'Hunger makes a sweet sauce. Doesn't it, Elizabeth?'

She ignored him and continued with her feasting. All she wanted was to stay alive and well enough to rejoin her children. If having to endure his insults and insinuations was the price she had to pay, then so be it.

Carey must have learned the reason of her disappearance from Charles and, for now, was either ignoring it or planning his revenge. As their sole benefactor, they were all, particularly Elizabeth, answerable to him. Though she was aware of his influence over Charles, she had yet to discover how absolute his power was.

Over the next few days Elizabeth was left alone. With the aid of

Thomas, she carried the luggage trunks down from the attic and set about packing the children's clothes. The items would probably be outgrown by the time they met again, but the work kept her mind occupied and she took comfort from breathing in the scent of each child as she folded the various garments.

The rest of her time was spent wandering within the grounds of the Hall. She would not venture outside again, not after witnessing the horror of the roads. She moved automatically, as though between worlds and suspended in time. Days and nights tumbled in slow motion, one into the other.

The Hall was a much darker place now, the grand chandeliers hung with cobwebs and the rooms had an empty, neglected feel to them. It was impossible to keep such a place clean without adequate staff. Annie did what she could, but Thomas was now so weak he could barely shuffle his way between the kitchen and dining room.

Elizabeth avoided Charles and Black Jack as much as possible; she still locked her door at night although there had not been any unwanted visits since she had returned. Sometimes, late at night, footsteps would stop outside, pause for a moment, then carry on down the gallery. She wasn't sure which of them it was, though they sounded too steady to have been Charles'. She knew that Carcy was playing a game of cat and mouse with her, but she had to hold on a few months more. Every night she lay there thinking of her girls adrift on the high seas and prayed for their protection. She usually fell asleep as dawn was approaching and the emptiness of the new day spread before her.

———

The tapping at the main door startled her. She was on her way to the drawing-room to fetch a book and was unsure what to do. Thomas was well out of earshot.

Tentatively, opening the door a crack, she peeped outside. An old woman with a bundle at her feet was peering back at her.

'Yes, may I help you?'

'I'm Mrs Carey. My boy Jack lives here.'

'I'm afraid he's out at the moment. Please call back later.' She moved to shut the door, but the old woman's hand shot out and grabbed her wrist.

'I'll wait inside, if you don't mind, dear?'

Flustered and wanting to be rid of the claw that held her, Elizabeth stuttered, 'Of course, I'll show you to the drawing-room, but you'll have quite a wait I'm afraid. Your son doesn't usually return until late.'

Picking up her bundle, the old woman followed her inside and sank into a gilded chair. 'It doesn't bother me, the wait. I know my boy works long hours, but then,' she sniffed, 'he was always a hard worker. Gets that from me, you know?'

'Really?' Elizabeth had no idea how to deal with the woman, who peered out at her from beneath the folds of a harsh, wool cape, like some large bird of prey. 'If you'll excuse me, I have to get on with my duties. I trust you'll be all right alone?'

'Yes, my dear. You run along, I'm used to being alone.'

Elizabeth walked away and in her hurry almost collided with Thomas.

'Beg your pardon, my lady, but I thought I heard voices.'

She told him about their visitor in a whisper. 'Perhaps you should go and see if she requires anything?' Relieved, she left the woman to Thomas, who had so much more experience in dealing with such people.

She waited for evening to approach and the sound of the horse hoofs that always heralded the men's arrival. She opened her door and listened to the voices below. Once she heard the slam of the drawing-room door, she edged her way to the rail and looked down. Charles and Thomas were both staring at the door as sounds of battle came from inside. This was the first time she had heard Carey lose control. There were screams and the sound of furniture being overturned.

When a lull came in the fighting, she could hear the pleading cackle of his mother.

Charles looked upwards and saw her at the banisters, but he just shrugged and wandered off to the dining-room. The battle seemed to rage for hours and growing tired, she knelt on the floor, so great was her fascination with the fight. When Carey emerged from the room he was flushed with anger. Not wanting to risk him seeing her, she crawled across to her room and had just made it inside when his footsteps sounded. Her door was flung open and he stood there, panting.

'Well, Elizabeth, I hope you found that to your amusement.'

'I have no idea to what you are referring, Mr Carey, and in future kindly knock before you enter my room.'

'Don't you mean my room?'

'That's as may be, but while I occupy it, I request that you knock. That's not asking too much is it?'

The calmness of her voice threw him.

'We have a new house guest.'

'Don't you mean *you* have a new house guest?'

He turned and walked away without answering. The unwelcome presence of his mother was a great disappointment and reminded him of his background.

Soon it would be time for dinner, and for the first time Elizabeth was looking forward to it. Carey's discomfort was obvious the minute she entered the room. His mother was sitting across from Charles, who appeared to be taken aback by her.

'This is Elizabeth.' Carey spoke to his mother, who smiled, showing a mouth full of rotting teeth.

'We've already met. Haven't we, my dear?'

'Yes, we met this afternoon.'

During the meal the woman's conversation became louder and more animated, as she downed one glass of port after another. Charles was incapable of speech. Carey tossed in his chair and picked at his food.

Elizabeth, seeing the opportunity to embarrass him, asked, 'Is the food to you liking, Mrs Carey?'

'It's grand, dear, but call me Agnes. I'm sure we are going to be great friends.'

'Yes, indeed,' Elizabeth smiled. 'I'm sure we are.'

Carey had now taken to kicking the table leg nearest to him, causing port to splash from the glasses with each thud. Neither Charles nor his mother took any notice of this, it only made them drink faster, in order to save the precious liquid.

'How are the people faring on the land these days, Agnes?' Elizabeth asked and, before her son could stop her, Agnes was in full flow.

'Oh, it's awful, my dear. The amount that's homeless would frighten you. They wander the road in their thousands and …'

'Enough!' The shout and the sound of Carey's fist banging on the table made them jump. 'Not another word, woman, or you'll find yourself back where you came from.'

'I meant no harm, son, just telling the truth. There are many that brought it on themselves, no disrespect to you.'

'Enough, I said!' He was shaking with anger.

'Perhaps we should change the conversation?' Elizabeth ventured.

'Perhaps you should go to your room,' he said.

She could hear him shouting as she went upstairs, and smiled. He was getting a taste of his own medicine for once and not liking it one little bit.

———

Carey's mood did not improve over the next few weeks. The very sight of his mother sent him into a rage. Elizabeth quickly became familiar with the woman's character. She could cause trouble in paradise. Even Thomas and Annie were at each other's throats as a result of her carrying tales and lies from one to the other. It seemed Agnes could only be happy when surrounded by misery. She had overheard her, on one occasion, asking her son why Elizabeth was still there. Luckily, his hatred for his mother was such that he ignored this. From then on Elizabeth avoided her as she would a rabid dog.

Seeing this as a snub Agnes complained to her son who, for once, listened to her. He questioned Elizabeth about it after dinner that night. When she was returning to her room, he followed.

'A word please, Elizabeth.'

'Yes?'

'My mother says you've been ignoring her.'

'No. I merely do not choose to seek her out and spend every day listening to poisonous gossip.'

'I'm sure she means no harm.' His words were spoken through gritted teeth.

'And I'm sure she does,' Elizabeth answered. 'Her very trade makes her a dangerous woman, don't you think?'

'Ah, it's pointless talking to you. Even now, though you have nothing, you still insist on acting as lady of the manor.'

'I have my pride and morals, but those are qualities you would know nothing about.'

'Get out of my sight,' he hissed, 'and remember this; your days here are numbered.'

'As you wish.' Her calmness denied the terror she was feeling, and she had angered him more than she had intended with the mention of his mother's profession.

For the next few days Agnes ignored her, sniffing and making remarks under her breath when they passed, but otherwise leaving her alone. Slowly, the old woman managed to snake her way into her son's confidence, and they could be seen whispering together. It all came to a head one night during dinner.

Carey was in one of his evil moods and it was evident that everyone was going to suffer. But Elizabeth could never have imagined the extent to which he would go. The table setting gave her the first suspicion that something was wrong. Charles' place was devoid of a drinking glass. She could tell he had been without alcohol all day from the surly way he'd returned that evening. Now, his hands shook as he tried to use his knife and fork. Carey drank more than usual, holding the crimson liquid up to the light and remarking on the superb quality of the port. Charles wiped away the saliva at the corners of his mouth with the sleeve of his jacket, and Elizabeth was disgusted to see him acting so coarsely. She offered her glass.

'Perhaps you would like my wine, Charles? I have no stomach for it.'

Carey stopped her.

'He's to have none of it. If you don't want it, leave it.'

She was glad when the meal finally ended and she could escape to her room.

Later that night she heard arguing downstairs and crept out to the landing to listen. A distraught Charles was begging and pleading with Carey to give him a drink. She almost cried in mortification for her brother-in-law. Then, with growing terror, she heard Carey's words.

'How can you repay me, Charles? You have nothing left that I want. I own everything you once had. Not as much as a blade of grass belongs to you any more.'

She couldn't make out Charles' answer and turned to go back to her room, when, suddenly, the dining-room door flew open and Charles came out with Carey following behind him. When she saw they were coming towards the stairs, she ran. Throwing her dressing gown on a nearby chair, she jumped into bed. Then, she realised with dismay that she had forgotten to lock her door. At that moment it was thrown open. Charles stood there, gasping for breath, and holding Carey's sleeve, 'Do you still say I have nothing you want?'

The men looked at one another and Elizabeth watched as Carey took the key to the cellar from his pocket and handed it to Charles.

Her heart was beating wildly as Carey locked her door and stood looking at her, with his back against the wood.

'No, please no,' she pleaded, shrinking against the headboard.

Her screams echoed throughout the house. Annie and Thomas
crossed themselves and silently prayed for her. Agnes looked up from
her knitting and cackled, while, in the cellar, Charles soothed whatever
guilt he felt with the first bottle of port.

There was stillness within the house the next day, the hush of death.
No one spoke and, for the first time, Carey rode out without Charles.
Annie crept up to Elizabeth's room after he had left and found her
huddled whimpering in a corner, covered only by a sheet. Her nightgown lay in tatters on the floor and the bed was in total disarray.

'Come my lady, let me help you up,' the old woman reached down
and touched her. 'That's right,' Annie spoke as to a child. 'That's a good
girl, you're safe now and he's gone. Come on, up you get.'

Once Elizabeth was on the bed, Annie left for a moment to fetch
some fresh water and returned to find her sobbing uncontrollably.

Wringing out a cloth in the water, Annie tried to wipe her face, but
her hand was brushed away.

'Don't touch me, I'm dirty, diseased, I want to die,' Elizabeth
wept.

'There, there, my lady, don't take on so. This is not your doing and
you can't allow him to destroy you.'

Elizabeth nodded and her crying ceased. The woman was right;
she could not let Carey win.

'There now, my lady, let's clean you up.' Taking the hair that was
flowing loosely around her shoulders, Annie drew it back and tied it
with a ribbon. Only then was she able to see clearly what Elizabeth
had suffered. One cheek was swollen and already darkening to a bruise.
Her lower lip was cut and caked with dried blood.

There were bruises on her shoulders and breasts and something else, some kind of indents, on the skin. Looking closer, she was horrified to find these were bite marks. She washed them as best she could and tried not to cry, when she saw he had broken the skin in places.

'Lie back now, my lady.'

Elizabeth lay down and allowed her to remove the sheet. The woman never spoke as she washed her mistress' body. Not even when she rubbed gently at the dried blood on her thighs. Turning her over, she could see more bite marks on her buttocks and the marks of his fingers were clearly visible on her back. When she was finished, Elizabeth sat up, and pulled the sheet around her once more.

'He really hurt me.'

'Yes, my lady, he did.'

'I have to get away from here before he returns. But, where will I go? I have no one to turn to.'

'There's always your father's house.'

'No,' Elizabeth knew she would not be welcomed there.

'The only place open to you then, dear lady, is the workhouse. He'd never think to look for you in that place. Though God knows things are bad there as well. There's fever raging and barely enough food to feed those inside.'

'I'll take my chances. I'd rather die than let him touch me again. This will be my life from now on if I stay here.'

They both knew she was right, although the old woman wondered how her mistress could possibly survive in the workhouse. She helped her to dress and, taking a carpetbag, filled it with a few items of clothing.

Before leaving the house Elizabeth told Annie about the letter she was expecting from America and made her promise to look out for it and keep it safe. After swearing that she would, the old woman led her down the back stairway and out into the kitchens. Thomas, who was sitting in front of the fire polishing Carey's boots, jumped up when they entered.

'I'm so sorry, my lady.'

'I know, Thomas, and I thank you.'

When he heard of her plan he was aghast. But there was no stopping her. Annie was crying and even Thomas dabbed at his eyes as she turned to go.

'Just one more thing, Thomas,' she asked. 'Will you please give something to Carey for me?'

'Of course, my lady.'

She handed him a note. It read, 'You will pay for this. I promise. E.F.'

SIXTEEN

August 1846

Seventy people a day were dying in the workhouse. Up until now Timmy had protected the children as best he could, but slowly, steadily, silently, with the vicious intent of a snake, it struck.

'My throat hurts and I'm too warm.' Timmy woke up to find Peter beside his bed and even in the half-light he could see the child was flushed. Picking up Katie, who was as always sleeping beside him, he carried her to another bed. The only isolation he was able to offer the sick child was his own bed. There was no use going to the workhouse infirmary, because it was already full to capacity. People were even lying on makeshift straw beds in the corridors outside his room. He rushed out to the well and brought back fresh, cold water that he urged Peter to drink. But the boy's throat was too sore and after a few sips he lay back wanting to sleep.

The fever had taken hold and he knew there would be no stopping it. It hung in the air like a black cloud, swirling and merging into a dark spectre that moved from bed to bed. He blinked, rubbing his eyes, but he could still see it, though fainter now. Had he inherited the gift of sight from his mother, or was it just his foolish imagination?

Peter slept fitfully, tossing and turning, calling for his ma. Timmy ran to the kitchens and asked Nora, who had been so kind to him in the past, for something, anything, to help the child.

'There's nothing, lad,' she told him. 'No medicine, no food, nothing. I've been promised fresh supplies today, but that will only be cornmeal and perhaps a little milk. If his throat's that sore, he'll never be able to eat it anyway.'

'I'll go up to the infirmary, then.'

They both knew he would be in serious trouble if he was found wandering around the sick rooms, but he didn't care. He had to get medicine for Peter.

'Be careful,' Nora warned, 'and I don't just mean of the guardians; the fever is worse up there. Tie this around your mouth,' she handed him a piece of cloth, 'it might help keep you safe.'

He tied it securely over his mouth and nose and turned to go.

'Timmy, this isn't your fault, lad. You cannot stop it reaching the children. They pass the sick and dying every day in the corridors. You've done your best.'

He nodded, feeling tears well up, but these were his children and it was up to him to protect them. He went into the yard and raced along in the shadow of the garden wall that hid him from prying eyes, the way it had once sheltered the vegetables. Now the soil lay bare.

He stopped short on reaching the infirmary, edging back until his shoulders came in contact with the cold bricks of the wall. Although the infirmary was within the workhouse grounds, it was set apart, and this was the first time he had seen it. He had seen many frightening things over the past two years, but this was the fabric of nightmares.

A long plank reached from an opening at one end of the gable to the ground. Heaped at the bottom lay ten, perhaps more, corpses. A nearby cart was already full and being led away. The loaders went indoors to await its return. The air, though cold with the sting of winter, hung with the smell of putrefaction.

Timmy wondered what the plank was for. Bodies were piled against the gable wall. Carefully picking his way over, he looked up into the door at the top. He decided it was just a black hole, and was just about to walk away, when a warning shout from above made him look up. The body of a small child came sliding down the plank and landed with a thud against him, knocking him off his feet. He opened his mouth to scream, but no sound came out, and he scrambled away in panic from the cold, glazed eyes. Finding it hard to breath, he pulled at the cloth around his face. He retched, unable to vomit, as his stomach had been empty for almost two days. The violent retching hurt his ribs and throat.

'Timmy, lad.'

He looked up to see Nora running towards him. She didn't ask any questions, but led him inside and sat him by the fire. The heat helped to soothe his fear as she wiped at his face, brushing away the tears with one hand, holding him tightly with the other.

'There were so many bodies,' he looked into her eyes, willing her to say he had imagined it.

But Nora shook her head. 'It's the fever. They're burying them by the scores every day. No one in the country has been spared. The children are the worst. They're too weak from hunger to fight it.'

'I'll fight it.'

'I dare say you will, or die trying.'

'I can't die.'

'We all have to die sometime, even you.'

'No, I promised my ma that I'd stay alive and look after my sister and brothers. So you see I can't die.'

'You're not an orphan then?'

'No.' A few months before he would have been afraid to tell anyone that he'd lied to get in, but now he didn't care. 'I had the fever,' he explained, 'and my da was afraid to let me back in the cabin, so I came here. I'm going home again though, one day soon.'

He was about to get up and go back to check on Peter, when she stopped him.

'Stay sitting a while longer, lad. You've had a bad fright and I'll make you a drop of tea as soon as I get a new helper. You'll have noticed most of the others are gone?'

He had been wondering where everyone had disappeared to.

As if reading his thoughts she answered. 'The fever; it's taken most of them and I'm blue in the face from asking for help. I've been promised someone today, though I suppose there's not that much to do now, with many too sick to eat this muck,' she said, banging the ladle on the side of the pot. 'Peel's Brimstone, the people call it and bad luck to him. It goes through you like a dose of salts, and those that can stomach it get no nourishment.'

The door opened and she looked up. 'Have you been sent to help me?' she asked.

Timmy heard none of the conversation; his mind was in turmoil trying to think what he could do to save the children. A hand on his arm startled him, and he looked up to find Nora was speaking to him.

'I'll go and check on the child while you have your tea. It won't be long brewing and will help calm you.'

He nodded and went back to staring into the fire. Soon a cup was held under his nose, he took it and sipped. He could feel the warmth run all the way down into his stomach. He smiled, looked up to thank the giver and threw the cup in the air almost scalding himself.

'My lady!'

'Timmy, I can't believe it, Timmy, is it really you?'

'Yes, it's me.'

'You're alive, I can't believe it. I've though of you often, but I never expected … come,' she led him to a table and sat down beside him, 'tell me all that has happened to you since we last met.'

They sat like old friends and exchanged news. She told him about her girls, their leaving, and how Black Jack was now in charge of the Hall. He listened wide-eyed to the news and could understand why she was there. Anything Black Jack touched turned bad.

Still, he cheered up when she told him about the expected letter and her plans to join her girls. He begged for news of his family. She had none, and explained that she never left the Hall, but would check the next time she went there.

'I have to explain something to you,' she whispered. 'I told them I was a ladies' maid and had been turned out. Things would be very bad for me, if they found out who I really am.'

'I won't tell anyone, my lady, I promise. I said I was an orphan.'

'Aren't we an awful pair?' she smiled. 'And remember now, my name is Elizabeth, don't forget.'

'I won't my ... I mean Elizabeth,' he blushed at being so familiar.

Nora returned with the news that Peter was still sleeping, but burning up. They took turns sponging him down and trying to make him drink. Elizabeth charmed one of the doctors into coming out to see the child ... anyone who entered the infirmary now left by way of the plank. After checking Peter thoroughly, the doctor shook his head.

'It's typhus all right. See the rash starting on his stomach?' He indicated red pinpricks on the skin. 'By morning this will cover most of his body. There's nothing I can do for him. Medical supplies are sparse. The best thing you can do is to try and get him to drink.'

'But his throat is so very sore,' Elizabeth said, 'is there nothing at all you can do?'

Taking her aside, he whispered, 'Within a day or two the child will die unless a miracle happens. If, and I say if, the fever breaks and you manage to get him to drink, he might make it, but I can't see that happening. I've seen seven die since daybreak. I'm sorry. I wish there was something I could do.' He shook his head and she could see the lines of fatigue etched deep in his face. 'Is the young lad his brother?'

'No, but as good as.'

'It'll be hard on him then.'

She thanked the doctor. It wasn't his fault that the child would die. It was this dreadful famine.

The kitchen was almost empty save for Timmy's group and the occasional other child scattered here and there. It was the same at the adult mealtime. Where the room had once seated over two hundred at a time, there was now perhaps twenty. Many of the adults were too ill to come for the food, while others just couldn't stomach it. The huge pot of meal was almost untouched and would be reheated the next day. There was no need to steep any more corn, as Nora had been doing, in the hope of making it more digestible. The two women had been working in silence, each lost in their own thoughts, until Nora spoke.

'He'll take it very bad you know.'

Elizabeth nodded; she had been thinking of nothing else.

'I'll sit up with Peter tonight to relieve Timmy and maybe he'll get some sleep,' she said.

'Won't you be missed, if you don't sign back in?' asked Nora, knowing that once Elizabeth signed herself into a workhouse she became a prisoner of the state.

'No,' Elizabeth told her, 'there are so many going over the walls these past few nights to escape the typhus that they've stopped all that.'

Many escaped late at night and Elizabeth knew she would soon have to do the same. She had calculated that the letter should arrive in another three weeks or so, and had been listening to the inmates as they compared escape routes in whispers. Her route was planned, all she had to do was to wait.

Timmy was still hard at work washing Peter down. Despite his best efforts, the child seemed even hotter than before, and his face and throat were very swollen. Elizabeth tried trickling water between his parched lips, but he choked on the slightest drop. The others sat in silence; even the youngest sensed something was dreadfully wrong. Hours crawled by, night fell, and the room became colder.

Elizabeth tried to persuade Timmy to lie down on one of the other beds, but he refused. They spent the night praying and taking turns to wipe Peter's fevered face. The flesh on his wasted body burned beneath Elizabeth's hands, and at times she almost cried out in frustration and anguish. She had been in the workhouse for over four weeks and seen many horrid and disgusting things during that time; senseless fighting over food and bits of clothing, parents climbing through windows and over high walls during the night, abandoning their children to the system, rats feeding on corpses in the hallways and on some that were not yet dead, but nothing could compare to the horror of a child dying.

'Do you think he'll get better?' Timmy startled her out of her reverie.

'It's in God's hands now. We just have to wait and see.'

He nodded and went back to wiping Peter's body. The boy tossed and turned, calling for his ma. In his quiet periods, they sat watching him, willing him to live, but it was useless. As the first fingers of dawn crept slowly across the sky, the atmosphere in the room changed. A cold stillness descended, rousing them both from their thoughts and striking fear into their hearts. Sitting on either side of him, they each held a hand and stroked the bony fingers. Peter eventually opened eyes that were glazed over with fever and, just for a moment, smiled up at Elizabeth. He was seeing what he wanted to see, and managed to whisper, 'Ma?'

'Yes, darling,' she sobbed, 'Ma's here.'

Timmy was crying too, but he didn't make a sound. He had never seen anyone die before and was expecting something dramatic to happen. Surely, an event such as death would warrant a fanfare of trumpets, something to warn the watchers. But it was nothing like that. Peter pulled away from him, turned on his side and cuddled closer to Elizabeth. She brushed the wet blonde curls from his forehead, murmuring little words of endearment between sobs, and with just a brief sigh he drifted into death.

'No,' Timmy looked at the still form. 'He can't be dead.'

'I'm so sorry, Timmy. He's gone.' She didn't know what else to say.

Running over into a corner, Timmy scrunched down, folding in on himself, wanting to disappear. He couldn't face the awful pain, the sense of loss.

Elizabeth got up from the bed, covered the body and went to fetch Nora. She found her sitting alone in the kitchen, staring into space. The woman looked up hopefully, but Elizabeth shook her head.

'How's Timmy?' asked Nora.

'Overcome with grief,' she said, sitting opposite. 'What do we do now?'

'We'll have to take the body to the burial cart. No one will come for it otherwise. There are dead and dying lying side by side all over the place, and no one to give them a Christian burial. God be with us all this day.'

'Amen,' Elizabeth whispered.

'Well, no use just sitting here,' Nora said. 'We'll carry him between us; God knows he won't weigh much. It's best he's gone before the others wake.'

Elizabeth followed her back to the deathbed. The only sound came from the steady, rhythmic breathing of the sleeping children, and the muted sobbing of the boy in the corner. They wrapped the small body in the blanket and were about to lift it from the bed when Timmy stopped them.

'Where are you taking him?'

'To the funeral cart,' Nora said.

'They'll just throw him in a grave and I'll never see him again.'

'There's nothing we can do, lad,' Nora bent, once again, to pick up the dead child.

'No,' Timmy stopped her. 'I'll take him.'

They stood back as he slid his arms under the bundle and lifted it. They followed him in silent procession through corridors, up to the main door and outside into the crisp morning air. They could tell from the movement of Timmy's shoulders, that he was crying as he walked. They stayed well back, but vigilant in case he should fall under the weight of his terrible burden. The loaders were already at work and the cart almost full, even at this early hour. Seeing Timmy and the women, the men stopped for a moment before one of them gestured to the bodies stacked up by the gable.

'Throw it there. We'll see to it later.'

'This is Peter.'

'What?' The man looked puzzled.

'This is a little boy called Peter,' Timmy repeated.

The men looked from one to the other, unsure of what to do, until the man leading the cart came forward.

'Give Peter to me, lad, I'll take care of him now.'

Timmy allowed the bundle to slip from his hands and into the waiting arms. They watched, as he laid the child on top of the pile of bodies that already filled the cart and, taking the reins, he led the horse away. With the movement, the blanket came loose and one small, white hand appeared. The jogging of the cart over the rough ground made it look like Peter was waving one final goodbye. Timmy, over-come with weakness, sank to his knees. Elizabeth and Nora supported one another as the cart passed. No one moved until it was out of sight and Peter's tousled, blonde curls were lost to them forever.

The horror of that day was to be relived over and over as the children succumbed to the fever. It spread rapidly within the confines of the room. Soon Timmy, Katie and Elizabeth were the only ones to remain untouched by it. Nora had disappeared, going over the wall one night within a week of Peter's death. The trip to the burial cart became a daily occurrence, but they no longer cried. Seeing so much suffering numbed them, and they developed a resignation that each day would be filled with sorrow.

No one besides Timmy, Elizabeth and the doctor, would come near the children. They huddled together, vomit forming a thick crust on their clothes, waiting for death. Even Timmy's stories brought no relief to them. All were living skeletons, many blinded as eye infection spread from one to the other. So they lay, in the freezing cold, watching the dark shapes of carers moving around them. They never moved, never cried, as they waited for death. Timmy and Elizabeth were exhausted and in very real danger. The constant minding of the children, coupled with lack of food and sleep, left them open to the fever.

A sad little procession returned to the room after the last child died. They gazed at the empty beds, each lost in private thoughts. Katie held tightly to Timmy's hand and he could feel her shivering from fright and cold. That one so young should witness such heartbreak was beyond understanding. Queues no longer formed at the workhouse gates, as people chose to die on the land or in their makeshift shelters. Others were too sick and weakened by hunger to make it that far. Most of the guardians had died, and there was no longer any order or organisation within. Neither was there any food.

The corridors were strewn with corpses, floors so matted with blood that the worn soles of their shoes stuck as they walked. Drainage gullies outside were packed and stinking with human waste. The air was heavy, cloying and the stench reached everywhere.

'We have to get out,' Elizabeth said, adamant they would take their chances on the land. Her cousin's letter should have arrived by now, and there might even be enough to pay the passage for Timmy and Katie. It was only because of her genuine concern for the boy and little girl that she had stayed so long in that dreadful place.

They saw no one throughout that day and it was a great relief when twilight fell. It was freezing and they needed warm clothing. Timmy and Elizabeth crept about the corridors and rooms taking whatever they could from those no longer in need of them.

They both knew where they would go. Timmy thought of nothing else, but seeing his family, and Elizabeth would go straight to Maycroft.

All was quiet as they crept away. Keeping well into the shadows, they moved under the archway and towards the gates. No one noticed their going … not even when the gate groaned loudly as they squeezed through. The town was quiet as they walked along, buildings casting dark shrouds across the dead bodies on the road. From somewhere far off came the sound of rifle shots. Later, they would learn the soldiers were shooting at dogs feeding off the corpses. Soon, they were on the outskirts of the town and the road lay bare and open before them. Despite his hunger Timmy wanted to run, to jump for joy. They were free and he would soon be back with his family.

SEVENTEEN

October 2003

Within weeks the first complaints started to filter through to the developer's office. There was nothing specific, no talk of building flaws, as he might have expected, just an overall feeling of uneasiness within the houses; freezing draughts that could not be explained, doors banging for no obvious reason. His men came back puzzled. They could find no reason for any of it. Windows and door seals were tight. The whole thing was bewildering.

Still ... no, he brushed the fleeting image of the graveyard from his mind. That was stupid. The dead were dead. He decided he was dealing with a hysterical group of nutters. Upwardly mobile shitheads and aging hippies, who liked nothing better than causing trouble.

He stopped his jeep outside number 26 and consulted his notes. Mr and Mrs Byrne, oh, yes, how could he forget, the brash ex-army sergeant and his timid little wife. He had met them when they put a down payment on the house. Mr Byrne was one of the more persistent complainers; best dealt with first. Everyone else would be a doddle compared to this loudmouth.

He forced a smile as he rang the bell. Byrne, holding tightly to the leash of one of the ugliest dogs he had ever seen, opened the door.

'Ah, Richards, about time. I'm sick of the endless trail of cowboys you keep sending. Come in.'

Bob Richards edged his way past the dribbling dog, his back to the wall so that it was in sight at all times.

'Never mind old Brutus here,' Byrne reached down and scratched the ears of the dog. 'He'll not bite you. Not unless he's ordered. Will you old boy?' The dog glanced up at his master, but there was no pleasure in the look. Brutus had been beaten during training and had not forgotten.

Richards was ushered towards the lounge with the dog so close behind that he could feel its breath on the back of his legs. He sat down without being asked, opened his folder and started shuffling papers about.

Christ, the atmosphere in the house was stagnant. The air felt heavy, cloying. He wrote note after note, barely pausing to look up, wanting to be done. He left with promises to call back with a team of specialists, who would check the drains and whatever else they thought might be causing the cold.

It was with great trepidation that he approached number 27. Already he could hear the shrill voice of the woman inside and the whimpering of a small child. Taking a deep breath, he rang the bell. The door was thrown open and a look of anger disappeared from the woman's face, to be replaced with a coy, welcoming smile.

'Mr Richards. Do come in.'

He remembered this one all right. Too sweet to be wholesome had been his first impression on meeting her. She had arrived on the arm of a much older man who was, he learned from her gushing endearments, her new husband. He had seen it all before. Men like her husband were easy targets for these women. And she had been showing all the usual signs of desperation. Neckline almost meeting hemline and make-up applied with a trowel.

'Good morning Mrs Mahoney.' He swept past her, but could not fail to notice the tear-stained face that peeped between the banisters. He winked up at the child and she tried to smile.

'Do come in and sit down.'

He hurried into the lounge, wanting to be out of smelling distance of the perfume she wore. It was overpowering and, although probably very expensive, applied in much the same way as her make-up.

'Now, about these problems.' He went through the same routine as before, taking down complaints, asking questions. Once he almost laughed aloud when, despite her advanced state of pregnancy and ridiculously tight dress, she tried to cross her legs suggestively, and almost slid off the couch.

There was a distinct lack of warmth about the place, not just the usual chill of morning. Small footsteps pattered down the stairs and along the hallway towards the back of the house. A door clicked shut. He smiled at the woman, who shrugged and returned his smile.

'Children,' she simpered, 'they can be so trying at times. Do you have any of your own?'

'No. I never married.'

There was that smile again. He now knew how a mouse felt under the deadly gaze of a cat.

'So despite the cold and doors banging, have you noticed anything else?'

'Well, my husband says I'm imagining things, what with the baby and all,' she patted her stomach, 'but I hear whispering and feel as if someone is touching me.'

He had been right, a nutter.

'How strange,' he tried to look concerned. 'I'll certainly check this out with the other residents and get back to you if I hear anything similar.'

He knew she was watching as he walked down the path. He had met only two of the residents so far and both were head cases. He went towards the next house thinking there must be an easier way to earn a crust, and wondering if he was too old for prostitution.

Once she was safely outside the back door, Jenny ran as fast as she could. There was nowhere to go, except through the bushes at the end of the garden. She crawled through a small gap and into the next field, where the grass was high, and it was hard to see where she was going. The ground felt lumpy and her foot slipped a couple of times into small holes. She wondered if they were rabbit burrows. She would have liked a rabbit or a kitten or puppy. But her mother said animals were dirty, disgusting things and would not allow her to have a pet. The thought of her mother made her scowl. She hated her mother. She hated when she shouted, hated the way her nails dug into her arm when she was angry. Most of all she hated the way she looked when she beat her. Then her face would look like a witch's.

Her mother had been so angry that morning that Jenny shivered, remembering. She went to use the bathroom unaware that her mother was already in there. When she opened the door the wind had whipped all her white powder off the sink unit, and she had screamed bad words, naughty, nasty words. Then her mother dragged her back to her room and hit her. On the head, in the face, scratching, screaming and punching. Her mother had only stopped, when the doorbell rang.

'Stay there,' she'd warned, wiping the white powder from her nose. 'Don't move until I get back.'

But she knew better. She would hide until Joe got home. Then her mother would be different. She never hit her in front of him. And it was quiet here, she could dream about starships and rockets to the moon.

'Ouch,' her foot slid into another hole. Deeper this time and something hard rubbed against her shin. She sat down to survey the damage, rolling down her white knee-sock. Her ankle was skinned. Small strips of flesh bunched here and there, and a trickle of blood stained the sock. That was the last straw. She curled up as tight as she could, her head against her knees and howled.

'Is it the hunger?'

'What?' Jenny looked up towards the voice, and shuffled backwards in terror.

'We've all felt it too.'

What was this thing? It was horrible and weird looking, a monster.

'Are you from up there?' she asked, pointing towards the sky.

'No, down there,' Katie touched the earth. 'We all live down there.'

'All who?'

'All of us,' replied Katie, gesturing behind her. Lots of other monsters crawled towards her through the grass.

'I ... I have to go home,' Jenny stammered in fright.

'Please stay and talk to us. We have no one to play with.'

They all nodded, clustering around her, and this started her crying again.

'Is it the hunger?' Katie repeated.

'Do you mean am I hungry?'

'Yes, we used to be hungry all the time.'

'No, I'm never really hungry. I hurt my leg,' she pointed to her reddened shin.

'I'll get Elizabeth,' one of the monsters said, before crawling away.

No one spoke as they waited for Elizabeth. The dead children were just as fascinated and uncertain as the living one. Soon, there was a shuffling in the grass and they turned towards the sound.

'This is Elizabeth,' Katie told her. 'She's nice.'

Jenny looked up at the woman standing over her and her crying started again. She didn't look nice, just scary like the rest of them. Cold fingers circled her ankle. Were they going to eat her?

'Have you a mother?'

Jenny peeped up through her fingers and nodded.

'She will need to clean this in case of infection.'

'I'm a bit afraid,' the child admitted.

'So are we,' said Elizabeth.

'You are?'

'Never mind,' Elizabeth said, straightening and casting a fearful glance around the graveyard. So far there was no sign of Carey. This was strange, as he must have been heard the child crying. They could hear every sound, no matter how far away. Timmy came strolling through the long grass. He had been wandering among the living, enjoying all the new sights and sounds. He stopped on seeing the child.

'Hello,' he smiled at her, but instead of answering, she cringed.

'I want to go home.'

'Yes, of course,' Elizabeth agreed. 'You go home, dear.'

'Really? I can go home?'

'Of course, unless you're lost?'

'Aren't you going to eat me?'

'Why would we eat you?' Timmy asked.

'Because you're monsters.'

'We're not monsters. Look at me. I'm just like you,' Katie bent down beside her, but the child squirmed away.

'Go away. You're horrid.'

Katie started to cry, and Elizabeth picked her up.

'Am I a monster, Elizabeth?'

'Not at all,' Elizabeth reassured her. 'You're the prettiest little girl in the whole wide world.' Turning towards the living child, she spoke curtly. 'Please go home now, child.'

The others backed away as Jenny got up, and limped towards the bushes. She turned before crawling through.

'I'm sorry. I didn't mean to make you cry.'

They ignored her, all busy fussing over the little girl. Except one, he was looking at her, the boy-monster.

'I'm really sorry.'

He nodded, and waved to her.

Jenny crawled into her own garden and looked back into the grave-yard. They had all gone, disappeared. She pulled the leaves aside to get a better look and came face to face with two glowing, red eyes.

'Hello, little girl.' Black Jack reached through the bushes and tried to grab her.

But she was too quick. She ran down the path towards the back door screaming for her mother, willing to trade one monster for another.

———

Bob Richards had just finished with his last complainant and was outside the door saying his goodbyes, when they heard the screaming. They ran towards the sound, just as other doors opened and the neighbours peeped out. No one answered the doorbell and they ran around the side of the house and through the open back door. They found the child huddled shaking and crying under the kitchen table, and the mother shouting at her to come out.

'What on earth happened?' Bob asked. He crawled under the table. Jenny remembered the nice man who had winked at her and allowed him to put his arms around her.

'What happened?' he asked, but she couldn't answer. She could still see the big, red eyes and the white hands that tried to catch her.

'She'll need a doctor. Something has scared her badly,' he said, noticing her blood-stained sock. His stomach lurched. Dear God, no! Surely she couldn't have been attacked. Not out here, in the middle of nowhere.

Helen's condition did not allow her to pick up the child, so Bob carried her upstairs to wait for the doctor. He tried to ignore the mother's feigned mutters of concern as she followed closely at his heels. Jenny was trembling and her small fingers gripped the sleeve of his jacket tightly. They had to prise her away from him, so the doctor could check her over. Bob went downstairs and waited with a few of the neighbours, each thinking the same thing, that this was the work of a paedophile. Already their idealistic little world was starting to crumble.

The sobbing from overhead filtered down to a gentle crying, as a sedative took effect. The doctor appeared, shaking his head. Bob got up and went to meet him.

'What happened?'

'Are you the father?'

'No, I'm ah … a friend.'

'Very well,' the doctor misconstrued his meaning of the word. 'She says she saw a monster.'

'A monster, are you sure?'

'Well that's what she said; very strange.'

'Yes, very.' Bob's mind was racing; freezing cold, doors opening and closing, and now monsters.

'I'll call back later.'

He realised that the doctor was speaking to him. 'Yes, yes, of course. Thank you.'

The neighbours had all filed into the hall, waiting for an explanation.

'She thought she saw a monster,' Bob told them. 'Probably fell asleep in the garden and had a bad dream,' he shrugged, smiling. 'Children, eh?' Then he realised he sounded as insincere as the child's mother.

The residents walked away in silence. Those with children would keep them indoors until the truth was known. Bob went upstairs and looked in on the sleeping child. Her mother was busy filing her nails, but looked up smiling when she saw him.

'Little terrors, eh?' she nodded towards the bed. 'I was having a lie down, I need my rest. It was her screaming that woke me.'

'Yes, gave us all a fright. Will her father be home soon?'

'Yeah, any time now. She's always had a very active imagination,' she jerked the nail file up at the rockets and spaceships dangling over-head. 'She'll be fine in the morning, don't worry about her.'

'That's good. I'll be off so.'

'Good of you to take the time.'

Nodding, he almost ran down the stairs and out to his jeep. He felt safer once inside and relaxed when he heard the comforting thunk of the locking mechanism. The place now seemed very quiet, even for a suburban housing estate where most of the couples went out to work.

A gust of wind sent a shower of leaves scratching against the window of the jeep and Bob almost screamed. The engine sprang into life as he turned the key. Easing the jeep away from the kerb, he reminded himself how ridiculous it was for a grown man to act this way. For a moment, just for a fleeting moment, he felt that if he looked in his rear view mirror, Jenny's monster would be staring back at him.

EIGHTEEN

October 1846

The journey home took two days. Their weakened state made the walking arduous, and it was a great relief when the tall chimneys of the Hall finally came into view. They separated, having made plans to meet again that evening.

Elizabeth needed to find somewhere to sleep before she made the trip back to the docks. She had to skirt around the outside of the Hall, afraid of seeing Carey, and crept along walls and behind sheds until she reached the kitchen. Opening the door, she peeped inside. Annie and Thomas were dozing in front of the fire, and it wasn't until she was almost on top of them, that they realised she was there.

'Get away at once,' Thomas said, struggling to stand.

'It's me, Elizabeth. Don't you know me?'

She had no idea how much she had changed, and would have been alarmed to learn that she had become one of the walking skeletons she so dreaded.

'My lady?' they gasped.

'The letter, did my letter arrive?'

'Yes, my lady. It came last week.' Annie eased herself up from the chair. 'Please sit and I'll get you something to eat.'

'The letter, Annie.'

'I'm sorry, my lady. The master took it.'

'No! Oh no! Please, this can't be!'

They helped her into a chair and covered her with a blanket. She had thought, after the workhouse, that she had no more tears left, but she was wrong. Sobs shook her thin frame and she held herself as she rocked.

'Please my lady, don't take on so,' Annie was crying too. 'I tried my best. I watched for it each day and when it came I hid it in my apron, but the master caught me and took it. He opened it in front of me and after reading the note inside took the money it contained. I'm truly sorry, my lady.'

'I know, Annie. It's not your fault.'

'My lady,' Thomas held out a piece of paper to her. 'I found this in the waste. Believe me, I have never done anything like this before.'

She looked up at him for a moment, not comprehending what he was holding. Her hands shook as she took it from him and read the words.

Andrew Farrell Esq.
14 Gardener Grove
Manhattan
New York
September 2nd 1846

My dearest Cousin,

I hope this letter finds you in good health and ready to start your journey to us. The children arrived here yesterday, tired, but in good spirits. Their ship had been held in quarantine for over two weeks, but they're none the worse for it. They arrived in the company of a sailor. A most agreeable fellow who refused to take anything for his trouble and asked to be mentioned to you when I wrote, which he strongly urged me to do as soon as possible.

I enclose the sum of forty pounds to cover any travelling expenses and assure you of the warmest welcome when you arrive. The children will write as soon as they are rested.

My dear wife, Martha, is overcome with joy at having them, and they seem to have taken quite a shine to her as well. A ship sails for England tomorrow and from there to Ireland. So weather permitting you should be here with us before Christmas.

Fondest regards,

Andrew

They were safe, her girls had made it to America. As long as they were all right, she could take anything life would throw at her.

'Here, my lady, try to eat,' Thomas put a plate of stew and a glass of milk in front of her.

The smell of the food was overpowering. She ate slowly, believing nothing had ever tasted so good. Annie dabbed a handkerchief to her eyes. Their mistress had no idea how bad she looked, and smiled, when she caught them staring.

'I'll be on my way soon.'

'You'll wash and change first, m'lady?' The servants acted as though she had just come in from a walk and would need to change before dinner.

'Is he here?'

'He's not expected back until late. You'll have plenty of time to change. His mother is snoring drunk by the fire. She'll not bother you.'

She followed Annie up to her old room. The bed had been remade, and there was no longer any sign of the atrocity that had been committed there. Her brushes and comb lay, as always, on the dressing table. Her dressing gown was draped across a chair and the fire had been set, ready for lighting. It was as though she had dreamed the last few months.

A gentle tapping on the door heralded Thomas' arrival with a pitcher of warm water. Annie poured some of the contents into a bowl on the washstand and helped Elizabeth out of her rags, stifling a gasp at the skin stretched tightly over her ribs. The only sign of flesh was on her belly, which was slightly swollen. The dress Annie was holding was much too fine for what she required, so she asked for something simpler.

The older woman returned with one of Elizabeth's better wool, riding dresses. Elizabeth was surprised to find two sixpenny pieces and several pennies in a drawer. These would come in handy when she paid for the next letter to Andrew. During all this time, she listened for a warning clash of hoofs below. When she was finally ready, she pulled on a heavy wool cape and ushered the old woman back to the kitchen. She would find Timmy and perhaps get shelter from his parents, until she decided what to do next. She would have to write back to Andrew soon. Thomas had left a flour sack on the table for her.

'It's just some bread and cheese, m'lady, but it will keep the hunger at bay.'

'You are both so very kind. I can't thank you enough.'

'Do you know where you are going, m'lady?'

'It won't be far, for now, and I'll be back from time to time.'

'The door will always be open to you, m'lady,' Thomas assured her. 'You will always be mistress here as far as we are concerned.'

Elizabeth was afraid she would cry again at their kindness. Picking up the sack, she began to walk away, and then paused, 'Thomas, do you remember the stable boy, Timmy?'

'Yes, m'lady, a small dark-haired boy, I remember him.'

'Do you know his family?'

'Yes, indeed. That was very tragic.'

'Tragic, what do you mean, Thomas?'

'It's the same all over, m'lady.'

'Do you mean …? Surely not!' Without another word she was out the door. 'Timmy,' she whispered, running across the yard and out towards the fields. 'Oh, dear God, no.'

———

Once they had left Elizabeth, Timmy and Katie walked across the fields that skirted the Hall. He had told her so many stories about the place that she begged him to stop for a moment, so she could see it properly. They were on a hill high above it, looking down at the main house. The watery afternoon sun glistened on the early frost and the Hall seemed to shimmer.

'Is it a castle?' Katie asked.

'No, it's just a very big house.'

'I wish I lived there.'

No you don't, he thought, not now that Black Jack owns it.

'Three little girls did live there once. Do you want me to tell you about them?'

'Oh, yes please!'

'Come on then. I'll tell you while we walk.'

They set off hand in hand towards his home. He tried to ignore the numerous ruined cabins of his neighbours, but when he came to his best friend, Martin's, he stopped. The thatch on the roof had been burned completely, as had the shutters and doors. Debris littered the front yard. He picked his way carefully into the shell of the cabin, almost expecting the family to still be living there. Even the whitewashed walls had been blackened and scarred by the flames. He closed his eyes for a moment and remembered the laughter, and Martin's father's look of love and pride. He felt a lump rise in his throat. Then a feeling of panic took over – if this had happened to them ... Rushing back outside, he grabbed Katie's hand and hurried her onward. Just a few more yards and his home would come into view.

'Please God, let them be safe,' he whispered, as they rounded the final bend. 'Aw, God no. Sweet Jesus, no.'

Dropping Katie's hand, he ran forward towards the pile of rubble that had once been his home. Unlike Martin's house, this one had been torn down. He had only been away for perhaps six months, what could have happened in that time to cause this? Perhaps they had gone to a different workhouse? He would wait for Elizabeth and ask if she had learned where they had gone. Sitting down on the garden wall, he lifted Katie up beside him.

'Where's your ma?'

'I don't know. We'll wait and see if Elizabeth knows. Don't worry she'll soon be here.'

'It's very cold.'

Despite the layers of clothing she shivered, and he knew they would need to find somewhere more sheltered to sleep. Above all, he mustn't panic. There was a simple explanation for his missing family, and if finding them meant a couple of more days walking, then so be it. Standing up on the wall, he shielded his eyes and looked across the fields to see if Elizabeth was coming. He thought he saw movement among the trees, but wasn't sure.

'Look, horses,' said Katie, pointing towards the horizon.

He spun round to see two riders approaching. His heart skipped a beat when he recognised Black Jack. It wasn't until they were almost upon him, that he identified the other rider. It was the master, but looking very different from when he'd last seen him. He was balding, and his skin seemed to have a yellow tinge, but Timmy thought that might be caused by the glare of the setting sun.

'Well, what have we got here?' Black Jack looked down from his horse, as Timmy pulled Katie closer to him.

'Well I'll be damned, if it isn't the little stable boy!'

Timmy saw that Black Jack looked very different in fine clothes and was even speaking differently, like a gentleman.

'Where have you been, boy?'

'The workhouse.'

'The workhouse, sir.'

Timmy looked up at him with raised eyebrows.

Hiding his annoyance at the boy's impudence, Black Jack continued, 'You might as well return there, boy. There's nothing here for you now.'

'I'm trying to find my family. Do you know anything of their whereabouts?'

Black Jack turned to Charles with a laugh, 'Perhaps we can be of some assistance to the boy.'

'Indeed, we can,' responded Charles.

Timmy looked from one man to the other.

'But first,' Black Jack said, 'a question for you.'

'Yes, anything.'

'Did you see anyone in your travels; the mistress, perhaps?'

'I've been in the workhouse. The mistress would hardly be there.'

Black Jack looked at him for a moment before deciding he was right. He had checked for her name on their register, she wasn't there. Pulling his horse's reins, he was about to ride away when Timmy stopped him.

'My family, what do you know of my family?'

'I know you have something they haven't,' Black Jack sneered.

'What do you mean? What have I got?'

'Life, boy, life, your family are dead. You're standing in front of their tomb.'

Timmy turned to look at the pile of rubble.

'I believe your mother was the last to go. They say her screams could be heard for miles.'

'No, you're lying. My mother is not dead.'

'Ask around, if you can find anyone. I did them a favour, saved them from a pauper's grave. You should be thanking me.'

'Lying cur!' Timmy launched himself at the man's legs, trying to pull him from the saddle.

'Get off me, boy. Let go!' Black Jack kicked out, sending him flying.

Timmy landed with a thud against the wall and sat there for a moment, winded. Picking himself up, he tried to renew the attack, but Black Jack was too fast for him and veered the horse out of his way. The boy fell flat on his face and stayed that way, sobbing into the grass.

'And get off my land!' Black Jack called over his shoulder, as he rode away. 'I won't be so understanding next time.'

Elizabeth had been hiding behind a tree and witnessed this exchange. As soon as the riders were out of sight, she ran forward and knelt on the ground beside the fallen boy. 'Come on, get up,' she tried to lift him.

'Did you hear?' he sobbed.

'Yes, I heard.'

'I want to die. I've let my mother down. I said I would live for the children, that I would protect them, and now I can't.'

'Timmy, listen to me. Your mother was speaking about all children. Not just your sister and brothers, but every child you come in contact with. You said yourself that she was a woman of vision and you were right. You helped the children in the workhouse, didn't you?'

'Yes, and they all died too.'

'Katie didn't. She's here now because of you, and there will be many more. You're not like most boys, you know. You're different, special.'

'How?'

'You've a fire and goodness in you that I've never seen in anyone.'

Sitting up, he looked across at the burial mound.

'Look what he did.'

'He may have been responsible for the death of your family, but don't let him kill you too. You have to be strong, fight back.'

She was right. He would fight back, he would stop Black Jack in any way he could. Pulling free of her arms, he stood up.

'We will have to find somewhere to sleep tonight.'

It was almost dark, and they would never survive in the open.

'We could try one of the sheds in the Hall,' he suggested.

'No!'

'We must get out of this cold,' he persisted, holding the shivering Katie close.

'Let's walk to my father's place. There are numerous buildings there where we can take shelter.'

They set off across the fields; the grass was heavy with frost and crunched beneath their feet as they walked. Her old home appeared deserted. No light shone in the windows and there was no movement about the yard. Keeping well into the shadows, they crept across to the barn. She was surprised to find that it held some livestock. A cow grazed in one stall, and there were two sheep in one of the pens.

'Let's climb into the loft. There's plenty of hay up there and it will help keep us warm,' said Elizabeth.

They made themselves comfortable, nestling together in its softness. Elizabeth took the bread and cheese from the sack and divided it between them.

'Why aren't you eating?' Timmy asked, breaking his share in half and holding it out to her.

'No, thank you, I've already eaten at the Hall.'

Suddenly, overcome with weariness, she lay back and covered herself with her cape and some straw. Katie, who had finished eating, cuddled close to her and within minutes they were both asleep.

Timmy sat for a while, staring into space, his heart aching with loneliness and sorrow over the loss of his family, but tiredness soon overcame him and he moved as close to Elizabeth as he thought decently possible. Reaching out, he took hold of a piece of her cape. The wool felt soft beneath his fingers, and he cried when he realised that she would be leaving them. He might never see her again after tomorrow. He was losing everyone he cared about.

———

Timmy awoke just as the prongs of a pitchfork pierced the hay a hair's breathe from his face. Scuttling to the edge of the loft, he looked down to see an astonished man staring up at him.

'Get down out of there,' the man shouted, waking Elizabeth and Katie.

Timmy helped them climb down the rickety ladder, and it wasn't until Elizabeth had brushed both Katie and herself free of straw, that she looked at the man.

'Mick! What are you doing here?'

He moved closer to get a better look at her.

'Miss Lizzy, is it?'

She took his look to be one of surprise at seeing her there and not one of revulsion.

'Yes, it's me,' she clapped her hands in delight. 'Can you believe it?'

'No, Miss Lizzy, I can't.'

'How are you, Mick?'

'As you can see I'm well, but let's not stand here. Come inside where it's warm and I'll fix you something to eat.'

They followed him into the kitchen where a huge fire was blazing. Elizabeth sat down beside the fire, in what once had been her mother's chair. Mick scooped some fat from a bowl into a pan and placed it on the stand over the fire. She watched it melt and bubble and heard the sizzle, as he placed thick rashers of bacon into it. He looked at her now and then from the corner of his eye, but she never noticed. Memories were flooding through her. She saw, in her mind's eye, her mother bustling around the room. She could smell the fragrance of the rosewater she had used, and her heart swelled with longing. It became a physical pain within her and soon burst forth in a series of gasps and sobs.

'There now, Miss Lizzy, dear, you're safe. Don't go upsetting your-self like that.'

He tapped her lightly on the shoulder. Katie pushed by him and climbed onto her lap.

'Don't cry, Elizabeth. We are going to have something to eat soon.'

Food could solve everything according to Katie.

'I'm all right now,' she assured them. 'I was just remembering.'

She smiled at Mick and for a moment she was Miss Lizzy again, and not the wasted creature she had become.

He told her, as they ate, how her stepmother had died some months before. Being an unfriendly woman, and without any living relatives, no one had wondered at her disappearance. Like so many others she had caught the fever and was dead within days. Everything of value in the house had already been sold for food, and the only things remaining were the few animals. He'd moved into the house, and it was only by slaughtering an animal when necessary he had managed to keep himself alive.

'And what's the harm in that?' he asked. 'I looked after her while she lasted and buried her as well I could. Who's more entitled? Besides you, I mean,' he patted her hand. 'I tried to find you. Went to the Hall and was warned off. Then I heard about the children going to America, and I thought you'd gone with them.'

She explained what had happened. Timmy stopped eating and looked up in awe when she came to the part about the letter. So she wouldn't be leaving after all. He felt pleased and then ashamed at finding pleasure in her disappointment.

'Well there's no need to worry any more on that score,' Mick assured her. 'I'll sell the cow and sheep. That'll be enough to pay your way.'

For a moment her heart sang, but then, looking at his kind face and the worried faces of the children, she knew she could not allow this to happen. She could not deprive them of their only means of survival for her own selfish needs. Thanking him, but refusing his offer, she assured him that Andrew would send more money on hearing of the loss. At least now she had a safe address for it to come to.

'Well, you know what's best, Miss Lizzy,' he got up sighing. He'd loved her since she was a girl, and though he could never tell her, he would gladly die for her.

She spent the rest of the day exploring and rediscovering the house and farm, and was pleased to find baskets full of apples in the cold store, along with turnips and large slabs of bacon preserved in salt. This would last for quite a while.

That night, for the first time in more than sixteen years, she slept in her old room. Katie was cuddled up beside her, refusing to sleep alone, and Timmy shared with Mick.

The coming weeks saw a vast improvement in their health. The children regained their colouring, their cheeks were rosy, eyes clear and sparkling. Elizabeth felt and looked much better, but not all her weight gain was due to good food. She could no longer deny the swelling of her stomach and the light fluttery sensation within. She was pregnant with Black Jack's child, a child that had been conceived of rape. Soon it would start to show and everyone would be aware of her great shame.

They had already had to slaughter a sheep. She tried to stretch the food as far as possible, but it was difficult. Now that he was feeling better, Timmy tramped the roads each day and brought home every child he found. They now had five extra mouths to feed, and she might well have one more, if her cousin didn't write soon. She knew that many of the ships had been delayed or held for months in quarantine, so she didn't know when to expect a reply to her letter.

It would soon be Christmas and despite the horror all around, she wanted to make it special for the children. Mick was an excellent carver and was making dolls for the girls and little ponies and carts for the boys. Elizabeth was making the clothes for the dolls from scraps of material. Mick had hidden himself away in one of the sheds and spent hours planing and sanding the wood to a smooth finish. She sometimes sat with him as he worked. This was her favourite time of the day. The smell of the wood hung in the air and tiny curls fell at her feet as he skimmed.

Today she was going to tell him about the baby. The weather had turned bitterly cold. Frost hung like silver cobwebs from trees and hedges. A thin layer of ice had formed over the little pools of water in the yard, and she stopped to break one of these with the heel of her boot; anything to put off the inevitable. What would he think of her? She walked on towards the shed. The turmoil in her stomach was now caused by something other than the quickening in her womb. Her cheeks burned in shame.

'Another cold day, Miss Lizzy,' said Mick, looking up from his work.

'Yes, indeed. It's been a very hard winter this year.'

She sat down and laced her fingers together in her lap.

'Is something wrong?'

'I'm in trouble, Mick.'

'I don't understand. What kind of trouble?'

She could not, dared not, look at him. 'I'm going to have a baby,' she heard his sharp intake of breath.

'Who's is it?'

'That doesn't matter.'

'Of course it matters!' For the first time in her life she heard him raise his voice. 'Is it a child of love?'

'No.'

'Then whose?'

She began to cry and he put his arms around her, 'Ah, Lizzy, I'm sorry.'

He held her, rubbing her back and telling her it would be all right. Then her name was suddenly called from outside, and there was no more time to talk.

Timmy noticed the change as soon as they sat around the fire. No one spoke. Usually, at this time, when the children were all in bed, they would swap news and he'd tell them tales of the roads and what he'd seen. Both Mick and Elizabeth seemed to be miles away from him, each lost in thought.

Mick left them early, making the excuse that he was tired and had an early start next day. Elizabeth's eyes were haunted, and once he was out of ear shot, Timmy asked her what was wrong.

'I'm going to have a baby.'

'Whose is it, Mick's?'

'No, it's not. Why would you think that?'

'Oh, because of the way he looks at you.'

'What are you talking about? What way does he look at me?'

'Like this,' he fluttered his eyelashes at her.

'Oh, he does not!' she laughed, smacking him playfully on the hand.

'Yes, he does. He thinks you hold the moon.'

His next question startled her.

'Is it Black Jack's?'

'Timmy,' her eyes filled with pain, 'never speak of that again.'

'It is, isn't it?'

Her refusal to answer was confirmation enough.

'Does Mick know?'

'No, and he must never find out. I don't know what he would do, if he knew the truth.'

Timmy nodded, she was right. Mick would go off in a temper, and he would be no match for that animal.

'When?'

'When, what?'

'When will the baby be here?'

'Sometime in April, I think.'

'That's a good time. The weather will be warmer then.'

'Yes.' She smiled, realising how accepting children were.

Mick came around to the idea after a while. His mood was down to old-fashioned jealousy. Timmy had begun a one-boy crusade against Black Jack and followed him everywhere, watching and waiting. Mick slaughtered the last sheep. Now there was only the cow left. She provided them with milk and cheese, and was their most valuable asset. Elizabeth looked up when he entered.

'That's the last,' she told Timmy.

He nodded and thought how tired she looked. He hated leaving her alone with the children each day, but he had to do what he was doing. He had to have his revenge.

Timmy hadn't walked very far when he found a small girl crying over the frozen body of her father. She allowed Timmy to lead her away and never spoke as they walked, never even looked at him. She reminded him of his children in the workhouse, a brave captive of a terrible faith.

Elizabeth was shocked when she saw the child. This was by far the worst of all the children he had brought home. Unlike the others, she refused to eat, but allowed herself to be bathed. Elizabeth, at first, was afraid to touch her. She was afraid the slightest pressure would cause her bones to snap. Then slowly, carefully, she rubbed the cloth over the wasted body. Just once the child looked up at her, and in that look was etched all the misery and hopelessness of the famine. Something told her that it would be wiser to let the child sleep apart from the others. This was proven so next morning when she found the child burning up with fever. Timmy and Mick had already left to bury her father.

'It was hard to bury him,' Timmy told her, when they returned. 'He was completely frozen, and so is the ground.'

'Change your clothes and wash thoroughly. Do it now,' she commanded.

They looked at one another and shrugged, she wasn't usually so bossy. She had a thin stew made for lunch; it held very little meat and was mostly turnips and cornmeal. But it was hot and welcoming on their cold, empty stomachs. The children had already eaten and were playing outside in the orchard.

Timmy told her how Black Jack had designated a field to be used as a paupers' graveyard. She knew where he was talking about. A hillside far away from the Hall and not somewhere Black Jack would pass each day and be reminded that he helped put the poor souls there.

'They even have men guarding the field.'

'Why on earth would they have to guard a graveyard?' she asked.

'They've opened a mass grave and want all the bodies thrown into it. They don't want to waste land burying everyone in separate graves.' Mick shook his head. 'It's worse it's getting. The bodies were piled high. I've seen these mass graves before, and the dogs digging up and eating the corpses, they were buried so shallow.'

How could she bear the horror of it all?

'The girl is sick,' Elizabeth announced. They stopped eating and turned to look at her. 'The young one from yesterday is sick.'

'Is it the fever?' Mick asked, putting down his spoon.

'Yes.'

'I'll take care of her. You stay away,' Timmy said to Elizabeth. 'You have that ...' He nodded towards her expanding waistline.

She knew he was right. She had the baby to think about and he seemed to have somehow developed a resistance to the fever. His vigil was a short one; the child died the next morning. This time he set off alone, the small body in the wheelbarrow wrapped in a blanket. Timmy was beginning to believe that he was cursed.

NINETEEN

Christmas 1846

As was its way, the fever took hold. By Christmas four more of the children were dead. While their going brought about a sad sense of loss, it was the death of Mick that really devastated Elizabeth and Timmy. For four days and nights he had suffered, tossing and turning, wild with imaginings.

Timmy truly believed that Mick's death would bring about Elizabeth's own. She mourned and cried from morning till night, finding comfort in nothing. Timmy had become used to creeping into the graveyard at night. The mound-filled field held no terror for him, as it did for many. He had fashioned a small hand-sized shovel from a piece of old tin. It was easier to manage. Although it took him twice as long to dig a grave, it offered him more protection. He could kneel while he worked, and was less likely to be seen by the guards, who were now there by night as well as day. The earth was hard from the frost and snow, and his cheeks stung from the cold. His hands were cut and badly marked from the toil, and although Elizabeth rubbed them with sheep fat it did little to ease the pain. In a way he was glad of this. If he could feel pain then he was still alive, although sometimes, he wasn't sure about this, as the reality of the famine had a nightmarish quality about it.

He heard tales of as many as seven ships a day leaving Ireland weighed down with cattle, butter, grain and eggs. How could there be famine if so much food was being sent to England? They had been digging a grave when he first asked this and he could remember Mick's face and the sadness in his eyes as he answered.

'This famine is the work of man, lad. There is plenty of food for those that have the means to buy it. They're wiping us out, clearing the land to make way for better things. That's all we are to them, cattle for the slaughter.'

They had laid the child, a girl called May, into the deep hole. Mick tucked a doll into her lifeless arms, an early Christmas gift for a child who would never again look forward to that season. He had done this with every child, boy or girl; all faced the unknown with a toy clasped in their hands. Now Mick was gone too. The whole country was at death's door.

Thankfully, Elizabeth rallied. There were even nights when she slept, and he no longer had to lie awake and listen to her sobbing. The child within her was growing daily and he wasn't sure if it was this, or the needs of Katie and Daniel, one of Timmy's strays, that had brought her back to life. They had been forced to slaughter the cow. Once that was eaten they would have nothing. Worried by the dwindling food supply, she made him promise not to bring any more children home. It was a request that went very much against everything she believed, but she had to make it.

He felt he had indirectly brought about the death of Mick and the others, and promised he would do as she asked. It was hard, and he tramped the fields crying in anger and despair. She didn't see the things he saw. She didn't have to pluck away a baby still suckling at the breast of its dead mother or watch children grazing like beasts on the grass.

The coming of the New Year brought none of the hope and expectation as before. For the first time Timmy really noticed the hollow in Elizabeth's cheeks and the thinness of her shoulders. The swelling in her belly belied what was happening to the rest of her body. He didn't know why, but he was suddenly crying.

'Timmy, what's the matter?'

He couldn't speak.

'You poor boy,' she stroked his hair. 'It's all been too much to bear. No one should have to shoulder so much suffering alone.'

'I'm sorry, Elizabeth, I'm so sorry.'

'There now, dear, you have nothing to be sorry about. You're a good boy, Timmy, the best I've ever known.'

'I'm sorry.'

'What are you sorry for?'

'Everything; being mean to you, bringing the fever into the house, killing Mick.'

'Timmy, please listen to me,' she took his hands in hers. 'You did not kill Mick or anyone else. The famine did that, not even God himself saw fit to stop the suffering. What can one boy do?'

'I'm so angry.'

'Of course you are, and when you feel like that you use me to vent it on. That's all right, I understand. There's no one else.'

'You never do that to me.'

'No,' she sighed. 'I kick gates and trees instead.'

'I see so many sick and dying. Sometimes I get frightened and hide when I see them approach. Sometimes, when they look really bad, I feel sick.'

'Timmy, listen to me. I have been frightened every day since John died.'

'You have?'

'Yes, sometimes I wonder how I will carry on.' As if to remind her, the baby inside kicked hard, and Timmy felt the thud against his leg. 'There's my answer,' she laughed.

Before he could walk away she caught his hand. 'Promise me you will stay away from the Hall.'

'I can't.'

In everything else he had obeyed her, but this was different. If he knew of Black Jack's plans, he could forewarn his intended victims.

'I see him in the distance, sometimes.'

There was no need to ask whom she was talking about.

'He'll not come here,' Timmy said.

'How can you be sure?'

'I've put out that this place is overrun with fever. He'll not dare.'

'I hope you're right.'

What were they to do? The food supply had almost run out. They were down to a few turnips and the cornmeal Timmy got from the relief officer.

It took him two days to walk to town with the wheelbarrow and return with one small sack. Now the sack was almost empty again, and the flour was gone. The letter from her cousin had still not arrived, and it had been many months since she'd written to him.

———

Spring arrived, but winter refused to loosen its grip on the land. Trees which should be well in bud, lay covered with snow. The winter had been one of the worst that anyone could remember. The temperature rose slowly. Snow turned to slush on the ground and, although it remained in the hedgerows until the middle of March, nature eventually had her way and the countryside began to blossom.

Timmy spent most of his time at the farm helping Elizabeth. Her movements were slower now that her time was near. The number of evictions shrank when Black Jack was forced to take to his bed. Despite her fear of Black Jack she forced herself to visit the Hall. This was how they had learned of his illness. Timmy hoped it was the fever, and that he would die a slow agonising death, but no such luck. A bad cold that developed into pneumonia kept him indoors for weeks, but he recovered.

Annie and Thomas were, as always, glad to see their former mistress. If the sight of her impending baby shocked them, they never said. Though very thin, she was not looking as unhealthy as the last time they'd seen her. The reason for her visit was twofold. She needed another source of food, and also requested Annie's services as a midwife. The woman was glad to help and gave the little food she could, without Black Jack noticing. Of course Elizabeth had to tell them where she was living, but knew they would guard her secret. In the final two weeks of her pregnancy, Annie called daily to make sure all was well. Now that Elizabeth had regular company, Timmy felt free to return to his wanderings. He hung around Black Jack's men and picked up all the news, including that of coming evictions.

When Black Jack recovered, tenants regularly disappeared into the night, leaving nothing behind. He still torched their cabins, but the act did not provide the same surge of power he'd grown accustomed to. As yet there was no news of Elizabeth. He thought she had managed to get away to America, or she had hidden herself somewhere. No one was telling him anything. After crawling his way to the top, there was no one to applaud his success. He'd earned what he now had and was used to hearing the people curse him, but his first loyalty was to himself. He had always known he was destined for better things, and now that he had them, his only companions were his mother and Charles Fitzwilliam.

Now, to top it all, he had received a note from a secret society warning him to leave the tenants alone. There were many such groups in the country and three landlords had been shot over the past few months. They were picking on the wrong one with him. He would seek them out and see them all hang before giving in to their demands. But first he would have to prove how bad an enemy he could actually be.

Timmy heard of an eviction planned for the next day. He knew the family, a widow with two daughters, and set off after dark to warn her. The cabin lay dozing deep in a hollow. Curls of white smoke rose from the chimney, a sign that someone was still awake. Only the fire lit the interior, and he could see a shape moving about. Knocking gently, he waited for the door to open. There was movement behind and the top half opened a crack.

'Who is it?'

'It's me, Mrs Ryan, Timmy Walsh.'

'Ah, Timmy, lad, its grand to see you, but don't come any closer. We have the fever. My two young ones are nearly dead from it.'

'I came to warn you that Black Jack Carey's coming at dawn to evict you.'

'God help us all,' she said, tightening bony fingers on the lower part of the door. 'What am I to do?'

'You have to get away. There are abandoned sheds not far from here. You can hide there.'

She studied him for a moment. 'I was sorry to hear about your people.'

'Thank you, ma'am.'

'Be off with you now like a good boy, and mind yourself.'

'But I'll help you move your things.'

'There's no need, we'll be all right. God speed you, boy,' she said, closing and latching the door.

The sound sent shivers through him. It had become the custom that the last surviving member of the family, when all hope was gone, would latch the door. He would come back before dawn, hoping she would have changed her mind.

The morning found him hidden in the thick foliage of a nearby tree. Black Jack, accompanied by his men, arrived at first light. The woman inside must have heard the clatter of horses in the yard and the shouts from Black Jack to come out. When she made no attempt to answer, he sent one of his men inside. The man returned with a handkerchief held over his mouth.

'It's the fever, sir. Both the children have it.'

'Go back inside and tell her to come out.'

The man hesitated, not wanting to put himself to further risk.

'Do as I ask, man, or you'll soon find yourself in her position.'

Grudgingly he went back inside and returned, dragging the woman behind him.

'You've not paid rent in over a year, Mrs Ryan,' Black Jack informed her. 'I want you out this day.'

'We've nowhere to go and my young are sick with the fever.'

'That's not my concern.' He motioned to his man to go inside. He returned carrying a blazing sod of turf.

'You have five minutes to leave before I set the thatch on fire.'

'Very well,' she went back inside.

'Throw it on the roof,' Black Jack ordered the man holding the sod.

'But, sir ...!'

'She's had her chance. I'll teach these people not to mess with Jack Carey. Throw it, man. Now!'

The frightened man flung the blazing sod onto the roof. Stumbling back in horror at what he had done, he called, 'Missus! For the love of God, come out!'

Her only answer was the clink of the latch on the door. The thatch, though wet with dew, soon caught light. Within minutes it was blazing, the straw crackling and hissing.

Timmy watched in horror from his hiding place. There was nothing he could do to rescue the unfortunates inside. The thatch started to give way and fiery clumps fell into the cabin setting the interior alight. Then the screaming began. Timmy tried to block his ears as the cries gave way to agonised howling. Black Jack's men, now truly frightened, crossed themselves and started to back away from the sacrificial fire.

This was the great show of strength Black Jack had wanted. After all, a man who would burn a woman and her sick children was capable of anything and best left alone. But there was no look of triumph on his face. He had paled and was urging his horse away from the flames.

His men had remounted their horses, wanting to be away from the terrible sight and sounds.

All at once the last of the roof swooned inwards, one final howl heralding the end for those inside. Then nothing, even the crackling of the straw became a faint echo. Somehow this was worse, Timmy thought, as the finality of a funeral quiet descended.

The trees about them started to sway as the wind whipped up into a frenzy. Leaves were torn from branches and swirled into the air. Timmy was forced to hold tight as he was tossed about on the branch. He watched as invisible hands threw stones and bits of fallen twigs at the men below him. He saw their skin split open as the missiles struck home and blood crept from open wounds. Their coats and capes flew about them as they tried to fight off this unseen force, but it was useless. The very heavens cried out for vengeance in the voice of the wind, nature itself was offended. One by one the men were dragged screaming from their horses, and hurled against the walls of the cabin. They each clawed at the wind, calling for mercy, and were soon rewarded with the same amount of mercy they had shown their victims.

Timmy watched as each man flew backward through the air and heard the crack as his head hit the wall with such force that his skull was shattered. Soon there were three bodies slumped against the burning cabin wall. Each face wore a grotesque look of horror mixed with wonder. The wind died down as quickly as it had started, and quiet descended once more. Timmy's fingers were stiff and sore, so tightly had he laced them together.

What he had just witnessed was unbelievable, but why had God waited so long to help these people? After a few minutes he began to climb down the tree, and was on the lower branches, when he noticed a movement below. Someone was still alive. He watched as the man struggled to his feet, groaning, using the tree trunk for support. His heart pounded, waiting to see who it was, as the man straightened and brushed the hair from his face. Black Jack! He was still alive! How had he escaped the fury when all this was his fault? Timmy wanted to scream, to curse God or whatever forces had been so lax in their duty. It would never be over while Black Jack was still alive.

Reaching into his pocket, Timmy pulled out the small shovel he used for the burials. He would succeed where others had failed. Diving from the branch, he landed on Black Jack's back. The winded man fell beneath the small weight and for the few moments it took him to recover, Timmy managed to stab the weapon repeatedly into his back and shoulders. With a roar of pain, Black Jack tossed him off and he landed with a thump on the ground. Amazed at what he had actually done, Timmy lay watching, the bloodstained shovel still in his hand, as his adversary stumbled about trying to feel at his wounds. Black Jack pulled off his cape and moaned when he noticed the amount of blood that stained his hand and trickled between his fingers.

'You're dead, boy,' he spat.

Timmy got up and ran. The full horror of what he had witnessed, what he had done, struck him. He ran across fields, jumped ditches and leapt over gates as though the hounds of hell were in pursuit. He didn't stop running until he reached the farm. Elizabeth called out to him as he streaked past and into the barn, but he didn't hear her. He climbed into the loft and threw himself down in the hay. He felt safe there, remembering his first night with Katie and Elizabeth. He was shaking.

What if Black Jack survived? He would surely hang for what he had done. After all, the man's word would carry so much more weight than the word of a mere boy. He became aware of a rustling beside him.

'I'm not able for this climbing,' Elizabeth panted. Her stomach had grown so much in the past few weeks that she looked as thought she might fall over under its great size. 'Well, what have you been up to now?' she poked him gently in the back. 'Some sort of mischief, no doubt.'

'I'm in terrible trouble.'

'Now there's a surprise.' Everything was so serious to Timmy. She was not expecting to hear what he told her.

'Oh, my God!' she brought her hand to her mouth. 'What if he finds us? He's bound to want revenge.'

'I-I know.'

'How badly did you wound him?'

'He was b-bleeding v-very b-badly,' he stuttered. 'I-I think I killed him.'

'Could he have got away?'

'I don't think so. Th-the horses had all bolted, so he would have had to walk.'

'Tell me exactly where it happened.'

'No! You can't go there! What if he's not dead?'

'That's a risk worth taking. I have to be sure. If he's still alive we're all in a lot of trouble. Stay here until I get back.' She eased her way to the edge of the loft and climbed down. She would take the others with her. Anyone who saw them would think them homeless, and a woman with children in tow wouldn't arouse suspicion. There were so many like that walking the land.

'We're going for a walk,' she told the surprised children.

They had never been allowed outside the farmyard before. Though usually listless due to the lack of food, they were determined to enjoy this unexpected freedom. They explored hedges as they walked and leapt, running and hiding, through the high grass.

But their laughter did nothing to dispel Elizabeth's uneasiness. What if he is still alive, she wondered? What if I find him lying wounded and not beyond help? Could I allow him to live? No, he was dead, he had to be or, if not … was she capable of killing? Up until today she would never have judged Timmy capable of such an act. This famine had changed them all. Here she was, in her final weeks of pregnancy, thinking of killing the father of her unborn child. I have become more of a beast than a human; she choked with the realisation. Nothing is beyond me. No suffering too great and no act too cruel. Oh, please, she prayed, let him be dead.

She was sweating by the time the cabin came into view. Her skirts felt like weights around her ankles and her back ached. If he was dead, then the grass hid him and she would have to go closer.

'Let's rest a while,' she suggested. 'We've walked quite a long way.'

She led them to a tree and they sat on the grass beneath it. 'I need some time alone,' she said, one hand on the trunk, the other supporting her back. 'Please stay right here and don't follow me. Is that understood?'

'I'll keep him here,' Katie nodded at little Daniel. 'Don't worry, Elizabeth.'

'I know you will. You're a good girl.'

The child beamed.

'I'm a good boy, aren't I, Elizabeth?' Daniel lisped.

'The best, you are the two best children in the whole world. Now be good until I get back.'

The next few yards felt like miles. She craned her neck trying to see in front, waiting to see his dark hair appear amid the green grass. The air hung heavy with the smell of burning meat. She was almost at the wall of the cabin and there was still no sign of him. A cape lay abandoned by a tree and she walked towards it. Bending down to retrieve it, she noticed there were small pools on the ground. It was blood, his blood. She could see the trail of dark patches leading away from where she was standing. Without thinking, she draped the cape over her arm and set off to follow the track. The stains were larger and darker in some spots, hardly visible in others. She had walked quite a way when the trail suddenly ended and she had to search among the grass for more evidence, anything that would tell her where he was. There was nothing, he had vanished into thin air unless ... a horse, one of the horses must have come back. He had managed to get away. She hurried back the way she'd come as quickly as her bulk would allow.

Realising, for the first time, that she was carrying the cape, she stopped. It weighed so much. Turning it over, she examined the clasp and a wave of longing overwhelmed her. It was John's cape, the buckle engraved with his initial. Something not yet dead inside had recognised her beloved husband's cape. Carey must have taken it from one of the trunks in the attic. She had been unable to part with any of John's things and had stored them away. Back then, in that other time, when the world was still kind, she had somehow believed he would come back to her; that the parting was simply a respite in their journey through life.

How foolish she had been, she smiled, tracing her fingers along the engraving. Would it still carry his scent? It smelled of musk, slightly perfumed, but nothing familiar. That too was lost forever. She allowed it to slide from her arms, letting him go once again. The cloth would have come in handy in time, but the memories hurt too much.

She had avoided looking at the cabin as she passed, but now she was curious. Perhaps Timmy imagined most of what he had told her? Had a freak wind stirred the imagination of a boy and fooled him into seeing what he wanted to see? From the corner of her eye, she could see some shapes against the cabin wall. Leaning against the wall, she slowly turned round. Sweet Jesus, he had been right. Three men lay against the wall. Their staring eyes showing the horrific nature of what they had witnessed. For each man, the halo of blood, trailing to a point behind his head, pronounced him dead.

Elizabeth found the children asleep beneath the tree, and she roused them to set off home. What had really happened that morning? Timmy never lied, but what he told her was impossible. Murdered by the wind? It was madness. She badly needed to rest and to work out what they would do. They could no longer stay at the farm; Carey would come looking for them for sure. Not even the rumours of fever would keep him away, not now, not after what had happened.

TWENTY

October 2003

Jenny stayed in her room for the next two days. Her mother laughed at her story about the monster, saying it was a cat or wild dog she had seen. Joe was nice to her and said she had probably fallen asleep and dreamed it. But Jenny knew this wasn't true. It was a monster, and much scarier than the other monsters, the ones who had talked to her. The nights now brought with them terrors she could never before have imagined. She was sure there was tapping at her window, but when it happened she huddled fearfully beneath the covers rather than disturb her mother. When she did venture outside she stayed at the front of the house.

'Jenny, I have to go out for a little while. You go inside and lock the door.'

'Please, can't I go with you?' she begged, but her mother would have none of it. Her dealer didn't approve of children. Especially when funds were low and she had to pay in kind. Her growing bulk was only made bearable by the drug she craved and she would do anything to get her hands on it.

'Go on, now,' she called from the car, backing it out of the driveway.

Jenny looked around once her mother's car had disappeared from view. She would have to go inside and be alone. The monster would come for her then, she knew it. She locked the door, making sure the dead bolt was in place the way Joe had shown her, and ran up to her room and hid under the bed.

He was coming for her, she could feel it. She did not hear him walking up the stairs, and tried not to scream when his legs came through the door and he stood before her bed. She could see his shoes. They were torn and muddy, and the buckles were dull and spotted with rust. She hoped he couldn't hear her crying, and then maybe he would go away and not find her. The mattress sank towards her. He was sitting on her bed. Sweat dripped down her forehead and into her eyes, but she was too frightened to wipe it away. There was a soft clinking sound, and a necklace was dangled down before her eyes.

'It's a gift for you.'

She bit her lip; she wouldn't scream.

'I didn't mean to frighten you. I'm so sorry.'

Go away. Please go away, she prayed.

'I know I look frightening, but that's not my fault. I'm really quite nice. It's just that I've come from a time far away.'

'Do you mean from the stars?'

He almost laughed in triumph at the small, hesitant question. He would need this child. He could learn from her the things he didn't understand.

'Yes, from the stars. That's why I look so different. Please take my gift and say you forgive me.'

A tiny hand reached out and took the chain. 'Thank you.'

'Won't you come out and talk to me?'

She shuffled backwards and came out at the opposite side of the bed. He kept his back to her as she slowly made her way towards him. For a moment her eyes widened and she backed against the wall.

He really was very scary and smelly, but the more she thought about it the more she realised he was just different. Like the monsters she saw on Star Trek and other space movies.

'Do you like your gift?'

She forgot that she was holding the necklace, and held it up it front of her. It was old and dirty, and there were bits of mud caught in the links.

'It should clean up nicely.'

She nodded. Her mother had a special cleaner for jewellery.

'Now, perhaps you could do something for me? There is a lot I need to understand. A lot I have to learn. Will you help me?'

'Yes.'

'Very well,' he stood. 'You're no longer afraid of me, are you?'

'No.'

'I told you I was nice.'

Timmy watched from outside the bedroom window. Hanging suspended in the air, he listened to the conversation. After Jack had left, Jenny ran to her mother's room. Taking out a white plastic container filled with liquid, she removed the lid and carefully dropped the necklace inside. Wrapping the dripping necklace in a towel, she rubbed and polished trying to remove all traces of the ground in dirt. Then she hung it around her neck. The clasp was stiff from age, but she had no need to open it, as the necklace was long enough to slip over her head. She went back to her room and chose a book from the shelf. This was her favourite one, filled with Martians and monsters and daring adventures on other planets.

Lying on her stomach, she started to leaf through the pages, all the while playing with the chain around her neck. She pulled it towards her mouth, ran it between her teeth, licking and sucking on the metal. It didn't taste very nice and she spat out some of the bits of dirt that had come loose with her probing. The dirt was mixed with dried louse excrement. Some remained behind, trapped in her teeth, dissolving slowly to release a disease that had lain dormant for over a hundred and fifty years.

———

Sheila Ryan was preparing for bed. It was the first time she had to sleep alone in almost a year. She had mentally prepared herself for Tom's absence, but now that it had come to pass, she wasn't at all sure. The night seemed darker than usual, despite the streetlights, and she shivered as she drew the curtains. Too many horror movies, she thought, going through the house to lock doors and windows and switch off lights.

She looked out into the back garden. The darkness seemed absolute, deep and threatening. It was no use, she would have to take a sleeping pill. Filling a glass with water, she carried it to her bedroom. She took a bottle of the pills from the drawer, shook one into her palm and sat looking at it for a moment, undecided; she would need two, one would not be strong enough. Not when she was feeling so jumpy. She swallowed them quickly and got into bed. She had left the door ajar so the landing light could shine through. Closing her eyes she whispered a prayer for Tom's safe return. Within minutes she was sound asleep.

She moaned and arched her back as the hand between her thighs moved higher. His touch felt cold against her warm skin, and she smiled, happy that her husband had managed to get home that night after all. She tried to open her eyes, but it was difficult. The effect of the pills made everything fuzzy and, she realised, the room was in total darkness. The landing light had been turned off. The bulb in the streetlight must have blown.

'You're freezing, darling,' she mumbled, brushing at the hand that was roaming across her bare stomach, pushing her nightdress up. God, she was so sleepy and what was that smell? She tried to focus as the cold fingers kneaded her breast, digging claw-like into the soft skin.

'Ouch, that hurt,' she slapped at the hand, expecting the movement to cease. Instead it dug deeper, bruising and scratching. 'Stop it, Tom,' she tried to sit up, 'this isn't funny. You're really hurting me. Stop, I said!'

She was thrown back against the mattress so hard, it winded her. And the leg that was forcing itself between her thighs was so cold that it felt as though thousands of icy needles were stabbing her. She fought back as hard as her drugged condition allowed, scratching and pinching, pulling his hair. He was on top of her, forcing her legs apart, when the headlights of a car lit up the room. She was staring into the face of the devil. His red eyes blazing with lust and madness, his skin black and mottled with green and yellow, and his dark hair, which almost touched her face, was speckled with white, a whiteness that seemed to cling to each strand and move of its own accord, lice. Their small fat bulbous bodies filled with redness. She saw all this in the few seconds it took for the car to pass, before the room was plunged once more into total darkness. Only then did she manage to scream. A foul-smelling hand was clamped over her mouth, as her legs were forced wider apart.

'Jesus, no,' she sobbed, chest heaving.

'No! No!'

It was a woman's voice; one of the neighbours must have heard her. She pushed as hard as she could. Almost at the same time, he was grabbed from behind so his weight was instantly lifted from her. Jumping from the bed, she reached for the lamp while the sounds of a desperate struggle continued in the room. Her hands shook as she tried in her panic to locate the switch. The brightness was dazzling as she turned to help her rescuer. Elizabeth and Timmy were struggling with Black Jack, but were not strong enough to hold him for long. All Sheila saw were demons locked in some frenzied dance. One of them turned to her and shouted.

'Run!'

She was frozen. Her sobbing had turned to a tortured wailing, and Elizabeth had to scream to be heard.

'Run! Run now, or he will get you!'

She ran around the bed, but he reached out as she passed and caught her nightdress. Sheila felt herself sail through the air as he threw her back down onto the bed. He was on top of her again, pulling up her nightdress, tearing and scratching, laughing at her pleas for mercy. She felt his breath, the smell of death, noxious on her face. He no longer paid any heed to the pulling hands of the others. They had caught him off guard the first time, but now he was unmovable.

Timmy looked around for something, anything that would have an effect on him. Then he saw it. Black Jack cried out in terror as the noose went round his neck. It was the cord from Sheila's dressing gown. Elizabeth grabbed her, pulled her from beneath him and towards the door.

'Run. We can't hold him for long.'

Sheila ran. She didn't stop running until she reached the house next door. Hammering on the door, she collapsed with relief, when the hall light was turned on. The door opened and another ugly face was pressed against hers. She screamed again, backing away.

'Come on, now.'

Strong arms lifted her and carried her into the house. The woman she had seen through the window hovered in the background as he placed her on the couch.

'Old Brutus gave you quite a scare just then.'

'A man,' she cried. It was all she could say before dissolving into sobs again.

Only then did Mike Byrne notice the scrapes on her neck and the blood staining the lower part of her nightdress.

'Call the police and a doctor,' he ordered his wife. 'Brutus and I will sort that bastard out for you, miss.'

He charged through the open doorway of number 25 without a thought for his own safety. He was not brave, but this was different. He was angry; a woman needing keeping in her place by all means, even the odd slap was no harm, but rape! Now that was entirely different. Fucking perverts roaming the night and taking by force. No, that was just not on. He took the stairs two at a time and went towards the only room with a light showing. It was in disarray, but it was the smell that made his stomach turn. He'd never known anything as bad in his life. He turned to leave and noticed that the dog was gone. He found him scratching at the back door, trying to get out.

'He went that way, did he, boy?' He turned the key and let the dog go.

Black Jack was standing at the bottom of the garden, struggling to loosen the cord that Timmy had knotted around his throat. The man was unable to see him. But not the dog ... it stopped, terrified.

'He must have gone through the bushes,' the man spoke aloud. 'I'll have to go back and get my torch. Stay there,' he ordered the dog, but there was no need, as it was unable to move.

He was back in minutes, large black torch in hand, the beam lighting the bushes and field beyond. Pulling aside some of the brambles, he ordered the dog.

'Go on, boy,' but it refused to move. 'What's the matter with you,' he roared. 'Come on.'

The dog cast a fearful eye at his master, then at the struggling spectre glaring at him. That did it. The dog ran yelping through the house and out into the street.

'Come back here, you mangy coward!' yelled Mike Byrne, hurrying after him, 'I'll beat the living daylights out of you.'

He was still searching for the dog when the sound of sirens invaded the quiet, and the flashing blue lights appeared in the distance. The doctor followed the police. He examined Sheila's wounds, cleaned and dressed them. She refused to go to hospital, and assured him and the police that she hadn't been raped. Still, her story made no sense whatsoever. The doctor shook his head as he listened. First monsters, now demons.

The police searched through the gardens and into the neighbouring field, their torches like small meteors zooming across the dark sky. Anyone who tried to run across this field would have broken his neck. There were so many holes hidden in the grass that they were slipping and sliding as though walking on ice.

A dog yelping in pain made them hurry back towards the houses. Mike Byrne was kicking the hapless Brutus, who had just come skulking back. The police had to drag him away from the dog, and had he been wearing his usual steel-capped boots instead of slippers, the dog would have been kicked to death. He pulled away from the restraining arms and stormed inside, slamming the door.

'Mike, hush,' his wife brought her finger to her lips and pointed upwards. Sheila was asleep in the guest room. The sedative the doctor had given her ensured she would sleep through the night.

'That fucking dog stays out. Do you hear me?' he snarled, the spittle dripping from his mouth.

She nodded fearfully and was thankful when he stalked away to bed. They each had their own room. They hadn't slept together for years. She bored him. She knew this and was glad. He had made her what she was, beaten and nervous. Making sure that the house was locked up, she wearily climbed the stairs. The street was quiet again. The police and doctor had gone with the promise of returning the next day. She gazed out into the night before pulling her curtains, and it struck her as strange that not one of the neighbours had come out during the ruckus. Not a single light had been switched on in any of the houses. In a few short months this place had turned people from being friendly and outgoing, to strangers filled with distrust and interested only in self-preservation.

A dark shape crept across the lawn towards the house. Though she never liked the dog there was no need for such cruelty. Picking up her rosary beads from the bedside table, she knelt and prayed. For the safety of her children, for the souls of her long-dead parents and lastly, though she knew it was blasphemous, for the death of her husband. Sighing, she got into bed and turned off the light. She lay for a while staring up into the darkness. Mike had made three trips to the warring Lebanon before he retired. In that time better men than him had died and yet not one bullet had come his way. Damn it.

Black Jack managed to free himself from the cord. It was no use making another assault on the woman. Not while Elizabeth and the boy were watching. A rat scurried by with something in its mouth. He followed. Even the vermin's sensitive ears were unable to hear his approach. The rat ran into a tangle of bushes. The piece of meat in her teeth was intended for her babies. Black Jack pulled aside the branches. The mother rat bared her teeth at the intruder and leapt. Black Jack caught her by the throat, his grip getting tighter, choking her. He smiled as the thrashing body went limp. Then he turned his attention to the helpless babies who squirmed and clustered together, sensing danger. He stamped his foot down again and again, delighting in the feel of the soft bodies exploding. When he was finished and his bloodlust sated he wiped his shoe on the grass, cleaning away the bits of stringy bodies and gore. That had been easy, he was satisfied. And it was practise for the human vermin. Like that man that tried to set his dog on him and the bitch that escaped.

He was seething with frustration, as he now knew that his body had betrayed him. That the act he had intended to carry out on the woman was beyond him. Still the urge was there, and while the assault offered no release, he had to admit that he enjoyed the hunt, the thrill of the chase. He would attack her again, when the time was right. For now, he would concentrate on other things; the man for instance and his faithful dog. Jack laughed, as he imagined the man's confusion when the animal turned on its master, and it would. He would make sure of that.

Somewhere a woman cried out in her sleep, and he turned and walked towards the sound.

TWENTY-ONE

March 1847

Black Jack fell from his horse as he reached the main door of the Hall. His shirt was soaked with blood, and he was dizzy from the pain. Thomas came running out.

'Sweet Jesus,' he whispered, on seeing so much blood. He felt no concern for the man, it was just the sight that startled him. Black Jack was trying to get up and reached a bloodstained hand to him. Thomas was much too thin to bear the weight of the well-fed Jack, and ran inside calling for the master. They returned and lifted him into the dining-room. Annie and Agnes came to see what was happening.

They laid Black Jack on the dining table and Thomas cut the shirt from him to assess the damage. All the while Agnes cried and lamented the wounding of her son.

'Get her out of here,' Black Jack roared, and Thomas led the crying woman out into the corridor.

Annie brought water and cloths and set about cleaning the wounds. Once she had managed to staunch the bleeding, it became clear that none would prove fatal. Charles administered sips of brandy to the wounded man who cursed everyone to high heaven.

'What happened, old chap?' Charles enquired.

Thomas and Annie took their time clearing away in the hope of hearing his answer.

'That boy, that stable boy, Timmy. He jumped on me, stabbed me.' Noticing the woman and man cast sideward glances at one another, he asked. 'Do you two know something of his whereabouts?'

'No, sir,' they replied in unison and hurried from the room.

'Someone must know something,' he turned to Charles. 'He's obviously hiding out around here somewhere, and if he is, then God help him.'

Charles nodded.

'I'm going to lie down,' he lurched towards the door, weak from loss of blood.

Charles was relieved when he had left the room. Filling a glass of brandy, he sat down to recover. When Carey had arrived in such a state he had put it down to the work of one of those secret societies. They were getting closer by the day, and he knew he would be held responsible for the actions of Carey and his men. It was time to leave Ireland and he had never been one to outstay his welcome. He had some personal items that would fetch a good price and pay his passage, but not to England. There was nothing worth going back for. He would sail for America, New York. He'd heard they appreciated the gentry there and he could start afresh.

Thomas and Annie were very worried. Black Jack's injuries would not keep him inactive for long. It was only a matter of time before he began searching for Timmy and found the mistress. They decided that it was safe enough for Annie to visit the farm. They heard Black Jack go to his room and reasoned that the effects of the brandy, coupled with the blood loss, would make him sleep. His mother had also retired to the drawing-room and was drowning her sorrows in port.

Black Jack was restless … despite the weakness he couldn't sleep. The memory of his men's deaths was fresh in his mind. Not that he cared for any of them, but he couldn't seem to figure out what had happened. Walking across to the window, he leaned against the frame, mulling the events of that morning over in his head. His thoughts were interrupted by the appearance of a figure in the distance. He tried to make out who it was, and realised it was Annie.

Taking the few scraps of food she could gather, Annie had set out.

There was little enough in her basket to feed three growing children, but it was some offering. It was well into the afternoon and the air had become colder. She pulled her cape closer and was so intent on her journey, that she failed to notice she was being watched.

———

Elizabeth had grown tired of waiting for Annie to appear. She was terribly worried and needed to know if Carey was still alive. Ordering Timmy to keep the children safe until her return, she set out for the Hall. She had walked almost half the way when she met the old woman coming towards her.

'Oh, mistress,' Annie gasped on seeing her, 'have you heard?'

'Yes, Timmy told me. I couldn't wait to find out if he was dead.'

'Come, sit down.' Annie beckoned to a fallen oak, and they sat on the trunk.

It took Elizabeth a few moments to catch her breath. Her companion waited patiently, rubbing her back, making soothing noises.

'He's not dead, is he?'

'Barely a few scratches, he has the luck of the devil.'

'He'll come after Timmy.'

'What will you do m'lady?'

'I don't know. We could always find another abandoned farmhouse, I suppose.'

'What about the baby? It's almost due and you'll need help.'

'I don't know,' Elizabeth wiped her brow. 'I can't seem to think straight.'

Taking the food from Annie, she set off home. She imagined the surrounding area as she walked, trying to envisage other houses that would be empty. She could always send Timmy back to the Hall with a note when they found a place. She was so deep in thought that she almost walked into the horse and rider blocking her path.

'Who are you and where are you going?'

She was afraid to look up.

'Answer me, woman.'

She stayed looking down at the ground.

'I asked you a question.'

Oh, God help me, she prayed.

Tired of waiting he kicked out at her arm and only then did she look up. He reined back in horror.

'Elizabeth,' he gasped, unable to believe that this woman, this thing before him, was the great lady he had known. He dismounted and his eyes darted over her, taking in the swollen stomach.

'You are with child?'

'I would have thought that quite obvious, even to you.'

'Who's the father?'

'That is none of your business. Now, if you don't mind I'll be on my way.' She tried to walk past him.

'How could you have allowed yourself to get to this state? I would have kept you. You know that.'

'I'm well aware of it. But I am also aware that I was destined for much more than being your whore. Now, get out of my way.'

'The child, is it mine?'

'If I thought it was, I would have torn it from my womb.'

'It's mine. Tell me the truth.'

She could see beads of sweat forming on his forehead.

'Just tell me it's mine and I'll see that you are well taken care of. You can come back to the Hall, and I give you my word, I'll not lay a finger on you.'

'I can't. Let me pass.'

'The boy, is he with you?'

'What boy?'

He caught the look of fear that crossed her face. 'My God, he's with you.'

'Allow me to pass, please. I have no idea to whom you are referring.'

'Tell me where he is,' he said, shaking her. 'Give the boy to me, Elizabeth, and I will give you back your life.'

'Let me pass,' she said, drawing back her foot back and kicking him hard.

He let her go, swearing and she stumbled away from him. She tried to run, but had gone only a few yards, when he caught up with her. She wanted to lead him away from the farm, from the children, but suddenly the horse was beside her.

She stopped, exhausted, and the world seemed to spin as he circled her, warning and threatening. Bringing her hands to her face she tried to stop the dizziness, and when she looked again he was beside her, his leg in the stirrup, so close she could smell the saddle soap.

'Go away!' she shouted, hitting out at him, but staggered and fell to the ground.

Her shouts upset the horse and it sidestepped in terror, whinnying and thrashing about. Its hoof kicked her full force in the stomach. She screamed in agony as the child inside her jumped, trying to get away from the pain. She tried to rise, but fell back as pain ripped through her body. A warm wetness welled between her legs.

'Elizabeth ...' Black Jack was lifting her.

'Take me to the Hall,' she gasped before passing out.

But he chose to go to the farm, as it was closer. Even as he walked the few hundred yards he could feel the warmth of her blood against his legs.

Timmy jumped up as Black Jack came crashing through the kitchen door with the blood-soaked Elizabeth in his arms.

'Take her upstairs,' Timmy said, following them along the hall, sickened by the trail of blood she left in her wake. Once he had laid her on the bed, Black Jack turned to Timmy.

'I'll ride to the Hall for help.'

Timmy nodded. Black Jack's clothing, from his waist to his knees, was one wet, black stain.

'Timmy.' Elizabeth held out a hand to him and he crawled onto the bed beside her. 'I'm dying, Timmy.'

'Hush, Elizabeth.'

'Listen to me before it's too late.'

He tried not to cry as she continued.

'Bury me with the others. Mick and the children, promise me?'

'I promise.'

'I'm so proud of you,' she smiled at him. 'And I'll be watching over you always.'

'Please don't leave us, Elizabeth,' Timmy's cried, tears flowing as he laid his head on her breast. 'Stay with us, please.'

But it was already too late.

Annie arrived to find Timmy hunched sobbing over Elizabeth, while rivulets of blood ran down the sheets, staining the floorboards. Black Jack walked to the side of the bed and looked down at her body. Without a word, he turned, and ran from the room.

'You did this,' Timmy's screams followed him down the stairs. 'I hate you. I hate you.'

Black Jack rode like a madman. He stopped only when the country-side grew unfamiliar. His horse was sweating, and he was gasping for breath himself. Dismounting, he walked to a small stream. The horse drank deeply, and Black Jack washed the sweat from his face.

'Well, well. What have we here? If it isn't the bold Jack Carey himself!' He turned to find a group of men walking towards him. These were the so-called Ribbon men, a name given to all gangs that advised rebellion against the landlords. They held sticks, and one a rope, that he looped and ran through his hands.

'So you ignored our threats, did you boy?' the leader asked. 'Drove the helpless from their farms and burned those that were unable to leave. You're a brave man, Carey, when you've your men in tow.'

They moved as one and pinioned his arms behind his back. He allowed it to happen and made no attempt to escape. His life, now that

Elizabeth and his child were dead, suddenly seemed empty. The rope was looped around his neck and tightened. They threw the other end over a branch and lifted him onto the back of his own horse.

'We'll see how brave you are now, Carey,' the leader said. 'Turning against your own people, throwing widows and orphans onto the roads. Are those the actions of a man?'

'My only loyalty is to myself.'

'Brave words; be sure to give our regards to the devil when you see him.'

'I'd rather die by the noose than of the hunger,' were the last words Black Jack spoke as his horse was whipped into a gallop, and the life was slowly choked out of him.

They buried him that evening in the same graveyard he had allotted to the paupers. Carey was a rich and powerful man, and the discovery of his body would have meant death for them all.

———

Elizabeth was buried on the opposite side of the field the next day. The guards had agreed to allow her a plot of her own. They all knew her well and were saddened by her death. Timmy dug her grave, refusing the help offered. He dug until his hands bled and his tears watered the earth. It was a small group of mourners that stood around her grave. Timmy was holding Katie and Daniel by the hand. Annie, Thomas and the graveyard guards were the only ones present to pray for her eternal rest.

Over the next few weeks, Timmy did what he could to feed the children. The little ones constantly cried for Elizabeth and he joined in their tears. He took them along as he tramped the roads, using the wheelbarrow to push them in, as they tired easily.

He found his friend Martin, and his family, dead in a ditch, and returned by night with his wheelbarrow serving a different purpose now, as he trundled it towards the graveyard. The guards no longer paid him any attention, as they thought he had gone slightly mad since the loss of her ladyship.

Many of the children Timmy found were ill with typhus and the disease soon spread within the farmhouse. Now, almost four months since Elizabeth's death, there was only Katie remaining. Little Daniel had succumbed a week before, and Katie was ill and gasping for breath, her body covered by the red rash of the fever.

Timmy was also ill and sweat dripped from his face, as he sat beside the long-dead fire and rocked her in his arms. The house was eerily quiet, though sometimes he thought he heard the sound of children's laughter, or Elizabeth's voice calling to him. It was cold and dark, the last of the candles were gone. Katie stirred in his arms and he pulled the blanket tighter around her. Leaning back, he closed his eyes.

When he woke it was morning. The room was freezing and lit only by a watery sun. He felt too weak to get up, but he would have to find food for Katie. She needed all the nourishment she could get. He had taken to bleeding the cows of local gentry. Mick had shown him where to cut, how much to take and how to stitch the wound with a hair from the animal's own back. He mixed the blood with the corn to make a cake, and though it tasted vile, it kept them alive.

'Come on, sleepyhead,' he said, shaking the child in his arms, but she failed to respond. Gingerly he moved the blanket back from her face and cried out in pain and anger.

Timmy wrapped Katie in the blanket and placed her in the wheelbarrow. Sweat mingled with his tears as he wearily pushed her along. Crawling through a gap in the bushes, he pulled her behind him. He dug for what seemed like hours. Digging as deep as he could, he laid her in the dark hole and pushed the earth over her to form a mound.

He was now truly alone. He believed he had failed them all. His mother, the children, he had been unable to protect them. God, he was so tired, sick and tired, and worn out. He lay down beside the fresh mound and closed his eyes. He would sleep for a while, here, with his loved ones. This was how the guards found him a few hours later. One of them knelt down and felt for a pulse. There was none and he sent his companion to fetch a shovel. Timmy joined the others beneath the earth, and as the last sod was placed over him, the graveyard rang with a dreadful crying. The two guards crossed themselves in fear and hurried away.

'Isn't it strange,' one whispered, 'that in all the suffering, this is the first time we heard that?'

'What is it?'

'The Banshee.'

'That's not the Banshee,' his companion turned and looked back towards the graveyard. 'That's Mother Éire herself, weeping over the premature death of another great son.'

TWENTY-TWO

October 2003

Helen was floating, sinking deeper into the warmth, dreaming of sunshine and swimming in blue, tropical seas. The water lapped about her skin, caressed her thighs. Its touch felt as soft and familiar as a lover. The cocaine speeding through her blood heightened the effect. Surrendering to them both, she forgot, in her drugged state, about the massive bulk of her pregnancy. It was only when she tried to turn gracefully within the water, twisting sharply, propelling herself forward, that reality returned. She cried out as the pain speared her stomach, and the warm water ran from between her legs.

'Shit!' She threw back the covers, pulled at the bunched sodden mass that was her nightdress, and stared at the rapidly expanding bloody mucus staining the sheet. Her waters had broken.

'Joe,' she jabbed at the sleeping form beside her. 'Joe, get up.'

Her husband awoke with a startled grunt and looked at her with bleary eyes.

'My waters have broken. Get up quick.'

Her what? Had what? He had been a bachelor for far too long. Not even the antenatal classes had managed to seep through a brain that was designed for such sterile things as facts and figures. Somehow, he had always hoped that it would never come about. That he would be away on business when the event occurred. Watching the video of a birth, with all its gore and screaming had turned his stomach. And the sight of the head appearing, pushing its way through like a giant white slug against the glutinous red of the surrounding tissue, appalled him. Anyway, it was a month earlier than he had expected.

'Are you just going to sit there looking stupid or are you getting dressed?' she demanded, waddling across the room, pulling the wet nightdress over her swollen stomach and breasts. He would have preferred to sit there, but swung his legs onto the floor. He filled a case with the assortment of nightwear, baby clothes, perfumes and towels that she threw at him. Soon he was carrying the case in one hand and a still sleeping Jenny on the other arm, down the stairs, and out into the cold night air.

The street was quiet and shrouded in a mist. The car doors slamming resounded like thunder in the silence. The headlights pierced the night as the car pulled away, its tail lights — red cat's eyes — skulking through the white of the night.

Black Jack stood surrounded by the mist and watched them go. They would be back with another child. He knew about her pregnancy. It was easy enough to spot as the clothes she wore did little to hide it. She was not like the others in this place, her very tone denied this. Like Elizabeth, she had married out of her own class, but she found it hard to settle into her chosen life and would never be happy. She belonged to the streets and alleyways, this one, and no doubt her needs would take her back there. Though it pained him to think in such a way, they were alike, this woman and Elizabeth. She did not want the child within her. He had heard her say so often enough, when she spoke to her friends, and he knew that Elizabeth cursed him for her condition. But unlike Elizabeth she would be back and with a live, bawling infant, while he, Jack Carey, had to watch the blood of his unborn child drain from between Elizabeth's legs. He should have had a son and if that whore returned with one, then God help her. He walked along the pathway, misted street lamps revealing his shadowy darkness as he passed underneath.

He paused for a moment to look back at the house and up at the bedroom window where Sheila Ryan slept fitfully, sensing his presence, despite the strong sedative. He was tempted, really tempted, to make another assault on her body. The need raged within him and he licked at the dry, indented hollows on his lips. But sense outweighed his desires, as his eyes caught the motion of the many shapes that followed his every move from the darkness. He laughed, scorning the watchers, and strode into the deepening mist.

––––––

Sheila awoke feeling as though she'd been run over by a train. Her head throbbed and the fuzziness refused to clear. The heavy sedative on top of the two sleeping pills had been too much. She had forgotten, in her terror, to tell the doctor about having taken them. Stumbling towards the bedroom door, she felt her way along the landing to the bathroom. She could hear muted mumblings from below, and realised that her hosts were up and about. Sitting on the side of the bath, she reached over and turned on the taps. Once the water reached the desired temperature, she allowed it to fill. The reflection that stared back at her from the mirrored tiles seemed alien. Black-circled eyes and dishevelled hair made her look like a mad woman. Her skin felt raw and sore. Easing the straps of her nightdress from her shoulders, she allowed it to fall to the floor. Most of the dressings had come loose and she pulled the remaining bits of tape off. The white gauze was stained with blood, pus and a blackness that felt like dried earth when she touched it. Cringing, she dropped them into the waste bin beneath the sink. Surveying the damage, she gasped at the bruises and lesions that marbled her body. There were long red scratches on the inside of both her thighs.

She shuddered, remembering the talons that had raked through her skin, opening the flesh in their wake and shivered, despite the warmth of the water.

The events of last night seemed impossible. The demon-things, whatever they were, had to be part of some crazy nightmare. Drawing her knees up to her chest, she hugged herself. Tom would be home soon, and everything would be okay.

A gentle tapping on the door made her jump, and she climbed reluctantly from the bath, unwilling to leave its womb-like sanctum. Grabbing a towel, she wrapped it tightly around her, and leaning against the door, whispered.

'Yes?'

'Are you all right, my dear?'

'Yes, thank you. I'll be down as soon as I'm dressed.'

She wasn't sure if the woman had heard, because she never answered, and there was no sound of retreating footsteps. Was she still standing outside the door, waiting for her to come out? She shivered again, pulling the towel up around her shoulders, hoping to find some warmth within its folds. She couldn't stop shaking. After cleaning the bath, she sat on the side, delaying the moment when she'd have to face them.

'Sheila?'

The voice startled her for a moment, then ... 'Tom!' She was struggling with the lock on the bathroom door. 'Oh Tom,' she threw herself, sobbing, into his arms.

'My God, Sheila, I didn't know what to think. The police contacted me first thing this morning. I got here as soon as I could. Are you all right?'

She couldn't reply. The relief at seeing him was overwhelming.

After she had calmed down and changed into the freshly laundered clothes that Ruth had fetched for her, they talked. The four of them went over the events of the previous night. It was hard to believe, sitting in the bright kitchen of their next-door neighbours, that anything like that could have happened.

'Hooligans, that's what they are. Breaking into people's homes, attacking helpless women,' Mike Byrne's booming voice made Sheila jump.

'They weren't people, I keep telling you.'

He didn't seem to hear, or chose to ignore what she said. She was a woman after all, and he knew how they were given to flights of fancy.

'Call the army in. That's what they should do. Bring in a curfew, clean up the streets.'

His wife tried to shush him by patting him on the arm, but he slapped her away.

'Well,' Tom cleared his throat. 'We'll get back home.' He stood and held out his hand to Mike. 'I'll never be able to thank you enough for what you've done for us.'

'Glad to be of help.'

Mike Byrne's huge hand closed over his, and Tom could visualise the bones crunching as the man shook. His fingers were tingling and it took all his strength not to flex them, when he finally let go.

Tom was glad when they were safely back in their own home, but not Sheila, who looked around her as though expecting the 'things' from the night before to jump out on her. Her nerves were so on edge, she almost screamed when the doorbell rang. Tom answered it and came back followed by the doctor.

'Well, well, young lady,' he beamed, 'feeling better are we?'

He reached down to feel for her pulse, and she drew back.

'Still a bit jumpy, eh? Well, it's to be expected,' he sat on the sofa beside her and, using his briefcase as a desk, began to write out a prescription. 'Just a few sedatives to help calm your wife down; if you need me, my number's on the top,' he threw the prescription pad back into his case and snapped the locks. 'Keep those scratches clean,' he advised Sheila as Tom led him from the room.

She lay back against the sofa and tried not to listen to the whispered conversation between the two men.

Tom came back, smiling.

'The doctor says that salt baths are the best thing for you.'

She remained silent and he sat beside her, reaching for her hand.

'It's going to be all right, you know, darling. They'll catch who-ever it was, and Mike is calling a locksmith and alarm company as we speak. We'll make this place safe as Fort Knox. What do you say?'

'Would "go to hell" be plain enough?'

'Come on, sweetheart. Don't be like that,' he said, trying unsuccess-fully to lace his fingers between her limp ones.

'I know what you were saying to that doctor. "Sheila's always been a bit nervy",' she mimicked his voice.

'Listen, darling, I know what happened last night was awful.'

'Awful! Now that's a nice word for it.'

'What do you want me to say, Sheila?' He jumped up and paced the room. 'How do you think I feel? I leave home for one night and my wife is attacked and almost raped while I was gone. Don't you think I want to kill him?'

'You think I imagined it.'

'Christ, Sheila. I know you didn't imagine it. I can see that.'

'I mean about the damned demons – or whatever they were.'

'I'm not going to argue with you now. You're far too upset and need these,' he waved the prescription. 'It will take me an hour to get to the pharmacy and back. Will you be all right, while I'm gone?'

She nodded, not looking up, and only moved when the front door slammed. She wanted to throw it open, to follow him. Tell him she was sorry. Sorry that she'd been attacked, sorry for not understanding. Sorry, sorry, sorry. Instead she leant back against the door and allowed herself to slide to the floor, sobbing. Crying for her loss of innocence, because she would never again feel safe within this house, this dream home, and for the loss of her parents and the empty years that followed. For the need for psychiatric care, but most of all, the stigma that was attached to this; never feeling wholly trusted after that. Not by the few friends she had and now not even by her husband. She forgot in her grief to be afraid, until a gentle tapping startled her. She sat for a moment, frozen.

'Sheila, are you there?'

Oh, God, it was that woman from next door. Ruth, wasn't it? Tapping tapping, ever rapping, like Poe's *Raven*. She struggled to her feet and opened the door.

'I just called around to see if you were all right?'

'Come in.'

'Well, just for a moment,' said Ruth, dodging as if expecting to be hit. 'Mike called the home security company and they've promised to be here sometime this morning.'

Sheila looked at the woman before her. At her dark-circled, red-rimmed eyes and tight smile. Hands clasped tightly together as if she feared they would fly away. Such a small woman, she thought, to have such a big, angry husband. With this the tears started again, and she found the arms that went around her were surprisingly strong.

'There, there now, dear.'

Sheila allowed herself to be led into the kitchen and sat listening to the kettle being filled and the clink of cups.

'Sweet tea.' She took the cup from Ruth. 'Best thing for shock. Better than any of those new pills they pump into you.'

'Thank you.'

They sat in silence for a while, each lost in their own thoughts.

'What did you see? What did you really see?'

'You believe me?' Sheila was incredulous.

'Well, I'm not sure. I've seen some things that I can't explain.'

'I'm not sure now either,' admitted Sheila with relief. 'I know I had taken two sleeping pills, and that I was panicked, hysterical, but I couldn't be that wrong. Could I?'

'You said demons?'

'Yes, like … um …' she searched for the right words. 'D'you remember the video *Thriller*? Where Michael Jackson danced with all these zombies, corpses?'

'Sorry, my dear,' the woman shook her head.

'No, not your thing, I suppose.'

Silence descended again, until finally Sheila asked.

'What if I imagined it?'

'That's possible.'

'Yes, but what if I didn't?'

'Then God help us all.'

'Amen.'

Outside a car door slammed and they both turned towards the sound. If it was Tom, he was taking his time. Ruth got up and started to clear away the cups. A key turned in the front door, and Tom came into the kitchen clutching a white paper bag.

'Hello, Ruth,' he greeted the visitor. 'The pharmacist said to take one right away, Sheila.'

Without being asked, Ruth filled a glass with water and handed it to her. Tom shook a pill onto her upturned palm and they both watched as she placed it in her mouth and swallowed.

'Better now, darling?' he brushed Sheila's hand, afraid of rejection.

'Getting there,' she grasped his extended fingers and pulled them back to her.

The doorbell sounded again and Tom went to answer it. Sheila had to admit she felt better. It was probably the effects of the pill, but terror was gradually being replaced by a warm, fuzzy feeling. Tom returned to say the locksmith had arrived and was setting to work. Ruth excused herself, promising to call back the next day.

'Oh, before you go,' Tom said, 'I met one of our new neighbours, Joe Mahoney from number 27. His wife gave birth early this morning, a baby boy; he's a month premature, but doing well. That's got to be a good omen, right?'

The women glanced at each other and nodded, but the news didn't bring about the usual exclamations of pleasure.

'You'll get little rest today,' Ruth looked worried.

'I'll be fine. They can work around me.'

'See you tomorrow. You'll be all right?'

Sheila nodded, but turning towards her asked again, 'What if I'm right?'

Ruth crossed herself – the question was unanswerable.

In the graveyard Elizabeth and Timmy sat hidden by the grass. The children ran and played about them, and paid little heed to their whispering. Black Jack sat on the branch of a tree, idly swinging one leg as he watched the movement in the houses. Strange, he felt weakest during this time, invisible. His strength returned as the sun went down. Now and then he glanced across towards the grass to Elizabeth and the boy. He'd find a way to outsmart them. Leaning back against the trunk, he turned his attention back to the houses and the things he desired therein. Soon, it would be his time, the need burning inside would be satisfied. He smiled, closed his eyes and waited for the night.

TWENTY-THREE

Jenny kicked off her bedcovers. It was hot and her throat hurt. She sat for a while, blinking and rubbing her eyes. It was almost dark outside. Her time spent in the hospital waiting room had disorientated her. She was waking when she should be going to sleep. Sliding onto the floor, she was surprised when the room rocked, and she scrambled back onto the bed. She thought perhaps her toes had fallen asleep and wiggled them. They were fine. She was about to make a second attempt to stand, when her door was slowly opened and Joe stuck his head round.

'Hello, sleepyhead.'

'My head hurts.' She scratched so viciously at her scalp, that he was forced to pull her hand away.

'I imagine it does hurt if you're going at it like that.'

'No, I mean inside. It hurts inside, and I'm too hot.'

He laid the flat of his hand against her forehead and frowned. She did feel hot.

'What does your mother usually give you when you're like this?'

When she named the medicine, he scooped her up into his arms and carried her downstairs.

The house felt cold, and he made a mental note to turn on the heating. He should have done so earlier, as they were well into autumn. Icy draughts flowed from beneath the doors and he shivered. So did Jenny when he placed the feverish child on the cold marble work surface. It felt like a block of ice on her bottom, and she suddenly needed to pee.

'Quick, let me down.'

He swung her onto the floor and watched as she hurried towards the downstairs cloakroom, hands clasped tightly between her legs. She was back in moments.

'Did you wash your hands?'

She gave him one of her looks. He found the medicine she required, and was reading the side of the box as she climbed up on a stool beside him.

'Two spoons.'

'What?'

'You have to give me two of the white spoons,' she directed, taking the box and pulling out a small, white, plastic spoon.

'Oh, good, well done,' Joe said, relieved not to have the worry of measuring the dose.

She sat waiting, mouth open, as he tilted the bottleneck towards the spoon. The liquid was thick, and once moving, fell from the bottle in a torrent, over the side of the ridiculously small spoon.

'Shit,' he exclaimed, throwing down the bottle and placing a hand under the spoon in a vain effort to stem the flow. 'Quick!' He thrust it towards the waiting mouth.

The bloody stuff was everywhere, stuck between his fingers, so that when he opened them they resembled crimson webs, on his shoes, on the floor, sliding down the side of the stool. It had a life of its own.

'Will I take the next spoon by myself?' Jenny smiled at him.

'If you would, please, Miss Know-all,' he grinned. Rinsing and drying the spoon, he handed it back to her.

Jenny poured with professional ease, and he shook his head in awe as the liquid flowed neatly onto the curve. She swallowed without losing a drop and handed the spoon back to him, raising her eyebrows a number of times.

'Yes, yes, I know.'

'Then say it.'

'You are the greatest, the most powerful living being on this planet. Now get dressed. We have to visit your mother.'

She climbed from the stool and went upstairs. He had a list of things to do before Helen came home with the baby. He had thought that she would spend at least a week in the hospital, but she had insisted on coming home the next day; not being a first-time mother her doctor allowed it and there seemed to be no problem with the baby, despite the fact that it was a month premature. Come to think of it, none of the doctors or nurses had remarked on this and it was only Helen who told him that this was the case. Anyway, he wouldn't dwell on it now, there was too much to do. Jenny returned dressed and holding a hairbrush.

'You have to tie up my hair,' she climbed onto the stool, handing him the brush and a velvet tie. After numerous attempts to gather her abundant tresses together, he gave up. 'Let's just leave it hang down, straight.'

Jenny shrugged, taking the brush from him. Her mother didn't like it that way. She said it reminded her of rats' tails, but that was Joe's problem. Her mother would have to shout at him over it. She still felt too hot, and struggled as he made her put on her coat.

'Come on, Jen. Be good and I'll take you for a meal after the hospital.'

'A real grown-up place?'

'Would you settle for a Chinese?'

'Cool!'

He steered her out the door, turning the key twice so the deadbolt fell into place. She ran ahead of him and was struggling with the safety belt when he reached the car. Placing the bag of goods for Helen on the back seat, he got in beside her. She had managed to lock the belt into place and was sitting hands in lap.

'Ready, Miss Jenny?'

'Ready.'

She couldn't see over the dashboard, and instead watched the streetlights as he backed out of the driveway. She usually liked going backwards. If she closed her eyes it felt like falling. But tonight it made her tummy feel sickly. It was not as bad when they started moving forward, and she pulled a lock of hair into her mouth, sucking on it. Her head felt so itchy, she scratched it again with both hands.

'You okay, Jen?'

'Fine, I think I'm hungry.'

'Will you be all right until after we visit your mother?' he asked. 'Don't tell her that I haven't given you anything to eat, okay?'

'I won't.'

Joe reached across and patted her hand. Sometimes she seemed so much older and wiser than he was. They drove the rest of the way in comfortable silence, as Jenny wondered what the small bumpy things were that she could feel in her hair.

———

The hapless Brutus had finally been allowed back indoors. He sat shaking in his basket, more from fear, than from his injuries. His master had not fed him that day as punishment for his cowardice. Ruth sat staring at the television screen feigning interest in the war documentary her husband was watching. She had no stomach for such things, and prayed for the victims and their families. He would accuse her of sulking or not enjoying his company, if she tried to retire too early. She wanted this day to end, to get away from his endless nagging and complaining. You would think it was her fault that Sheila had been attacked. The insults had started over dinner.

'Of course, that Sheila is a fine-looking woman,' he'd remarked, leering across the table at her. She had continued picking at her food, knowing better than to answer.

'You'll have no worries in that way. Not unless the attacker is blind or desperate.' Nothing was omitted.

He sneered at her flat chest, her sagging stomach; even the dryness of her skin didn't escape his attention. Through it all she remained still, trying not to cry. No wonder he needed his collection, he'd said. This so-called collection was no more than a stack of smelly, dog-eared, porn magazines that he kept under his bed. She was forced to view them each time she vacuumed, pouting, lip-glossed girls thrusting their breasts and other parts up at her as she worked. When the programme was over, he flicked from channel to channel. There were some things she would have liked to watch, but dare not ask, as he would only ridicule her taste. It had been great when he been working or away. She loved the morning shows and the smart self-assured women she saw, speaking of equality and rights. She had forfeited any rights the day she married Mike. She longed to have her own car like Helen Mahoney, and nice clothes and the freedom to enjoy them.

'Better let the dog out.' He rose, clicked off the television and walked into the kitchen.

Ruth sat staring at the blank screen. Tonight, for some reason, she felt worse than usual. More depressed, desperate. She heard him swearing at the dog, shouting at him to go out. Walking over to the door, she peeped through. Brutus was cringing inside the patio door and every hair on his body was standing on end. He whimpered and growled at whatever it was he saw in the darkness. Ruth brought her hands to her chest in terror. He was out there, in the dark, whatever it was that attacked Sheila was back.

'Get the fuck out.'

She cried out as Mike kicked the dog, lifting it off its feet and propelling it into the darkness. Its howl of pain and terror echoed around the kitchen and she found, to her surprise, that she was crying. Even though Mike had slammed the patio door shut, she could still hear the creature howling.

'What's wrong with you?' he demanded.

She didn't answer.

'I asked you a question?'

'It's the dog.'

'Speak up. What about the dog?'

She wanted to tell him how she pitied the helpless animal. To beg him to let it come in, but before she could say anything, he roared.

'Oh, I get it. The dog might upset the neighbours with his howling. Well, fuck the neighbours, and fuck you.'

The fist that smashed into her face sent her flying. She fell onto the floor and stayed there waiting for what was to come next. It was the increase in howling from outside that saved her.

'Right, that's it!' Mike stormed towards the kitchen. 'I'll finish that fucking dog off for good this time.' He stopped in the doorway and looked down at her. 'I'll deal with you when I get back.'

Ruth sat up, feeling her face. Her mouth was filled with the coppery taste of blood. She climbed to her feet, using the couch as support, and looked in the mirror that hung over the fireplace. Her bottom lip was already swollen and badly cut. The blood had run down her chin and stained the collar of her dress. She hoped it would wash out.

She had very few clothes and couldn't afford to lose this dress. She had no thoughts of Mike's attack on her or the consequences when he returned. Her mouth felt raw, meaty against her tongue. Mike was crashing about in the kitchen looking for something to beat the dog with. Perhaps, when he was finished with the animal, his bloodlust would be sated, and he'd forget about her. God help me, Ruth prayed. Give me the strength to endure what happens next.

Elizabeth watched the blood that trickled down the woman's chin, and shook her head in disbelief. Even here, in this new century, women still suffered at the hands of men. She had thought that things would be different, but that was not the case. The women in the other houses were not like this one. They moved with a sense of purpose, and she knew by the way they held themselves, that they would not allow this to happen to them. Perhaps it was only women like Ruth, who relied on a man for support, who were beaten. Not much had changed.

TWENTY-FOUR

Mike had found an old hurley belonging to his son. Nothing was ever thrown away in the Byrne household. He tore open the patio doors and stalked outside towards the howling. The light from the kitchen lit the garden half way. From then on it was in shadow. He forgot, in his haste, to turn on the outside light and had to stop and allow his eyes to adjust to the darkness. The dog was somewhere at the bottom of the garden. He could just make out its shape over by the tree. His grip tightened on the hurley. That dog had never been any good. He'd get a new one, a better breed. Might just as well do the same thing with the wife, she was as useless as the dog. He smiled at his own joke. Suddenly the howling stopped.

'Where are you, boy? Come on now. Good dog. I'm not going to hurt you. Just beat you to death,' he mumbled beneath his breath.

'He's over here.'

The voice from the dark made him jump.

'Who's there?' he spluttered. 'Come out, show yourself.'

'Why don't you come and find me?'

'By Christ, I'll find you all right, and give you the dog's dose. I'll teach you to trespass on other people's property.'

Black Jack was leaning against the tree. The dog was hiding on the other side of it, unsure of which of the men he was most afraid of. Jack liked the animal, it was prepared to strike at the most vulnerable of targets. It had no sense of loyalty. A rope hung from one of the branches and formed a small loop on the ground. Mike was almost in front of him, but he was still unable to see him. Black Jack watched as he turned this way and that, searching for the owner of the voice, all the while willing him closer, closer.

Mike's right foot landed inside the snare. He had no time to react as the noose tightened and his feet shot from under him. He yelled as the world turned upside down, and his head, a couple of feet from the ground, bounced painfully off the trunk. Blood rushed to his head, pounded in his ears. He felt nauseous as the grass spun beneath him, and he brought his hands down to steady himself. The tips of his fingers barely touched the ground. Sweat matted his hair to his head.

'You were saying?'

Mike tried to turn towards the voice, but the movement caused him to rock.

'Just what do you think you're doing?' he gasped. There was no way he was giving in to this thug. 'Ruth,' he called towards the open doorway. 'Ruth, come out here.'

'I don't think she can hear you. Call louder.'

'When I get down from here you're dead!' His blood chilled at the reply.

'I'm already dead.'

'Bastard, rotten, stinking coward. It's easy to be brave when I'm tied up like this. Let me down and fight man to man.'

'Oh, I have no intention of harming you in any way,' the voice said. 'Let's just say I'm lengthening the odds, for someone who is not as strong as I am.'

The man was obviously a lunatic.

'Ruth!' Mike shouted, now that he had recovered his breath. 'Ruth!' Something brushed by him, something solid that he was unable to see. The stench, Christ, it was rotten, putrid. He could hear the dog growling, a low warning growl and then the voice.

'He's been a bad master. It's time for revenge. Come now.'

The thing brushed by him again, and moments later he was amazed to see Brutus standing in front of him. The dog looked different, its eyes vicious.

'Get Ruth!' he commanded. The dog refused to move. 'Go on, get her, I said.'

Brutus growled, a deep threatening sound that echoed in the quiet of the garden.

'Don't you growl at me.' Mike looked around for the hurley. It lay nearby and he ran the fingers of one hand across the grass towards it. Making contact, he inched it towards him until he could get a proper grip. The fingers on the other hand kept him from swinging too much. The hurley was almost in his grasp.

'Jesus Christ,' he yelled as teeth sank into his flesh. The dog's incisors scraped bone as they buried themselves deeper in his skin.

His voice seemed to enrage the animal further, and he shook and tossed the hand as if killing a rabbit.

'Ru-u-u-th!' Mike screamed.

Next door, Tom Ryan shook his head in wonder. That poor woman, how did she put up with all that shouting? It was hard to see anything, but he thought he could make out the dog running backwards and forwards in the back garden. What a time of night to start playing with a dog. He pulled the curtains closed against the noise, hoping it wouldn't wake Sheila. She had slept fitfully through the day. Now, finally, with the aid of a sedative, she was sound asleep in bed.

'Stupid man,' he muttered, closing the kitchen door.

Ruth had washed her face and put on her nightclothes. The stained dress was steeping in the hope of dislodging the blood. Her body ached from the fall, so she turned on the water heater and set about collecting the few things she would need for her bath, when she heard her name being screamed from outside. She walked slowly down the stairs. It was best to get it over with, whatever it was. There was no sign of Mike and she stood uncertainly for a moment. The dog was snarling, as she flicked on the outside light. The garden lit up and she had to shield her eyes from the sudden glare.

'Ruth, you stupid bitch, help me!'

She looked towards the voice and gasped. Her husband was hanging upside down from a tree. She almost laughed, until she saw what was standing beside him. It was a man, no, something that had once been a man. His eyes blazed red in the harsh, white light as he stared at her. His hands were folded before him, his stance arrogant. Brutus had stopped his attack, and he too was staring at her.

'Will you stop standing there with your mouth open, woman, and get me down!'

She turned towards her husband and noticed the blood. His hand was covered in it, and the grass beneath him splattered scarlet. A movement behind the tree made her look away, and she watched in wonder as a child, or something resembling a child, leapt up onto the branch holding the rope. It seemed to be trying to cut through it, trying to release her husband. The man-thing followed her gaze, and growled in frustration.

He jumped up and tore the boy away, flinging him through the bushes. Ruth watched it all thinking, this isn't happening. It's a nightmare. I'll wake up soon and be safe in bed.

'Will you hurry up?'

She turned again towards her husband's voice.

'Are you listening to me? Hurry up! Get a knife, cut me down.'

Brutus growled.

'So help me, Ruth, if you don't move I'll beat the living daylights out of you when I'm free! Get a sharp knife and get it now!'

Ruth was turning to walk towards the house when the thing spoke. She watched it as it scooped up the blood-spattered hurley.

'Come near,' the thing waved the stick at her, 'and you will share in his fate.'

She didn't bother to answer. Instead, she went inside and closed the patio door. The last thing she saw as she drew the curtains was the dog and the man-thing turning back towards her husband.

Mike Byrne screamed just once. He was unable to do more as the dog sunk his teeth into his face, tearing his lips and tongue away with one bite. He tried to call out through the white of his exposed teeth, bleeding gums and frothing blood, but all he could manage was a low moan. The wind had suddenly whipped up. Its shrieks and moans mingled with his. The disembodied voice spurred the dog onwards. He felt his ear being ripped from the side of his head. The teeth sank into his forehead and pulled. His scalp peeled backwards, and he felt each single hair as it was torn from its roots. The pain was absolute. He was now more dead than alive and groaned almost with pleasure as the teeth sunk into his neck, locating the main artery. He heard the yelp of surprise as blood spurted into the animal's face. It released him, shaking its head and splattering Mike's clothes with his own blood. Warm blood coursed down his neck and lodged in the cavity that had once been his ear. He hung like an animal on a butcher hook as it quickly drained from him. His last thought was of his wife. She had balls after all. He would have smiled, if he'd had any lips.

———

Ruth walked back upstairs and pulled the plug out of the bath, allowing it to drain. She shivered, imagining how nice the warm water would have felt on her chilled skin. He was probably dead now. Dead, gone forever; she giggled hysterically at the thought. Would he go to heaven? Despite being a total bastard he probably would. He had been murdered after all. By that man-thing, the dog and even she had played her part in his death. He'd be there to greet her on the day of judgment, there was no doubt about it.

Her footsteps, though muffled by the carpet, sounded thunderous as she descended the stairs. The silence of the house buzzed in her ears, and her hands shook as she reached out for the curtains on the patio door. Mike was still hanging from the tree, though motionless now, his face a red mask. She didn't dare step outside, in case the thing was lurking somewhere. It was only fitting that she cut him down, but it would probably be wiser to wait until first light. Taking the sharpest knife she could find, she sat at the kitchen table and waited for the dawn.

As the hours ticked by, she thought about the endless years of torment that had been her life. Her nerves had become much more frayed since the move, but she had put that down to the unfamiliarity of her new surroundings. Holding her hands out in front of her, she gazed at the thin, gnarled fingers that seemed to vibrate to the pounding of her heart. A dark shadow slunk past the patio door and she drew the knife closer to her chest, finding comfort in the cold steel.

'Go away,' she screamed at the darkness outside, but the shape returned, drawn by the sound of her voice.

The noise of its clawing on the glass made her moan in terror, and it wasn't until the familiar whine of the dog reached her that she realised what it was – Brutus. Her knees shook when she stood up. Flicking the switch on the outside light, she waited for the bulb to blink on. The urgent scratching of the dog's nails had left red tracks on her clean glass. Her stomach turned at the sight of her husband's blood and her eyes strayed to the dog, whose face and chest was covered in blood. The hairs on its chin stood out in dark, dried tufts and its footprints lined the patio slabs, daubing the white granite with crimson blotches. The dog whined again, begging to be admitted.

'Go away!' Ruth screamed, flicking off the light and pulling the curtains closed. It was too much, she could not bear any more suffering. Holding the knife close she climbed the stairs. Once on the landing, she opened the hotpress and turned on the emersion. Now that there was no one to berate her for wasting money, she could do as she pleased. As she waited for the water to heat, she went into the back bedroom, the one she had designated as a guest-room for her grandchildren. While they would never come to stay, terrified of their grandfather, she had always hoped that someday ...

The garden below her was empty, except for the figure that still swung from the tree. Opening the window an inch or so, she looked out into the night. The only sound that marred the silence was the creaking of the rope as it moved in the breeze. She looked towards the bushes at the bottom of the garden and her heart began to pound once again at the sight of the dark shapes that moved behind the trees. A sudden yelp from the dog made her slam the window shut. Had the thing returned? She wondered about this as she walked into the bathroom. Turning on the taps she allowed the bath to fill, testing the water with shaking fingers. Laying the knife on the side of the bath, she climbed in.

The warmth soothed her and she closed her eyes. Her mind was filled with images that refused to be ignored. Some were from the past, the nightmare of her childhood at the hands of a drunken father and her own stupid decision to marry Mike and allow the terror to continue. Once, when Mike had phoned her from Bosnia to say that he was coming home, she had attempted suicide. It had been a rather half-hearted attempt and her stomach had rebelled at the pills she had swallowed. The aftermath was nothing more than a slight feeling of nausea and light-headedness. Throughout her marriage she had consulted numerous doctors on the condition of her nerves. The only results were prescriptions for various tranquillisers, none of which worked. But it didn't take an expert to tell her what was really wrong and the cause of her nervousness had finally been removed.

Lord I'm tired, she thought, brushing a strand of greying hair from her forehead. But it was not just an end-of-day tiredness, or the effects of the pills she had taken to deaden the pain of Mike's beating. This was a mind-numbing weariness that only death would relieve.

Her religion had taught that suicides go to hell. She could live on happily without Mike, except for one thing, a fear that consumed her. What if she were to have an accident? She could be just out shopping or even crossing the street and get knocked down and die. Then she would surely go to heaven and be back once again in the clutches of her husband. No, she could not bear the thought. She would rather run the risk of eternal damnation than meet him again. Could the devil be any worse than Mike?

She winced as she traced the blade along the dark vein on her left wrist, watching the blood pump from it in time to her heartbeat. Black, then red, it gushed between her fingers, making the knife difficult to hold. Plunging her wrist beneath the water, she washed away the blood from her fingers. She would be quicker this time and so she sliced through the vein on her right hand, rather clumsily, but with the same results. Throwing the knife onto the floor, she lay back in the warm, bloody water and waited for death. She felt light-headed and wasn't sure if that was from loss of blood or the sudden feeling of total freedom. She could feel her heart slowing, taking longer between beats. She muttered a prayer, but it was no act of contrition. For a moment, just as her eyes closed, she thought she heard the faint beating of wings. A dark angel was coming for her. She smiled and slid into the blackness beneath the crimson water.

TWENTY-FIVE

The next day was like any other in a modern suburban housing estate. The morning began with the usual banging of car doors and shouts of children, hurrying for their rides to school. The air was crisp and cold, but not as cold as the undiscovered bodies of Mike and Ruth Byrne.

At number 25 Sheila Ryan was struggling awake. The two days since the attack were a blur. Tom left for work hours before, in the hope that an early start would mean he could finish earlier and be home before dark. Sheila shivered; despite the central heating, the room felt chilly. She went downstairs in her dressing gown and slippers. She walked to the sitting-room and switched on the log-effect gas fire, which glowed instantly to life and then stood in front of it, relishing the heat. Sheila wondered if Tom would remember to ring the school and make her excuses. It didn't look too good to be ringing in sick, when she had been there so short a time.

Sipping coffee, she realised she felt safer and better now that the alarm and new locks had been fitted. Tom was right. Perhaps, in her drug-induced slumber, she had imagined that her attacker was a monster, a demon of some sort. She really would have to gather her wits.

'This is the twenty-first century,' she reminded herself, 'and I'm living in a new house, not some creaky, old Victorian mansion filled with family ghosts. What I have imagined is the stuff of nightmares, or the imagination of some thrill-a-minute horror writer.'

It was time for action. She would shower, do some grocery shopping, and they could enjoy a leisurely dinner together when Tom got home. He would be relieved to find her looking well ... or as well as cosmetics would allow. She could feel the hollows beneath her eyes and knew that they would be dark. She had not yet drawn back the kitchen curtains, wanting to keep the heat from escaping. Now, with a feeling of renewal, she pulled them back, allowing the watery sun to flood the room. It was just like any other day. The trees were still green, the sky was blue and there was no sign of anything out of the ordinary.

Her eyes wandered towards next-door's garden. She wanted to invite Ruth to lunch, and although the thought of having to meet Mike Byrne filled her with distaste, she would brave it for Ruth's sake. There was something swinging from a tree at the bottom of the garden. She leaned across the sink and pressed her forehead against the window, trying to get a better look. It was some sort of upside-down scarecrow. That horrible man couldn't even leave the birds alone.

Sheila was glad she had worn a jacket, even though she was only going next door. The wind was cutting and she dug her hands deeper into her pockets as the doorbell chimes echoed inside. There was no answer, and she frowned. The car was still in the driveway and usually the dog would kick up a racket. She peered through the letterbox. Not a sound, no movement, nothing.

She rang the bell again. Perhaps they had gone out into the back garden. She walked around the side of the house; there was no sign of either of them, so she rapped hard on the patio door. This was strange, the two of them missing at the same time. She had only ever seen Ruth going out in her husband's company on a Friday for the weekly shopping. She turned to walk away. Then, remembering the scarecrow, she went towards it. It would give Tom a good laugh when she told him about it this evening. The breeze had swung it around so its back was towards her. It was very lifelike, even if the head was pulpy and misshapen. She leaned over and touched its legs, swinging it round to face her.

Her screams brought the neighbours running. A couple of women led her home. Her throat filled with bile and her stomach heaved at the horror. She didn't make it inside in time, and had to stand over her freshly planted flowerbeds as the coffee she had so recently drunk spewed from her. To her immense embarrassment, the force with which she vomited, made her wet herself. She could smell the warm urine as it coursed down her legs, forming a pool at her feet. The women fussed and reassured her, helping her to slip off her sodden shoes. She felt she would never get over the mortification as they led her, childlike, upstairs to the bathroom. The shocked man, who rediscovered Mike's body, was running around in panic, screaming for someone, anyone, to call the police, an ambulance.

Sheila was trying to wash the dirt from her body under the spray. The urine was easily soaped away, but her hand, the hand that touched him, she scrubbed repeatedly, as she sobbed her distress. Blue lights were flashing around her bedroom when she emerged from the shower. In the street below uniformed police moved swiftly, taping off next door's garden. Her sedatives were on the bedside table and she quickly, without the aid of water, swallowed two of them, almost choking on their dry chalkiness. She dressed, mechanically, tugging at the clothes that stuck to the still, damp patches on her body.

'Are you all right, my dear?'

She turned and nodded. 'Yes, I'm fine now, thank you.'

The woman's eyes strayed towards the open pill bottle.

'Such a terrible shock for you. Would you like me to call your husband?'

'No, I'll be fine, thanks, and he's very busy.' She could do this. She could face this demon alone. What had happened next door was real. There were witnesses to that effect.

'Well, if you're sure.'

'Yes, thank you.'

'I'm Betty Regan, by the way,' she held out a hand to Sheila, who stared at it blankly. 'It's a terrible way to meet, but I live at number 17, and I'll be there until lunchtime, if you need me.'

Sheila, who desperately needed to be left alone with her shame, managed to nod. The woman was just turning to go when a crash from next-door made them jump.

Betty leaned out of the bedroom window.

'The police are breaking down the door.'

The thought of her kind neighbour spurred Sheila into action. She raced down the stairs after the woman. She tried to run past a police officer standing by the splintered front door, only to be grabbed from behind and steered away.

'Come on now, miss,' a plain-clothes detective led her aside, holding firm despite her struggles.

'You don't understand. I'm her friend.'

'Yes, yes, I understand. But I just want to ask you a few questions.'

The mutterings of the assembled crowd came to a sudden stop. The silence hummed as she watched the small procession emerging from the side of the house. Two figures in white overalls, stretcher-bearers struggling under the weight of Mike's body. Gasps and shudders came from the crowd, as the stretcher passed by them, and the black body bag was loaded into the waiting ambulance.

'Is Ruth all right?' she asked the detective. 'Is Ruth all right?' she repeated. 'Tell me.'

'I'm afraid not.'

'Oh God, no, what happened?'

'We don't know for sure yet. The coroner will fill us in later, but it looks as though she attacked her husband, and then committed suicide.'

'No, that's not possible,' she whispered, watching a technician carrying the blood-stained hurley, encased in plastic.

'We'll be in touch,' the detective informed her.

'It's just not possible,' she whispered, thinking of the small, frail woman who had befriended her. Mike must have weighed at least a hundred kilos more than his wife ... how could she possibly have strung him up like that?

z

236

A van marked with the lettering of the ISPCA drew up and its driver, leash in hand, hurried down the side of the house. He re-emerged with Brutus in tow. There were more gasps from the crowd when they saw the dog. His coat was matted with blood and he had to be helped up into the cage that sat behind the van. Sheila moved closer to it, gripping the wire mesh.

'What happened to you, boy?' she whispered. What was happening in this place?

'Move aside, please miss.' A police officer ushered her back from the van, and she watched until it disappeared from sight.

'The dog must have witnessed it all', the whisper ran through the crowd, until a movement in the doorway caught their attention. The stretcher-bearers appeared once again. This time the black bag was too big for the body inside. It could have been a child. Many of the women in the crowd started to cry. The sight of such a tiny figure encased in its black plastic shroud was too much to bear, even for the most morbid among them. Sheila cringed as the ambulance doors slammed shut. It moved slowly away from the kerb, followed by the police and coroner. The blue lights had been switched off. The couple inside the ambulance were beyond help. Sheila went back indoors and lay on the couch in the sitting-room. She had forgotten to switch off the gas fire, and the room felt hot and stuffy, but she didn't turn it off. Still in her coat, she closed her eyes, huddled into a ball, and waited for Tom to come home.

———

'Jenny, will you please come away from the window?'

This was the third time he'd asked and Joe Mahoney was losing patience with his stepdaughter. He was rushing about trying to get the house ready for Helen and the new baby's homecoming. The events of next door, though chilling, were not the most important thing on his mind. He had already missed two days from work. An absence that was unplanned for with the baby arriving so early, and at one of the busiest times too.

'Jenny, I won't tell you again.'

Jenny climbed down from her perch on the window seat, scratching her head. The people next door must be very sick. There was an ambulance and police cars and everything. She felt quite sick herself, and was still feeling too hot and her throat hurt. She wanted to tell Joe, but he was so busy.

'I'll go up and clean my room.'

'Good girl,' he smiled at her, as he struggled with the vacuum cleaner.

Jenny could hear him muttering and grumbling as he tried to steer the machine across the carpet. Her bed was easily made. She just pulled the quilt into place and ran her hands along it. She would tidy her books next. Sitting cross-legged in front of the bookcase, she was soon lost in pictures and words.

'Are any of those books on the afterlife?' She turned to find her alien friend sitting on her bed. He really did smell very bad.

'What's an afterlife?'

'It's the life after death. Do you have any books on that?'

'How can you be alive after you're dead?' Jenny knew all about death. Her goldfish, Jerry, had died and her mother flushed him down the toilet. Her mother said when you're dead, you're dead, and that was that.

'Never mind. Just find me some books that deal with that subject.'

'Where will I get them from?'

'Where do you normally get books from?'

'From the shop or the library.'

'Then get them from there.'

'Okay, but I can't go today, because my new baby brother is coming home from the hospital.'

The whore had a son after all. Black Jack paced around the room, angry at having to wait.

'Then go tomorrow. Go to your library and get me the books I ask for.'

'Yes, I will.'

'Jenny!' She jumped as her name was called. 'Jenny, get ready. We have to go and collect your mother and the baby.'

'Okay, I'll be down in a minute.' She quickly tidied the remaining books. Her mother would be angry if her room wasn't neat. She almost forgot about her alien friend in her hurry.

'Don't forget what I asked of you,' he said.

'I won't. I promise.'

Black Jack was left to wander the house once the front door had slammed shut. He pulled the books that Jenny had so carefully tidied, from the shelves and threw them around the room. The clothes from the airing cupboard were scattered along the landing and down the stairs. He wanted the books and he wanted them now. There had to be some way to escape this place, this limbo. He had seen the pictures on the talking box, heard others speak of an afterlife. Going into the main bedroom, he pulled the covers from the bed, tore open drawers and tipped their contents into a pile. The whore's clothes smelt sickly-sweet. Like Elizabeth she had elevated her status by marriage to a rich man, but this one was not finding the transition easy and he would make sure that her new-found lifestyle would not last. Downstairs, he made just as much mess. In the sitting-room he yanked cushions from their covers, ripping the material in half, allowing foam to spill along the seats and across the carpet.

The kitchen was next. He flung food from the larder, fridge and freezer; cutlery drawers were upended onto the pile. When he was finished the house was a shambles and Black Jack, for now, was satisfied.

The journey home from the hospital had been an uneasy one. Helen was suffering withdrawal symptoms from the cocaine. The few grams she had taken with her had soon gone and she had been prevented from stocking up by the sudden onset of labour. Jenny knew her mother was angry the minute she saw her. Joe made her wait in the car while he went inside the hospital. He returned carrying a case and bags. Her mother marched grim-faced behind him, with a nurse by her side carrying the wrapped bundle. The fighting started the minute Helen entered the car. She sat in the front passenger seat, and waited for the nurse to place the baby in her lap.

'Don't you think it wiser, dear, if you sat in the back?' the nurse suggested.

'Mind your own business,' Helen grabbed the baby from her and slammed the car door.

'She is only thinking of your own good and that of the baby, dear,' her husband said, patting her arm.

'And who asked you?' she turned in her seat and deposited the baby into the car seat.

'Do up the harness,' she ordered Jenny, who could hear her mother's nails drumming on the dashboard, as she strapped the baby in.

The baby made small sounds as they drove and Jenny kissed his face and whispered to him. In the front her mother and Joe were arguing. Her mother was saying nasty things, and Joe's eyes looked bright and shiny when he looked back to check on Jenny and the baby. She wished that her mother would go away and be dead like the goldfish.

When they reached home, Helen jumped from the car almost before it came to a stop. Joe took the baby from the car seat and opened the door. Helen stormed inside and screamed. Joe hurried after her, and Jenny, not sure what was wrong, peeped into the hall. Towels hung from the lamps and banisters. Bits of coloured foam were sprinkled like fairy dust across the carpet. Joe stood looking around him in a daze. Jenny could hear her mother fumbling around upstairs. She looked into the kitchen. It was as bad there. Food had started to defrost, and small puddles dotted the tiles.

'Nothing has been taken as far as I can see,' her mother's voice came from the hallway. She stood with numerous gold chains and rings draped across her fingers.

'There's no point in calling the police out then,' Joe said.

He had placed the baby seat on the couch, and was looking around the room, running his fingers through his hair in disbelief. He went throughout the house checking the windows and doors for some sign of entry. There was none. No broken glass or a door kicked in. Jenny had started to clean up the mess. She was on her hands and knees picking up the bits of foam and dropping them into a waste bin.

'Leave that for the vacuum,' her mother said, stepping over her and going outside to the car. She returned with her case and bags.

Jenny could hear her talking to Joe, who was also on his hands and knees in the kitchen.

'But why do you have to go out?' he asked. 'It's ridiculous. You've just come out of hospital. What's so important? I don't understand.'

Jenny was still there, when her mother emerged from the kitchen with a bottle of baby formula.

'He'll need feeding in about an hour,' she thrust the bottle at Jenny.

'Oh, okay.'

Joe came from the kitchen and grabbed his wife by the arm.

'Stay here.'

'Let go,' she pulled away, 'I'll be back as soon as I can.'

They stood mute in the hallway, as the car roared to life and she drove away.

'Well, Jen,' Joe tried to sound cheerful, 'looks like we're on our own.'

Jenny nodded and shrugged her shoulders. She was used to her mother's strange mood swings, and, apart from the baby, everything was normal to her.

Helen drove away from the house cursing under her breath. When she was clear of the estate, she stopped and fumbled in her purse for money. Straightening the bundle of notes she had tucked in there. The money she had taken from Joe's dresser drawer. She pulled down the sun visor and checked her lipstick in the mirror. Soon she would feel better. Her dealer had magic to stop the shaking and lift her mood.

Black Jack stood a few yards away watching her. He would have come closer, got in beside her, but he was tied to this place. He had tried to leave in the past hidden in the back seat of numerous cars as they left, but was always tugged back as though an invisible cord held him.

Helen was at the end of her tether. Her dream of a happy life was rapidly falling apart. She had just given birth to a child she did not want, and by a man she did not love. She had a right to be happy, to feel young and free again. Still, there was the rush of the drug to look forward to. Helen would not have looked so pleased with herself had she seen the look on Black Jack's face. There was more to fear than an angry husband.

TWENTY-SIX

Tom climbed from his car and looked in amazement at the tape around the house next door. He walked over to the policeman that stood guard and asked what had happened. The news sent him running for home. Sheila lay huddled on the sofa. The room was stifling from the heat of the fire and he turned the switch down a notch.

'Sheila, are you all right?'

'I can't seem to get warm.'

He took her hands in his and was surprised at how cold they were.

'I just spoke with the policeman on duty. He told me what happened.'

'Poor Ruth,' she started to sob.

He held her, kissing her hair and promising that it would be all right. Though it was still only a little after two, the light was already beginning to fade and the room was deep in shadow.

'We have to leave,' Sheila murmured, stirring in his arms, 'we have to get away, before this place destroys us too.'

'It's not this place,' he assured her, 'it was just a terrible tragedy.'

'No!' She bolted upright. 'It's this place. Ruth knew it as well. It's cursed or the land is tainted. I want to leave, now.'

'Okay.' He wasn't sure if it was her nervousness that caused his sudden feeling of unease. 'We'll go and stay with my parents for a while. Stay there and I'll pack what we need.'

Elizabeth and Timmy hugged each other. They watched in silence as the man loaded suitcases into the machine. He went back into the house and came out with his wife. The woman could hardly stand and he was forced to hold her upright. Once the car doors slammed shut, Sheila closed her eyes and breathed a sight of relief. Tom turned the heater up as high as it would go.

'It'll soon warm up,' he said as he patted her hand.

'Thanks,' she replied, turning away so he could not see the tears that threatened.

As he steered the car out of the drive she looked back for the last time at what should have been their dream home. Elizabeth recognised the look of fear in her eyes. She too had been Black Jack's victim and her heart ached for the woman and for what she had suffered ... what she would continue to suffer for evermore.

Angry now, she looked down at Timmy.

'Where did he go?' He shook his head.

'We have to search for him, find some way of stopping him before he hurts others.'

———

Jenny grumbled, and tried to brush away the hand that shook her. She had been sound asleep and was too ill, too worn out, to want to wake up.

They had spent hours cleaning the house and taking care of the baby. When her mother finally came home, Jenny went to her room. Joe was angry, she could still hear them arguing as she drifted off to sleep.

'Stop, I'm too tired,' she pulled the duvet up over her mouth, trying to block out the stench.

'Don't forget my books,' Black Jack prodded her shoulder, hurting her.

'I'm not going to school,' she mumbled. 'I have to mind the baby.' Her mother had crept into her room before going to bed, and informed her of this.

That whore was getting in his way. Black Jack flew through the wall and into the bedroom next door. The nursery had been painted a sunny yellow. Cartoon characters dotted the walls and stuffed toys were lined up beside one another on a seat by the window. Helen had no hand in the decoration of the room, and it showed in its simplicity and brightness.

Black Jack gazed down at the sleeping child. Reaching out, he stroked the soft skin of its cheek with his thumb. A boy child, the whore had done well. The baby moved, irritated by the touch of coarse skin on his face. He mewled softly and tried to move away. Black Jack's face hardened as he continued to gaze at the child. His child was dead and unlike the whore he would have welcomed a son. He brought his hand down once more and covered the baby's face with his open palm, blocking its nose and mouth.

'It would have better if my mother had done the same to me,' he groaned.

Elizabeth wrenched the hand away. They had tracked him down just in time. She and Timmy tried to hold him, but were repeatedly thrown through the walls. Elizabeth ran to Helen and shook her awake.

'Your child is in danger.'

Helen, still high on coke, started to scream.

'Your child needs you,' Elizabeth, wrung her hands in frustration.

Joe, woken by his wife's screams, started in terror at the spectre beside the bed. Elizabeth, realising she was getting nowhere with the mother, turned to him.

'Your child needs you. He's in terrible danger.'

He shot out of bed and ran towards the nursery. The scene he encountered on opening the door would live in his memory forever. There were two more of these spectres involved in a terrible struggle. They both turned as he entered the room, and for a moment he froze.

'What's wrong?' Jenny stood beside him, rubbing sleep from her eyes.

'He was trying to kill the baby,' Timmy answered.

Black Jack threw his head back, laughing. He was having great fun tonight. The unholy sound broke the spell, and Joe rushed past him, snatched up the baby and backed away.

'I thought you were my friend,' Jenny looked at Black Jack and started to cry. He didn't answer her, just turned away and walked through the wall leading outside. He would get the child another night.

Elizabeth turned towards the man holding the baby.

'Guard your children well. He will return, he is not easily thwarted.'

'Yes, thank you,' Joe managed to stutter before the woman and boy disappeared.

He carried the baby and took Jenny by the hand, back to his room. The bed was empty, and he could hear Helen moving around in the bathroom. She had not witnessed what had just happened, and he was thankful for that. Jenny climbed into the bed and he got in beside her, cradling the baby on his lap. He was shaking from the shock, and the possible consequences, if the spectres hadn't helped him.

'What are they, Jen, those things that were here?'

'Aliens, I think; there are lots of them here.'

'Where?'

'Out there,' she pointed towards the window.

'You know them?'

'I know Black Jack. He was my friend, but now he's not. I don't like him any more. And I know Elizabeth. She helped me when I hurt my leg. I don't know the names of the other children though.'

'Children, how many children?'

'Lots,' Jenny managed to say, before she fell asleep.

Helen carefully lined up the cocaine on a small mirror. Taking the piece of plastic tubing she kept especially for the purpose, she placed one end in her right nostril and the other next to the line of powder and sniffed. Moving the tube to the left nostril she repeated the process. She sat on the toilet and waited for it to take effect. The chemicals were quickly absorbed into her bloodstream, bringing a warm flush of wellbeing.

Wiping the mirror, she placed it, and the tube, back at the bottom of her cosmetic bag. Hastily wiping her nose, with the back of her hand, she went back to her room. She was surprised to find Joe sitting in bed with the children beside him.

'I can't sleep with them in the bed.'

'Do you really expect to sleep tonight after what's happened?' Joe was amazed at her cavalier attitude.

'Why, what happened? I had a bad dream that's all.'

'Helen,' his tone was cold, 'that was not a dream.'

'It was real? The thing I saw was real? Aaagh!' She jumped in beside him, pulling the duvet up around her.

'It's unbelievable I know, but it's real all right.'

'What was it?'

'I have no idea, but I intend to find out.'

'Well you can find out alone. I'm leaving here first thing in the morning,' she shivered.

'This is our home, Helen. We have to fight to protect it.'

'You do what you want, I'm leaving.'

'What about the children?'

'What about them? I'm sick of the children and I'm sick of you. So, shut up.'

'Now you're being ridiculous.'

'I'm being ridiculous? I'm not the one who wants to fight with monsters, or ghosts, or whatever the hell that thing was. Now shut up and leave me alone.'

'What's that on your nose?' Joe reached over and brushed at the telltale white powder.

'Talc.'

'Taken to sniffing talc, have you?'

He'd had his suspicions of late. The huge amounts of money she spent weekly had to be going somewhere, and it wasn't into furnishing the house or grocery shopping. He'd made himself believe that a woman like Helen was expensive to keep. Not wanting to admit that her looks were a charade, that beneath her polished exterior, lay hardness and a glutinous craving for pleasure.

They sat quietly for the rest of the night, the silence broken only by the baby demanding to be fed, and Jenny's tossing and turning. The main ceiling light and the lamps at either side of the bed were all switched on, in the hope that their light would protect them from the things outside.

It was almost seven o'clock when the first fingers of dawn crept across the sky. Helen started to pack. Joe watched, sad, but resigned. For the first time since their marriage, he fully realised what a terrible mistake he had made. After another trip to the bathroom to satisfy her craving, Helen left the bedroom. The suitcase banged against her legs as she descended the stairs, causing her to swear. It was heavy, but she could not take the chance of leaving anything of value behind. Luckily, and unknown to Joe, she had kept the rent on her council house up-to-date. As an unmarried mother the rent had been nominal, and the council were still unaware of her change in marital status. Now she would return to her own kind. She had been a fool to imagine that her chosen life would satisfy her and Joe had not come out of it too badly. He now had the children he desired, so to her thinking they were all winners. Dumping the case on the floor in the hall, she stumbled into the dark sitting-room. Her head swam from the effect of the cocaine, so she lay down on the sofa to allow the dizziness to pass. The long night had been too much coming so soon after the birth, so she would rest for a while before trying to drive.

Black Jack lay face down on the nursery floor. His senses were so heightened he could see right through it. So, she was abandoning her children. Deserting the son she had never wanted. Spreading his arms wide, he allowed himself to be absorbed by the floor, blending into the soft carpet, the wooden floorboards and the yellow fibreglass insulation.

Helen's eyes opened wide as the ceiling above her bulged, taking on the shape of a man. She froze as a monster dropped towards her. He landed right on top of her; they were face to face. His red eyes stared into hers and she had not time to scream as a hand was clamped over her mouth. The smell of his skin was poisonous and she could feel the coarseness of his hair brushing against her cheeks. The cold from his body shot through her, chilling her to the very soul. She struggled, but it was useless, as all strength had left her body. She could feel his hand moving rapaciously over her skin, grasping and tearing at the flesh. The buttons on her blouse snapped beneath his fingers and she felt the chill intensify on her bare flesh.

A sudden sound from overhead made Black Jack stop and look towards the ceiling. The momentary lapse in concentration was all that was needed and Helen managed to roll from beneath him. Unaware that it was Joe's footsteps that had saved her, she ran into the hall and grabbed her suitcase. Sobbing she threw the case into the back seat and climbed into the car.

TWENTY-SEVEN

After the front door slammed, its noise echoed through the house and Joe felt truly lost. He looked towards the baby, who was already starting to move and fuss, and at the still-sleeping Jenny. First things first, the baby needed feeding. He had passed the night reading the numerous baby books Helen had amassed in her pretension of motherhood. Luckily, with Jenny's help, he'd prepared two extra bottles of formula, and these were stored in the fridge, needing only to be heated.

He would have to go downstairs to fetch one and that meant leaving the children alone. The fussing of the baby grew more urgent, and he sprinted from the room, down the stairs, almost skidding on the wooden floor in the hallway, and into the kitchen. Grabbing one of the bottles, he ran back upstairs and was overcome with relief to find the children still safe. Placing the bottle in the warmer, he opened the curtains, and allowed the milky, white light of early morning into the room.

Taking the baby from the crib, he laid him on the bed and reached for the bag that contained the diapers, creams and powders. He struggled with lotion and diapers, but eventually succeeded in changing the nappy. Then he took the baby in his arms and gave him the warm bottle. The infant stared up at him as he fed. Joe smiled at him, amazed at how dark his pupils were. Helen said babies could not see properly, but this little chap's gaze was mesmerising. Big silent tears coursed down Joe's cheeks.

He couldn't remember the last time he'd cried. Balancing the bottle under his chin, he wiped the wetness from his face. He felt lost, and had no idea what to do next, whom to ask for help.

'What are we going to do, eh, son?' he whispered.

The baby turned and looked towards the voice. Joe thought he understood what was being said, and leaning him back a little, looked into his eyes. 'We'll get by, won't we, son?'

The infant moved in his arms, smiled, and Joe felt his heart almost burst with love. This helpless little baby was his flesh and blood, and totally depending on him. He felt ashamed at his momentary lapse of weakness. Placing the baby back in his crib, he tucked him up. Jenny slept on.

Going into the en-suite bathroom, he shaved and washed at the sink. With the door left open, he could see both the children. He felt better after the wash, invigorated and ready to phone a few agencies to find a nanny. When he had finished dressing, he decided to wake Jenny. It would be easier if they were all downstairs, and he had the phonebook and pens at hand. Leaning over her, he smiled at her flushed cheeks and chubby face. She looked so angelic in her white cotton nightdress, so still and peaceful it seemed a shame to wake her. Too still, Joe suddenly realised, he could hardly hear her breathing.

'Jen,' he shook her arm, fear building as she failed to move. 'Jenny, wake up!'

He placed his hand on her forehead. She was burning up. He had to get help. Picking up the phone, his hand shook as he punched in a number.

'Ambulance,' he answered the query of the disembodied voice. 'My little girl won't wake up.' He wanted to scream, but he would have to remain calm for Jenny's sake. He gave his address automatically and was grateful for the soothing voice that assured him they would be there as soon as possible. He ran downstairs, no longer afraid of the monster from the night before, and took the last bottle of formula from the fridge. Pulling on his coat, he stuffed keys and wallet into his pocket. Within minutes he was back upstairs. After putting the bottle in the baby's bag, he wrapped him in a blanket.

Helen should have been there. He could understand her leaving him. It was obvious now that she had only married him for his money. But, to desert her children was unthinkable. He knew his anger was unreasonable in the present situation, but it was keeping him from going mad. The wailing of a siren sounded in the distance.

'It'll be all right now, Jenny,' he promised. 'We'll soon have you well again.'

The siren came closer, its noise shattering the stillness of the morning. He heard the ambulance draw up outside and the sudden silence, as the siren was switched off.

'We're up here,' he called through the window.

The paramedics thudded up the stairs and came into the room laden with a stretcher and equipment. They brushed by Joe, sensing immediately that their patient was very ill. Picking up the baby, he watched from the opposite side of the room as they worked on the small, still form. They threw question after question at him.

'How long has she been like this? How old is she? Is she allergic to any medication?'

He answered as best he could, but he had no idea of her medical history. A tube was inserted into her airway and an oxygen mask covered most of her face. One of the men picked her up and placed her on the stretcher, covering her and strapping her in.

'Will you be coming with us?'

'Yes, of course.' Joe picked up the baby's bag and followed them.

There were no spectators to watch their departure. Joe climbed inside the ambulance, once the stretcher had been loaded. He heard the driver radioing a description of Jenny's condition to the waiting hospital staff. Cradling the baby, he watched as the paramedic worked on Jenny; seemingly oblivious to the bumping and swaying of the ambulance, he took her blood pressure and checked her heart.

'Have you any idea what it is?' Joe asked.

'I'm afraid not. They're still trying to work this out.'

'Then there are other cases like this?'

'There have been twenty-four other cases in the last three days, all with the same symptoms.'

'These symptoms, what are they?'

'See,' the man pointed towards Jenny's face. 'The unusual swelling to the face, accompanied by a sore throat and fever.'

If only he had taken her to the doctor when she first started to complain; if he hadn't been so taken up with Helen and the baby, he might have noticed something was wrong.

'You couldn't have known,' said the paramedic, noticing the pain in Joe's face. 'It starts out like a chill and catches hold quickly. But children are very resilient.'

Joe forced a smile. She had to pull through. The children were all he had in the world. He did not know that out of the twenty-four cases he had just been told about, that two of them had already died, and both had been children.

———

The hospital bustled with life as Joe zigzagged his way along the corridor behind the stretcher, trying to avoid nurses, doctors and wheelchairs. After filling in the necessary forms, a nursing assistant ushered him towards the relative's waiting room.

'Someone will be with you shortly,' she promised. 'Your daughter is in safe hands.'

She hurried away and Joe was left to find a seat in a room that was already quite full. It was mostly couples sitting huddled together, all with the same anxious expression. They held tightly to one another, drawing strength from their closeness, praying and suffering, as only the parents of a sick child know how. Some of them looked at Joe and nodded. They all watched the door and moved to the edge of their seats every time it opened. The baby slept on, and he was thankful for this.

'Mr Mahoney?' a nurse asked.

'Yes, that's me,' Joe raised his hand.

'Come with me, please.'

He struggled to his feet, baby nestled in the crook of one arm and the bag in the other. Following her unquestioningly along the corridor, he walked by her, as she pointed to an office.

'Take a seat. Dr Peters will be with you in a moment.'

He sat and slid the bag onto the floor beside him. He felt the baby's hands to ensure he was warm enough, and didn't hear the doctor come in.

'Joe. How are you? It's been a long time.'

'Ted, my God. It's good to see you,' Joe held out his hand. 'Forgive me for not standing.'

'No bother, old boy. I can see you have your hands full; a grandchild, eh?'

'A son.'

Ted Peters had been his friend through most of his senior college years. He had moved to England to study medicine and they had lost contact, but Ted had hardly changed. He was a few pounds heavier and his dark hair tinged with grey, but his eyes and good-natured smile were the same.

'Sorry, me and my big mouth.'

'No problem. God knows I'm old enough.'

'And the little girl, her surname is different than yours, so I assumed.'

'My stepdaughter.'

'Ah, I see,' Ted sat down behind his desk. 'And her mother?'

'Left us, I'm afraid.'

'You can contact her? You know where she is?'

'I'm not sure,' he said, pausing at the urgency of the question. 'Is it that bad?'

'Look, Joe, I don't want to beat around the bush with you. Your daughter is stable at the moment. We're pumping as much fluid and antibiotics as we can into her, but the fact is, we really don't know what we're dealing with.'

'What are her chances?'

'We don't know. Over ten per cent of the cases we've treated have died. We have just been sent one of the leading bacteriologists in the country. She's working on it as we speak. I'll let you know as soon as we establish a link. Now, if you like, I'll take you to see your daughter.'

'Yes, thank you.' Joe shifted the baby onto his arm and picked up the bag.

'You can't take the baby, I afraid.'

'What can I do? I have no one to take care of him.'

'Your wife, perhaps?'

'She wouldn't want to know.'

Ted checked the baby over carefully and was relieved to find him in perfect health.

'Leave it to me,' he said, punching the numbers on the phone in front of him and speaking to a voice on the other end. 'How would you like to take care of a lovely baby boy for a while?' he winked at Joe, already sure of the answer. 'I thought you might. He'll be with you in the next half an hour. I'll explain later,' he said his goodbyes and turned to Joe. 'That was my wife, Anne. She misses not having someone to take care of, and a room is already set up for visits from our grandchildren. Your son will be in safe hands, for however long it takes.'

'I can't thank you enough.'

'No thanks needed. She's always complaining she hasn't enough to do. You'll be doing me a favour. I'll take you to see your daughter, then I'll drive you there myself.'

Joe nodded, too overcome to speak. Ted spoke again into the phone and within seconds the baby was being taken from him by one of the nurses and Ted was leading him to Jenny's room. She looked so tiny in the big hospital bed, and the tubes running into her small white arms were frightening.

'She hasn't regained consciousness, Dr Peters,' a nurse checking the tubes informed him.

Joe watched as Ted checked her vital signs.

'We'll leave her be for the moment,' he said, placing an arm around Joe's shoulder. 'She's not in pain, and that's a blessing.'

They collected the baby from the nursery and walked to the parking lot. Ted kept the conversation going as they drove to his house, trying to catch up on all the time since they had last met. Joe told him as much as he could about his life. Not that there was very much to tell, until his meeting with Helen.

'Yeah,' Ted laughed, 'marriage takes some getting used to.'

They drove down a tree-lined street bordered on either side with palatial houses and came to a stop in front of one. A woman emerged from the doorway.

'This is Anne,' Ted spoke with pride, as he introduced his wife.

'Nice to meet you, Joe,' she smiled, taking the baby from his arms.

The inside of the house was as magnificent as the outside. Anne had an eye for colour and decoration. Her taste was impeccable, and Joe wished for a moment that Helen had been like that.

'We'd better get back to the hospital.' Ted took his elbow.

'Yes, of course. Thank you very much,' he turned to Anne, but she was too busy fussing over the baby to take much notice of him.

They were walking back towards the car when she called out.

'What's his name?'

Joe looked at her, puzzled.

'The baby, what's his name?'

'He doesn't have one yet.'

'Never mind, I'll think of something.'

They returned to the hospital in relative silence and parted company once Ted had checked on Jenny. Joe sat beside her bed for the rest of the day, willing her to get better, and doing something he hadn't done since childhood, praying. He took no heed of the nurses, who urged him to get something to eat. He had no appetite, although his stomach felt hollow. It was after dark when he returned home. The taxi swept into the estate just as an ambulance was leaving.

The house was in darkness, the hallway an endless, black tunnel. All the streetlights were out, and he had to feel his way along the wall in search of a switch. He expected at any moment to feel another hand close over his own and he almost cried out with relief when he made contact with the switch, and light flooded the hall. Checking the answering machine, he was surprised to find a message from Helen. He wrote down the phone number she gave and dialled. There was no answer, but he left a message.

The house felt bleak and tomblike as he moved around it. He needed a shower after the warmth of the hospital and his own sweat from the worry. But first he would collect some more nightwear for Jenny, and books and toys, for when she was well enough to play. He packed a small bag with her stuff and went to shower. It had been very easy to be brave in the daylight. The dark had its own way of renewing fears. He listened above the noise of the water for any movement in the house. Finally, drying off, he went back to the bedroom. Two of the things from the night before were standing in the room, waiting for him.

TWENTY-EIGHT

The fine hairs on the back of his neck and arms stood on end. Goose pimples rose on his skin, fear crawled across his body like millions of tiny insects. He started to back away as they moved towards him. Managing to close and lock the bathroom door, he stared at its white panels. They could easily come through it, he had seen them do that. He could hear them whispering and brought his ear against the door trying to hear. The sharp rap on the wood made him spring back in terror.

'We mean you no harm. You know we are capable of walking through this door. It would not protect you, if our aim was to hurt you.' The tone was soft, a woman's voice. 'We have come to ask about the child, the little girl, and to help if possible.'

Joe was shaking. Pulling a bath towel from the rail, he tried to cover himself. They were waiting for him to come out. If he didn't go to them, then they would come to him. Clutching the towel, he brought a quivering hand to the door key and turned it. They were still there, standing across the room from him.

'Perhaps you would care to dress?' the woman suggested.

'Yes, thank you.' He gathered the clothes he had discarded, not caring that they were dirty. He pulled on his trousers, almost falling over in his haste. The shirt felt warm against his chilled flesh. Finished, he stood waiting for what was to come next. It was the woman who spoke.

'I am Lady Elizabeth Fitzwilliam. This,' she placed a skeleton hand on shoulder of the boy next to her, 'is Timmy Walsh. I apologise for our appearance. It is not, I take it, all that it should be?'

The voice was cultured, and had Joe closed his eyes, she could have been a character from a period drama.

'Y-yes,' he stuttered, 'it takes some getting used to.'

'Again I apologise. It is not of our choosing and I assure you, we mean you no harm.'

'Thank you,' he said, edging his way to the bed and sitting down.

'There is much sickness here,' the woman continued. 'It is all around you. The child, will she recover?'

'I don't know. God, I hope so,' Joe was momentarily unafraid, as he thought of Jenny. 'They don't know what it is, so it's difficult to treat.'

'It's typhus.'

'Typhus!' he whispered the name, as though saying it out loud would make it worse. 'I thought that had been wiped out years ago.'

'It comes from the past. It has lain hidden for over a century. You must go to your doctors, tell them it is here. Already we fear it is too late.'

She sat on the bed beside him and he no longer felt the need to back away. The boy came and stood beside him.

'How soon can you get word to them about the disease?' Timmy asked.

'Now, this minute.' Joe reached for the phone and dialled the hospital. Ted had left for the night and he had no idea of his home number. The nurse in charge refused to give him the number, repeating automatically, that it was against hospital policy to do so.

Finally, he asked if the new bacteriologist was still there, and without replying she put him on hold. A few short rings sounded on the other end of the line.

Finally, 'Hello, Dr Lucy Edwards.'

'Dr Edwards,' Joe asked. 'Are you the bacteriologist who's working on the unexplained fevers at the hospital?'

'Look,' she sounded exasperated, 'if you're a reporter, I have nothing to say.'

'No, please,' Joe begged, 'my little girl is one of your patients. I know what it is, the fever. I know what's causing it.'

'Go on.'

'It's typhus.'

'That's impossible. Typhus was eradicated generations ago.'

'Yes, I know it sounds impossible, but please believe me. It has resurfaced.'

There was silence for a few moments. He could hear a slight scratching as though she was writing.

'Okay, I'll test for it right away.'

'Oh, thank you,' he almost cried with relief. 'I'll be in later. Thank you so much.'

He was shaking when he put the phone down. But, this time it wasn't from the fear of the things beside him. If this doctor could find a cause, then Jenny would live. He turned and looked at his two strange visitors.

'She's going to test for it. I pray to God we're in time.'

The woman beside him held out her arms and the boy sat beside her. She cradled his head against her, stroking his limp, lifeless hair.

'This is it, Timmy. This is why we are here. Why God in his infinite wisdom chose you. Don't you see, child,' she cupped the boy's face, 'you finally have your chance to save the children.'

Joe watched, realising that these things were not monsters, but people. The sight before him was poignant. All the love he felt for his children was in that woman's touch upon the boy.

'I'm sorry,' he murmured, before the tears that had been long threatening started up. His body shook as sobs tore from him, and the hand that rubbed his back felt like dried twigs against his skin. 'I'm so sorry,' he looked up into the hollow eyes of the woman.

'There is no need to be. We also know what it is to lose those you love.'

Joe listened for over an hour as she told him of the famine. Of the suffering brought about by ignorance, prejudice and the slavery of a nation.

'Do you know of the famine? Do your people ever speak of it?'

'Oh yes, we know about it. It's called the Great Famine. It is remembered through books and plays, songs and poems, even great monuments. You have not been forgotten.'

'So,' she smiled, 'we are written about, facts and figures maybe, though none but those who were there could imagine the full extent of what we endured. I suffered because I was a woman unable to bear a male heir. Timmy, because his family lived in servitude to an unjust landlord, and the other children,' she waved into the darkness outside, 'because they were not allowed to rest. You cannot imagine what it is to be dead and yet walk the land. To know you are reviled and feared for a fate that is not of your making. But,' she sighed, 'you must go now. Go to your child and your doctors. Tell them of this place and the disease that lies here.'

'What about you? What will happen to you?'

'We will be fine,' she said, placing an arm around the boy.

They faded away, dissolving into mist. He wanted to cry out that he would find a way to help them, but the words stuck in his throat. How can the living help the dead?

The recent events had left him shaken, and not trusting himself to drive, Joe rang for a taxi. He changed into fresh clothes and was waiting at the door when it drew up. He didn't want to stay inside the house. He was no longer afraid of the woman and boy, but that other thing, the one they called Black Jack, was a different matter. The streetlights were all out, the road lit only by the few chinks of light that escaped from the houses nearby. In the twenty minutes it took the taxi to arrive, he saw two more blanketed casualties being carried to cars and driven away at high speed. This typhus, this killer, was spreading fast.

He breathed a sign of relief when he was safely inside the taxi, and scanned the trees and bushes as they sped past, expecting to see shadowy figures watching. It was impossible to be sure if the shapes and darting movements from the hedgerows were anything other than his fearful imagination. Until now he had never realised how truly black the night could be. Nothing could have prepared him for the terror brought about by the going down of the sun. The warmth from the car heater was comforting. He closed his eyes and didn't open them until they arrived at the hospital.

The bright lights and general hubbub of the hospital calmed his nerves. It was difficult to believe in ghosts in the modern, antiseptic hospital surroundings. Jenny had been moved to an isolation ward, still unconscious, swollen and flushed as ever.

'No change,' the charge nurse told him at his anxious inquiry.

He had been sitting beside her bed for hours, dozing off periodically, only to be jerked awake by the clattering of medicine trolleys, and the movements of the nursing staff checking on Jenny. It was almost morning when he felt the light hand on his shoulder, shaking him awake. He looked up bleary-eyed into the most beautiful face he had ever seen.

'Mr Mahoney?'

'Yes, that's right,' he said, struggling to get up, his muscles aching after the nightlong vigil.

'I'm Lucy Edwards. We spoke last night.'

'Yes, yes, of course, doctor.'

Her handshake was warm and firm, and he wasn't sure whether it was her smile or the fact that he hadn't eaten that made him dizzy. She motioned him to follow her into the corridor.

'Would you like to come down to the cafeteria with me? I've been working since early yesterday morning and could really do with something to eat. I'm sure you could use something as well.'

He nodded and set off beside her.

'I'll tell you all about my findings once we're seated.'

The cafeteria was quiet at that time of the morning, just the occasional white-coated figure drinking coffee or pouring over paperwork. Once they were sitting across from each other, she began.

'You were spot on with your diagnosis. It is typhus. Unfortunately they stopped making and storing the vaccine years ago, so a new batch has to be prepared, before I can inject you. We should have it soon. Until then we're pumping as much fluid and antibiotics as we can into the patients. I know how worried you must be. But, now that we know what it is, we're halfway there.'

'Thank you,' he smiled and searched for something vaguely intelligent to say. 'That's an American accent, right?'

'Yes, but I'm fifth generation Irish. My great, great, great, grandmother came from here, and I've always wanted to return. I came over on vacation last year and I was hooked. Couldn't seem to settle once I got back home and within seven months I'd sold up, got this job, and here I am.'

'Did your family mind your moving?'

'I've no family to speak of. My mother's happily married for the third time,' she rolled her eyes, 'and as I'm an only child, there was no real objection. I miss my friends though, and there hasn't been much time to make new ones yet. What about you? Tell me about your family.'

'That's a rather pathetic story,' he cleared his throat. 'I've been a bit of a fool.' He told her about Helen. Their hasty marriage, his growing suspicion about the drugs and how she'd finally deserted them. 'I suppose I should be grateful in one way. I have a son and stepdaughter so at least I'm not alone any more, not back where I started,' he said, fiddling with the grains of spilt sugar on the table.

'Perhaps she'll come back? Some women behave differently after they have given birth. The shock of responsibility of a new baby may have scared her.'

'No,' Joe shook his head. 'It's over. It should never have begun.'

'Tell me,' she asked, changing the subject, 'what makes you such a great diagnostician?'

'If I told you, you wouldn't believe me. I find it hard to believe myself.'

'Go on, try me.' She turned suddenly and looked towards the doorway. A white-coated figure was gesturing to her.

'Something is happening.'

She rushed from the room and Joe had trouble keeping up with her as they wound their way through the maze of corridors. Once they reached the isolation wards, she began issuing directions, as those that had been held in the grip of the fever started to rally. He ran back to be with Jenny, and within minutes Lucy arrived followed by a nurse pulling one of the clattering trolleys. She skilfully administered another shot of antibiotic in to Jenny's arm.

'What now?' Joe asked.

'We watch and wait. It's working on the other patients,' Lucy called over her shoulder, as she hurried from the room.

The next few hours passed slowly. There was the usual bustle in the corridors as the staff changed shift. The odd laugh and hurried calls of goodbye were more cheering than the hushed tones of night-time conversations. Joe walked to the window and watched the outside world continue as usual. Ambulances pulled into the bays below, deposited their cargo and were off again in minutes. The parking lots teemed with life, white-coated figures merging with the more colourful ones of the visitors and day patients.

'I'm thirsty.'

The hoarse voice startled him, and he hurried to the bed and felt her forehead. It was considerably cooler.

'Welcome back, Jen.'

She looked up at him, quizzically.

'Why? Where was I?'

'You were in a very deep sleep, but it doesn't matter now, you're back.'

She looked around the room in wonder.

'Am I in hospital?'

'Yes. Remember how sick you felt, how much your throat hurt.'

'Yeah, it still hurts a bit.'

'I'll get you some water, back in a minute.'

He went to the nurse's station, told them Jenny was awake and asked for a drink. The nurse ushered him back to the ward, and within minutes doctors surrounded them. Ted was delighted to see the child sitting up and drinking. Lucy followed shortly after, and reported that the same results were happening in all the other wards.

'I don't know what we would have done without your help,' she told him. 'It could have taken weeks before we found out what it was. By that time who knows how many would have died.'

'Glad I could help.'

Lucy stayed and talked with Jenny. Asking her where she played, what she had eaten the first time she'd felt sick, who her friends were. She noted down the information to check against her files, to look for a common link. Joe walked over to the window, gestured at her to follow.

'I think I know where the source is.'

'You do? That's great, where?'

'The estate where I live.'

'Not that I doubt your word, but what makes you think so?'

'Call it inside information.' He had no intention of telling her about the ghosts. 'The houses are new, but seemingly built on an old famine graveyard. You're just going to have to trust me on this one.'

She paced the room, lost in thought and fiddling with the heavy gold chain around her neck.

'Typhus was rampant during those times, but could it have lain dormant for so long?' Turning to Joe she asked, 'Will you take me there? I'll need to get a team working on the area as soon as possible. If we find the exact source we might be able to stop the spread.'

'I'd like to spend some more time with Jenny first.'

'Okay. It'll take me a few hours to get the equipment and manpower I need. I'll come back and let you know when I'm ready.'

TWENTY-NINE

Black Jack went to see what all the noise was about. Huge white tents had been set up just outside the graveyard. Thick black coils of electric cable snaked across the grass to shuddering, humming generators that powered giant searchlights and made the place bright as a summer's day. White-coated doctors, scientists and technicians moved busily around the place. It made no sense at all to Black Jack, but Elizabeth and Timmy knew exactly what was happening. Joe was still at the hospital with Jenny, whose condition was rapidly improving. As he had decided to stay with the child, Lucy and her team arrived armed only with his address and limited information about the place.

They spent the first day setting up the equipment. Her tent held all the microscopes, sterilizing units, incubators and general articles like gloves, masks and sterile suits. She intended to get started first thing next morning and a group of security guards were left to protect the expensive equipment.

It was dark when Lucy left the estate and she wondered at its empty stillness. One would expect to see a group of teenagers huddled somewhere, or perhaps neighbours gossiping over garden walls. It felt eerie, out of time.

———

The security guards were hard men. Most had criminal records for public brawling and were usually found working as bouncers at pub doors at weekends. Very few would challenge these four to a fight.

The main tent was filled with many articles Black Jack had never seen before. He picked up the delicate electron microscopes, turned them over in his hand, examined them, and then threw them over his shoulder. They made little sound as they shattered on the grassy surface. It was not until he started to destroy the incubators that he attracted the guards' attention. They arrived together at the tent and struggled to beat each other inside. There was something about the sound of breaking glass that excited them. They gaped in wonder at the scene of carnage. All the equipment lay broken on the grass. Glass crunched under their feet as they moved forward, open-mouthed and aghast that anyone would have the audacity to do such a thing.

'What the fuck happened?' one asked.

All sides of the site had been covered. No one could have got in without them knowing. An argument ensued and developed into a tussle, as each man blamed the other. It was only the dark shadow moving across the white of the tent that brought proceedings to a halt.

'There's someone out there.'

'Tell us something we don't know, dickhead,' another growled.

They moved in a pack towards the entrance, the shadow moved with them.

'I'll tell you something. He's a brave cunt.'

They were all thinking the same thing. Either that or he was very stupid.

Black Jack had been watching and listening to these men since their arrival. At first, their coarse language and boasts had fascinated him. They were fearless, their faces scarred and showing the signs of battle, but they were human carrion, mentally weak, pathetic. Because of this he could not approach them for information. They were un-educated and would be of no help to him. He could smell them in the same way he could smell the whore. They were vermin. But, unlike the rats, they might prove to be greater adversaries. There was fun to be had. They pounced out of the tent to be met by ... nothing. He stood watching, as they ran around in circles trying to find the intruder.

'Split up,' their leader called. 'The cunt must be here somewhere.'

He followed one to the hedge bordering the houses and watched as he shone his torch into the back gardens. Black Jack picked up a heavy mallet that had been used to hammer the tent pegs, and then carelessly discarded.

The crying in the trees started up. The wind tore against his body as invisible hands tried to pull him back, to stop what was about to happen. He swung the mallet with all his might at the back of the man's head. The force crushed his skull; splinters of bone were embedded in his brain. Blood splattered everywhere, dripped from the leaves and bushes and coated the head of the mallet.

It had been so easy, too easy; he needed the thrill of the chase. He walked nonchalantly across the site, the mallet swung over his shoulder. The men were too far apart to notice him, and he wanted to be done with them before the first body was discovered. He loved the element of surprise, crouching behind a clump of bushes, he waited for his next victim. When the guard was close enough to hear, he shook the bushes. Torchlight beamed towards the sudden rustling and the man moved cautiously forward. Black Jack stood up and revealed himself. Before he could act, before he could shout a warning to his colleagues, Black Jack caught the man on the side of the head. It took four more blows before his moans of agony ceased and his head was reduced to a bloody mass.

The remaining men were making their way back towards the main tent.

'What in the fuck is that noise?'

'Must be the wind blowing through some pipes or something.'

There was something unearthly about the sound, though neither would admit it, not wanting to be thought a coward. Black Jack was waiting for them at the main tent. He swung the mallet between his fingers as though it were a twig. Blood dripped from it and the head was covered in gore. The men stopped short. Like well-trained dogs their instincts were to attack, but this was like nothing they'd ever seen before.

'Look at his fuckin' eyes.'

'Contact lenses,' his companion sneered. 'Has to be, let's get him.'

'You're prepared to try your luck with me, are you?' Black Jack laughed. He liked their daring, their foolishness. 'Shall we commence, gentlemen?'

They nodded, signalling that they would attack at the same time. Pouncing straight at him, they collided into one another. Each shook his battered head, trying to clear it. Black Jack lashed out. The first few blows fractured shoulder bones and arms. They struggled to rise, only to be knocked back down again, screaming in agony as the mallet met with kneecaps and ankles, shattering them. Helpless, cowering, they tried to cover their heads with their useless hands.

'You disappoint me, gentlemen,' Black Jack swung the mallet, finishing off what he had started. The screaming of the men mingled with the cries all around them.

Timmy and Elizabeth watched as Jack toyed with the men. They, like him, realised what these men were, but they didn't deserve to be tormented in this way. It was only when the last man had been killed, that they returned to the earth. No one had a chance against Black Jack's increasing strength. Not even Elizabeth or Timmy.

Lucy and her team had to park outside the estate. Ambulances, police cars and the vans of news crews blocked the road, and they were refused admittance past the taped-off crime scene. Lucy tried to find out what was happening from one of the reporters milling around, but her inquiries were brushed aside as each vied with the other for news on the breaking story. She called to one of the policemen, introduced herself and asked to speak to whoever was in charge. She waited as he relayed the news along the line. Fifteen minutes went by, and she was becoming irritated at being kept waiting. She was anxious about her equipment. Had it been stolen? It was so frustrating not knowing what was going on.

'Okay, doctor, you can come through.' The policeman lifted the tape to allow her to duck under it and pointed towards a group on men. One of them turned on her approach.

'You, Doctor Edwards?'

'Yes, that's right.'

'Good,' he led her towards the tent. 'This was your site, your dig or whatever you want to call it?'

'Yes, we're checking the soil and water supply for bacteria.'

'Not today you're not.'

His attitude was beginning to annoy her.

'Can you tell me what happened?'

'Someone attacked the security guards,' he said. 'Made a right mess of them, their own mothers wouldn't recognise them.'

'And the equipment?' she cringed, knowing how heartless the question seemed.

'That got the same treatment as the men.' He didn't seem to be the least put out. 'It's all in bits.'

Her colleagues would have a field day when they heard about this. Four brawny security guards had been murdered, and thousands of euro worth of equipment had been destroyed. She'd have to grovel for more. Despite the gravity of the disease, they would be unwilling to finance her again, and may call in what they would term, 'a more experienced, local specialist.' The attitude here was completely different from back home. It had been hard enough to prove herself there, but here it was like stepping back into another century.

'When will I be able to get back to work?'

'When our investigation is completed.'

'And do you know when that might be?'

'Maybe later today.'

'Thank you. You have been very helpful.'

'No problem.' If he recognised the sarcasm in her tone, he showed no sign of it.

The team groaned as one when she told them what had happened. There was nothing they could do, but return to the hospital.

By nightfall the site had been searched and the detectives finished with their examinations. They would return in search of clues, but find nothing. Elizabeth, Timmy and the children grew used to hearing screams coming from the few houses that remained occupied. The police were constantly being called to the estate. Women were being attacked in their beds. The beatings and abuse they suffered was plain to see, but the stories of the thing that caused the injuries were crazy. The police were baffled and everyone, from the mayor to the police superintendent, was up in arms.

Hospital admissions with typhus were still increasing, and after demands from the medical council, Lucy and her team were allowed back on the site. By now ninety per cent of the houses had been abandoned, their owners either too sick or too scared to stay. Lucy was allowed to continue on the understanding the equipment was packed away each night. They collected samples of soil and water from different areas of the estate. Elizabeth watched in frustration as they worked. The disease was in the graveyard, and possibly in the soil on which the last three houses had been built. So far, no one had dug there. Lucy had to establish a viable link. Frustrated, she wandered the site, trying to figure out what was wrong. Elizabeth and Timmy watched as she came closer to the trees and bushes bordering the graveyard. There was something familiar about the woman, something that stirred Elizabeth's heart. Lucy stopped, sighing in despair, and tugged at the chain around her neck. Elizabeth cried out, as she recognised the locket that hung from the chain. It was the one she had given to her Lucy on the day she lost her and her other daughters, the day they had sailed out of her life.

She started to go to her, wanting to know who she was, how she had the locket. Timmy had to pull her back, whispering to her, urging her to be careful. But he too had been disturbed by the woman's appearance. She looked like ... somebody.

Lucy, hearing the cry, parted the bushes, but could see no one. Just an animal, she decided. Elizabeth wanted to call out to her. The longing and heartbreak she felt when that ship had sailed was now returning.

'Dear God, Timmy, what's happening to me?'

The other children felt her pain and sprang from the earth, running to her, trying to give what little comfort they could with hugs and kisses. Timmy watched the retreating figure and was unaware that little Katie was doing the same.

'Who's she?' she asked.

When Timmy didn't answer, she decided to find out for herself and flew through the bushes. She had to know why this person made her beloved Elizabeth so sad. Lucy was unaware of the child walking backwards in front of her, studying her face. When she had seen enough, Katie turned and ran back to the graveyard. Elizabeth sat weeping on the grass. Timmy and the others gathered around her, frightened and unsure of what to do. The smaller ones tried to cuddle her, but it was hopeless, she was wretched. She wanted her children, her own flesh and blood. To smell just once more the scent of their hair, feel their arms warm around her neck. There was no warmth here. She was sick of the dead.

'Elizabeth,' Katie crawled towards her, pushing the other children away. 'I saw you.'

'What do you mean?'

'Out there.' Katie pointed towards the next field. 'It was you, but then again,' she mused, 'it wasn't.'

Timmy hadn't wanted to admit it, but he had thought the very same thing. The woman looked exactly like Elizabeth had before, but how was that possible?

'Timmy,' Elizabeth called. She was walking towards him, her pain so visible, he felt he could almost touch it.

'Is Katie right? Do I look like that woman; did I once look like that woman?'

'Elizabeth …' No matter what he said he would hurt her.

'You never lie, Timmy. I know that. Please don't do so now.'

'Yes, she looks a bit like you. Only,' he stopped and forced a smile, 'you were, I mean you are, much more beautiful.'

'Thank you,' she walked to the bushes, hungry for one more glimpse of the woman. 'She's mine. I know it. We are of the same blood. Oh, Timmy, it's one of my children!' Hope rose like a light around her. 'God has sent one of my daughters back to me. Grown now, I grant you, but nevertheless mine.'

'Elizabeth, listen to me.'

'I will go to her,' she said, blending into the bushes, only to find herself being dragged back by Timmy.

'We've been dead for over a hundred and fifty years, Elizabeth. She cannot be your child.'

The cry from her lips was heart-rending. It reached Lucy and the other members of her crew, who were busily packing up for the night.

'What in the name of heaven is that?' someone asked.

They stood and listened as the crying echoed in the still air. It could have been anything, an injured animal, perhaps. But Lucy thought differently. She could feel its anguish in her heart, she wanted to call out, answer its cry, but that would be ridiculous. Her colleagues were already starting to give her funny looks. With all the samples reading clear, they already had enough ammunition to throw at her.

Timmy helped Elizabeth to her feet. Her crying had stopped, when he had whispered to her that she was frightening the children.

She looked at the small groups that huddled together and held her arms wide. Bony arms encircled her waist and curled around her arms. They may not have felt like those of her children, but that didn't matter. These were her children now and they needed her as much as any living child did its mother. She had been selfish to think that woman was hers. She had lost everything long ago, she would never again see her children.

'I'm sorry, Elizabeth.' Katie, as usual, managed to get closest to her. 'I didn't mean to make you cry.'

'You didn't make me cry, my pet. I did that all by myself. I was being very silly. Now run and play, all of you.'

They drifted slowly away from her and soon forgot what had happened, as they ran and played in the long grass. Elizabeth and Timmy watched, listening to their calls and the sounds of their laughter.

'Forgive me, Timmy.'

He turned to her and swallowed hard, as he watched the tears trickle down her cheeks. 'There's nothing to forgive,' he said, leaning his head against her shoulder.

'I was being foolish. My heart ran away from me.'

'No. You could be right. She could be your great-great-great grand-daughter.' He counted his fingers as he spoke.

'Do you think so? Oh, Timmy, do you really think so?'

'I do,' said a familiar voice.

Black Jack was behind them. In the intimacy of their conversation, they had failed to notice him approach.

He continued, 'I was wondering where I'd seen her before. Now I know. You're quite alike, my dear Elizabeth,' he laughed. 'Or I should say what you once looked like; such a rare opportunity.'

'What do you mean?'

They both looked at him and she noticed the children had stopped playing and they too were standing, silently watching.

'I had you, my dear Elizabeth, and now I am to have your daughter.

True, she is a few centuries removed from you, but still. I'm sure the flesh will feel the same, the taste as sweet.'

'Touch her,' Elizabeth snarled, 'and I swear by all that is holy I will kill you.'

'How? You can't kill a dead man.'

'I mean it, Carey. You lay one finger on her and you'll pay dearly.'

'This is not your time, my Elizabeth. You are no longer lady of the manor. I will do exactly as I please.'

They watched him stride across the graveyard, flicking at the children who stood in his path, knocking them aside. Elizabeth had never felt such fury. She wanted to rip him to shreds. Tear the blackened heart from his chest.

'Oh my God!' she turned to Timmy. 'What are we to do?'

'Pray.' His voice was full of anguish. He knew they could not fight Black Jack and win.

'Lord,' Elizabeth called to the sky. 'We accept that it was your will to leave us here. We have tried to help in anyway we could, but we are tired, Lord. We are tired and we want to go home.' Some of the children sniffled, others wrapped their arms around one another as she continued. 'Please help us, Lord. Help my child. Protect her from the evil all around, and give us at last what you promised. Give us eternal rest.'

THIRTY

Things turned out just as Lucy predicted. Her superiors, angry at what they saw as a waste of time and money on a whim, ordered her to move to another area indicated by red dots on a map, where more casualties had come from. She had no choice, but to do as they asked. Otherwise, they inferred, someone else would do her job. The message was disguised, but barbed. Jenny had been discharged while she was away. Lucy had been disappointed to find her room empty, but smiled when the charge nurse handed her a note from Joe. They had been invited to stay with Ted until she was finished her investigation and they could return home. She thought once again of that strange place, of the cry she had heard, and deep down she knew Joe was right. The disease was there. She rang the number on the note and was disappointed when no one answered. She left a message, and hoped he would get it soon. She was going back to the site to find the samples that would prove them both right.

It was dark when Lucy drove into the estate with minimal equipment; just some jars, a small trowel, a torch and some gloves. She could not have risked asking the stores assistant to sign out anything else. The place was deserted; not one light showed in any of the houses. She shivered, realising she was totally alone. It took a few minutes to adjust to the inky-blackness around her. As usual, the streetlights were out. Black Jack took a childish delight in breaking the bulbs, and the council had grown tired of replacing them. She walked about the site, concentrating on the play areas, the back and front gardens, anywhere she thought the children might have picked up the disease.

'Good evening, my dear.'

She looked up from her digging, and her smile turned to a look of horror, when she saw what was standing over her. It was some kind of monster, its eyes blazing red against the darkness around her. She tried to stand, but fell back in her fright. Sitting looking up at him, she slowly edged her way back, trying to get free, to tear her eyes away from his hypnotising gaze. She was on the borderline, where the estate meets the graveyard, when he struck.

Reaching down, he grabbed the front of her coat and tore it open. Before she could react, he was on top of her. Realising she had the small trowel still in her hand, she raised her arm and thrust it down towards his back, but only succeeded in hurting herself, as the sharp blade passed through him and embedded itself in her shoulder. She cried out in pain, and could smell her own blood as it mingled with the rotten, earthy smell of the thing that was almost on top of her. She tried to fight, but there was nothing there. Her hands seemed to pass through him, but he was there. He felt solid; he was capable of hurting her, why couldn't she hurt him back? She was sobbing, there was nowhere to run, and her back was against the bushes.

––––––

Elizabeth, Timmy and the others had long since returned to the earth. Elizabeth slept fitfully. Up to now her sleep had been dreamless, but tonight it was filled with voices. She could hear her husband John's voice. They were walking in the gardens at Maycroft, the sun felt warm against her skin, and she could feel his arm as it linked through hers. Her girls were close by, she could hear them laughing as they played and Lucy's voice.

'Mamma, help!' Elizabeth turned and smiled. The child had snagged her dress on a rose bush. 'Help me, Mamma,' she tugged at the trapped cloth, impatient to be free.

Elizabeth let go of John's arm and went to her rescue. The sky began to darken as she moved towards her child. The scene faded and she reached out in her sleep, trying to hold on to it, to bring it back. Still the cries continued. 'Help me! Please, help me!'

Her eyes flew open. She was beneath the earth, her family but a cruel dream. Then she heard it again, the cry for help. She soared towards the surface, her very soul crying out. Timmy was waiting for her.

Lucy was burrowing deeper into the bushes. Her hands clasped at her top, trying to hold the shredded pieces of cloth together.

'You'd do well to surrender, madam,' Black Jack warned, reaching for her again.

She beat out at the air, screaming for someone to help her. She felt hands encircling her waist, and instantly, she was being carried upwards and away from the thing before her. She sailed backward over the bushes, and landed on the grass on the other side of the boundary. When she looked to thank her saviour, she once again shrank back in terror.

'Don't be afraid,' said Elizabeth, reaching out to her. 'We are not like him. We were once what you are now.'

Lucy wiped the tears from her eyes, trying to get a better look. There was a woman and a boy. The voice was soft, no hint of danger about it, and it comforted her. This only lasted for a moment, and she began to scream again as all around her dark, wilted children sprouted from the earth. There was no time for Elizabeth to tell her who they were, what they were, before Black Jack appeared.

'Don't get in my way, bitch,' he growled at Elizabeth, as he advanced towards Lucy.

'Get her away!' Elizabeth cried to Timmy, before throwing herself at Black Jack.

He tried to toss her aside, but she held on, refusing to let go. She was a mother fighting for her child. Black Jack had never before encountered such fury. The children joined in, biting and kicking, but he threw them away. He was too strong for them and though some of them attacked him time and again, they were too weak to stop him. Elizabeth could hear the children sobbing all around her. Spirits that had hung helpless for so long in the trees, took to the air. Their cries echoing to the heavens, screaming for justice, they flew at Black Jack, but he beat them off as easily he had the children.

Timmy was trying to get the sobbing Lucy to move. She watched transfixed at the battle that raged before her, at the white spectral shapes that skimmed around the air above her. Every fibre of her being screamed to run, but something held her back. Something primeval stirred within her.

'There's nothing you can do,' Timmy called to her above the screaming. 'You have to leave this place.'

'No!' she shouted, no longer afraid. 'I have to help her.'

Black Jack had pinned Elizabeth beneath him, one hand around her throat. He was crushing her; she could hear her bones cracking under the pressure. Lucy tried to pull him off, but again, her hands met only air. Timmy joined in, tearing at Black Jack's hair, screaming at him to let go, only to be tossed aside. Black Jack reached out with his free hand and grabbed Lucy's ankle, sending her crashing to the ground. She kicked and struggled, trying to get free.

'Is she worth it, Elizabeth?' The pressure increased on her throat. 'Tell me, is she worth it? I gave you a chance to live once before, and you threw it in my face to save the boy. Look what you have become. Will you save yourself this time?'

Elizabeth struggled to speak and he released the pressure.

'There is nothing to take,' Elizabeth scratched at his hands. 'I am like you, I have no life left to give, but if I had I would give it to you willingly in exchange for hers.'

Black Jack roared in frustration. The bitch, the rotten bitch, damn her to hell. He had raped her, humiliated her, but she would never give in. His hand tightened around her throat. She looked towards Lucy who had, by now, stopped struggling, and was staring at her in despair. Elizabeth would gladly cease to be, if she thought that in doing so, she would save this woman, this part of her that had continued on long after she had become but a distant memory. Suddenly strong hands shot through the earth on either side of her. The pressure on her throat ceased as they grabbed at Black Jack's hands, tore them from her. She struggled up and towards Lucy who was watching wide-eyed, her mouth open in a silent scream.

'Don't be afraid. There is nothing more to fear,' Elizabeth put her arms around her.

Timmy and the other children watched in amazement, as Black Jack struggled with the men who held him fast. Mick was there, with Martin's father, and from around the graveyard others appeared and dragged him away. They had lain in wait, silent sentinels, watching over those they loved, waiting to appear until now when there was a real need of them.

'You're safe now, Miss Lizzy,' Mick called back to her.

They could hear Black Jack cursing as he was pulled towards his place in the graveyard and thrust into the ground. The men that had held him followed suit, diving in after him, the struggle continuing beneath the earth.

'Oh, Christ, this can't be happening,' Lucy sobbed. 'I'm losing my mind.'

'No, child, you're not.' Elizabeth rocked her, and the face that rested on her shoulder felt warm, the hair silky.

Elizabeth whispered to her, soothing and calming, as she had with her own daughter long ago. Soon the sobbing subsided and Lucy looked around her. She shrank back at first from the children, but as the woman told her of what they had suffered, why they were there, she relaxed.

'Then the typhus is here?'

'Yes, it's been here all along, and now you must put an end to it.'

'How?' Lucy looked up into the sunken eyes.

'With fire. You must dig up the bones of those who lie here. The disease is in their very marrow. Cleanse the land.'

'What about you? What will happen to you?'

'I, along with the others, will complete our destiny. But you must go now.'

Timmy handed Lucy one of her jars. He had filled it with earth from the graveyard. They walked with her towards the bushes, and held them apart for her to pass.

'I have to ask you something,' Lucy stopped. 'Why can I feel you, touch you and not that other one, the one that attacked me?'

'That is of our own choosing,' Elizabeth said. 'We can reveal ourselves when we chose, become part of the air when we chose not to.'

'I can't understand this,' Lucy shook her head. 'How can you be dead and still here? Everything I know, everything I have ever learned, tells me it's not possible.'

'You can't see the wind. But, you must admit sometimes it is powerful enough to knock you off your feet.'

'Yes, of course.'

'Will you allow me to ask a favour of you?'

'Anything.'

'May I see the image contained in your locket?'

Lucy opened the gold circle around her neck and, for the first time in over a hundred and fifty years, Elizabeth was looking into the face of her husband. She studied her own image, the face of a bright, happy woman, filled with hope. She tried not to cry as she asked.

'You know who they are?'

'Yes,' Lucy pointed to the portraits. 'This is my great-great-great grandmother Elizabeth and her husband John.'

'What became of them?'

'John died young, and Elizabeth was a victim of the Great Famine, just like you. But not before she sent my great-great grandmother and great aunts to America. She didn't have enough for the fare, and we know nothing about what happened to her after that. My family have tried to trace her on numerous vacations here, but without success. They say my great-great grandmother never gave up hope that one day she would arrive at her door. Lucy, that was her name; I'm called after her. She kept a light in the window until the day she died.'

Elizabeth had to lean on Timmy for support. Her heart was breaking. She didn't turn around as she asked.

'Lucy and the others, did they have a happy life? Did they prosper?'

'Yes,' she could feel this woman's sorrow. 'They lived well into their seventies, and had lots of children, I'm proof of that.'

'Thank you, child,' Elizabeth whispered. 'Thank you and God bless you.'

Before Lucy could reply they had vanished.

She hurried back to her car with the sample of earth clutched tightly in her hands. Just as she was about to get in another car appeared, its headlights cutting through the darkness.

'Lucy!' She recognised Joe's voice. 'My God, Lucy!' He stared at her torn clothing, her dirt-streaked face.

'I'm fine,' she assured him, 'but I'm glad to see you. I need to get this sample back to the lab right away, and I'm not sure I can drive.'

He helped her to the car and as they drove she told him what had happened that night. She was surprised he did not think her crazy. When he told her what he had seen, they drove the rest of the way in silence. The woman and the boy had touched them in a way they would never forget. She refused to change her clothing on reaching the hospital. Joe helped her to clean and dress her injured shoulder, before she threw on a lab coat and set to work. Joe watched, as she studied the sample of earth, injecting different substances into it, searching for results.

———

Neither Elizabeth nor Timmy returned to the earth that night. They sat waiting for the dawn. There was no sign of the men who had helped them, but Black Jack was back. He sat scowling on his grave, not daring to touch them. The children sleeping beneath were restless. They could hear gentle crying, and voices calling for their lost mothers.

'Why didn't you tell her who you were?' Timmy asked.

'It is better that she never knows. The living need to believe that the dead are at rest.'

The machines arrived at first light, the thundering of the Earthmovers now a familiar sound. Elizabeth, Timmy and the other children gathered together in the middle of the graveyard, and watched as the giant teeth scooped into to one section of the bushes, making a gateway for the others to follow.

'Oh, Elizabeth,' Katie buried her face against her. 'Will it hurt?'

'No, of course not; you won't feel a thing, I promise.'

Timmy's hand sneaked into hers and she held on. The machine drew back, and they were surprised when Lucy walked through the gap, followed by the man whose baby they had saved.

'Lord, have mercy on us,' they heard him say.

'That's what we are hoping for,' Elizabeth replied.

Lucy walked up to her. She no longer felt any fear at the sight before her.

'You found what you were looking for?'

'Yes, the digging is about to start. What do you think will happen?'

'That's in God's hands now, child, what is about to happen is not of your doing.'

'I know who you are,' Lucy started to cry.

'And I know who you are.' Elizabeth reached out and stroked her hair.

'What I don't understand is why you're here.' Lucy wiped the tears from her face. 'Didn't you suffer enough in the famine?'

'We are as puzzled as you are. Timmy is here, perhaps, because of a promise he once made to his mother to save the children, and I have been denied rest because of the hatred of one man. The others ...' she waved around the graveyard, 'perhaps it is the fate of those who die of hunger and disease, torn from their families before their time, to lie in restless sleep. The only good that has come from our torment is that the typhus has been found and Ireland will no longer have to bear its scourge. We may yet get our answer in heaven,' Elizabeth smiled. 'Now go child and remember us in your prayers.'

Lucy walked away, feeling as though her heart would break. She stopped at the edge of the graveyard, and stayed looking back as the Earthmovers passed by her and trundled to their designated areas. The drivers were unable to see the small group that stood before them, bravely awaiting their fate. The ground shook beneath their feet, and the children crowded tighter around Elizabeth. She closed her eyes, and waited for the end.

'Ma,' one of the children called, and ran from her.

She looked up to see the child running towards a woman who stood with her arms outstretched. There were people walking towards them from all around the graveyard and, one by one, children cried out with delight and ran to their parents.

The dead had come to claim their own.

Soon only Timmy and Elizabeth stood alone. Lucy watched from the edge of the field supported by Joe.

'Look's like we're on our own again,' Elizabeth turned to Timmy.

'You've kept us waiting for far too long, madam.' She spun round to find John and her daughters walking towards her. They all looked exactly as they had the last time she'd seen them.

'Mamma,' her girls ran and threw their arms around her waist. She kissed each of the upturned face and turned to her husband.

'I was delayed.' Her heart sang as his arms went around her. 'Timmy.' She wanted to gather him to her, but he didn't hear her.

He was holding too tightly to his mother to take any notice.

The men waiting to dig the field saw none of this. They were watching the woman who stood sobbing, and looking into the distance. They didn't see the Lucy the child, run to Lucy the woman with her hands outstretched.

'I promised my mamma that I would keep it safe until we met again,' she pointed to the locket.

'Yes, of course.' Lucy slipped the catch, and allowed it to fall into the waiting hand.

She had realised almost from the beginning that Elizabeth was a part of her.

'Thank you,' the child stood on her tiptoes and kissed her cheek, before running back to her mother.

Lucy watched as the locket was held out to Elizabeth, who shook her head and whispered something to her daughter.

'My mamma said I must return this to you. She had no further need of it, not where she is going,' the child held out the locket to Lucy. 'She said you must wear it with her love and asks that you remember her always.'

'I won't forget her,' Lucy felt the heavy gold chain being slipped into her hand, but she was crying too much to say any more. She watched as Timmy walked over to Elizabeth and hugged her before going back to his mother.

'I'll see you up there,' he pointed towards the sky.

'You better be waiting when I get there.'

The last thing Lucy heard was the sound of their laughter, as they dissolved into pinpricks of light. The spirits in the trees rushed to join them and they became one, a silver shower of meteorites that rushed upwards, towards the heavens.

'The sky will be brighter tonight,' Joe wiped his eyes.

Lucy nodded. She was no longer the same woman who had first come to the field. Nothing in science or medicine could explain what had just happened. It took the love of a mother and a young boy to teach her that life was eternal. That it never dies, only moves on.

'Do you think they'll be special in heaven?' she asked Joe. Only days before this question would have seemed foolish. 'I mean, do you think they'll be angels?'

His answer was exactly what she wanted to hear.

'They were already angels.'

EPILOGUE

It is still there, the evil. It has not been eradicated. The unrest, the destruction, continues. The housing estate lies empty. The once pristine buildings, some still furnished, stand cold and unused like giant doll's houses. No one who has been to this place remains untouched. Like the builder, who was found hanging from a tree in the estate. Some believe he was driven to suicide, by the generous amounts awarded by the courts to the angry residents claiming compensation. Others say that some unseen force murdered him. But everyone agrees, it is a place best avoided.

The graveyard has been completely dug over and a huge black square marks the place. No grass has grown there since that fateful day. It is a sad reminder to passers-by of the loss of those who once walked the land. At first, the place was a magnet for the curious or the derelict hoping to find comfort within the empty houses, but soon no one dared to go there, as body after body was carried from the place. The deaths served to warn the unwary, the foolish, to stay away.

Some believe the dark shadow they see on the hillside is nothing more than a trick of the light, but they are wrong. He is there. Not welcome in heaven, he lives in his own private hell. He has learned to be patient, and eventually they will come – they always do. Evil does not need to go looking. There are always those who will seek it out.

ACKNOWLEDGEMENTS

Thank you to everyone at Mercier Press, especially Eoin Purcell for his vision, to Patrick Crowley, Clodagh Feehan, Wendy Logue and Mary Feehan. To my agent, Jonathan Williams, for his guidance. To Seamus Cashman, for his kind comments and words of encouragement.

To David Rice and Kathleen Thorne of the Killaloe Hedge School of Writing, who held up the torch to light my way.

To my friends, Eileen Townsend for her kindness and unending faith in me, Dympna Moloney, who never failed to bring me treats, laughter and understanding. To my daughter Jessica, for reading and commenting on my work, my son Robert for his patience, and my taskmaster George, who made sure I was seated at my desk by ten each morning. My aunt, Kitty Murphy, for lending me her ear, and the members of the Killaloe Writing Group, too numerous to mention, but you know who you are.

Last, but not least, to my father, Jim Loughman – thanks Dad, for everything.